Breakaway

NATIONAL BESTSELLING AUTHOR
ROCHELLE ALERS

Breakaway

ARABESQUE®

Recycling programs
for this product may
not exist in your area.

BREAKAWAY

ISBN-13: 978-0-373-83182-1

www.kimanipress.com

Printed in U.S.A.

Dear Reader,

Breakaway is the fourteenth novel in the enduring Hideaway series, which continues the themes of family, sensuality and suspense.

In this book you will find out more about Celia Cole-Thomas, a witness to the hospital massacre that left her fiancé fatally injured. To recover from the tragedy, she travels to her vacation retreat in North Carolina while awaiting the trial. There she meets undercover FBI special agent Gavin Faulkner, who is in the area as part of a stakeout operation to apprehend his brother.

Breakaway has all of the hallmarks you have come to expect from Hideaway novels, but with an added bonus—intense, passionate and very sexy love scenes.

I hope that you enjoy the serenity and splendor of the Great Smoky Mountains, the beauty of Virginia's horse country and the sultry Florida heat as Celia and Gavin willingly risk everything for a newfound love and a future that promises forever.

Yours in romance,

Rochelle Alers

HIDEAWAY SERIES

Everett Kirkland - Teresa Maldanado - Samuel Cole - Marguerite Diaz[11]

Martin Cole - Parris Simmons[1]
- Oscar Spencer- Regina Cole - Aaron Spencer[5]
  - Clayborne
  - Eden

Tyler Cole - Dana Nichols[9]
- Martin, II
- Astra
- Samuel II
- Arianna

Nancy Cole - Noah Thomas
- Timothy Cole-Thomas - Nichola Bennett
  - Ynez
  - Grace
  - Malinda
- Celia Cole-Thomas - Gavin Faulkner[14]
  - Nicholas
- Diego Cole-Thomas - Vivienne Neal[13]
  - Samuel
- Matthew Sterling - Eve Blackwell - Alejandro Delgado[2]
  - Sara Sterling - Salem Lassiter[6]
    - Isaiah
    - Eve/Nona (twins)
  - Christopher Delgado - Emily Kirkland[7]
    - Alejandro
    - Esperanza
    - Mateo
- Joshua Kirkland* - Vanessa Blanchard[3]
- Michael Kirkland - Jolene Walker[8]
  - Teresa
  - Joshua-Michael
  - Merrick

Josephine Cole - Ivan Wilson[11]
- Gisela
- Esther
- Joseph
- Felipe / Ashley

David Cole - Serena Morris[4]
- Gabriel Cole - Summer Montgomery[10]
  - Immanuel
  - Anthony
  - Imani
- Alexandra Cole - Merrick Grayslake[12]
  - Victoria
  - Cordero
- Jason/Anna (twins)

LEGEND
* - Illegitimate Birth
1 - Hideaway
2 - Hidden Agenda
3 - Vows
4 - Heaven Sent
5 - Harvest Moon
6 - Just Before Dawn
7 - Private Passions
8 - No Compromise
9 - Homecoming
10 - Renegade
11 - Best Kept Secrets
12 - Stranger In My Arms
13 - Secret Agenda
14 - Breakaway

In loving memory of my mother for whom grandchildren are the crown of the aged, and the glory of those who are their parents.

He himself went on ahead of them, bowing to the ground seven times, until he reached his brother.
—*Genesis* 33:3

Chapter 1

*D*r. *Celia Cole-Thomas pulled back the curtain in the cubicle where she'd dressed the sutured forefinger of an elderly man. She immediately heard screams for help in English and Spanish coming from the E.R. waiting room. Her heart rate quickened when she saw two young men in blood-soaked clothing struggling under the weight of a limp body.*

"Bring him over here!" She shouted to be heard above the yelling and crying. She motioned to an empty cubicle. "Dr. Jones, help me out here," she said to the pediatrician who'd rushed over when he'd heard the commotion. Putting on a pair of latex gloves, she grabbed her stethoscope from the pocket of her lab coat, placing it against the chest of a boy whose breathing was becoming shallower with each passing second. "GSW to the chest, and he's bleeding out fast. Call the O.R...."

Whatever else she was going to say was drowned out by the sound of gunfire. There was one shot, then another—the rapid fire exploding like cannons shot through the emergency room of Miami's busiest municipal hospital. At that moment Celia realized the E.R. was under siege. The curtain of the makeshift room was ripped open and she stared into the barrel of a large-caliber handgun. The young boy, gripping the semiautomatic with two hands to steady it, winked at her and her gaze went to the distinctive tattoo on the back of his left hand.

"Step off, doc," he ordered through the white bandanna covering the lower portion of his face.

It was as if everything was happening in slow motion. The first bullet hit the chest of her patient, the impact causing his body to jerk several inches off the gurney. The second knocked Dr. Yale Trevor-Jones backward. He collapsed on the floor like a rag doll before Celia felt the impact of another bullet slamming into her midsection. The fire in her side spread throughout her body. She placed her right hand against her ribs as blood— warm and acrid-smelling—spilled through her splayed fingers. The shooting and screaming continued as she lay sprawled on the tiled floor, shutting out the sights and sounds of carnage tearing through the E.R. In less than a minute, four people had been injured and six lay mortally wounded.

Celia sat up, her heart racing uncontrollably. Placing a hand over her mouth, she cut off the screams caught in the back of her throat. Rocking back and forth, she cried without making a sound. The nightmare had returned. It'd been almost a year and yet she could not stop reliving the horror of the night that so many innocent people had lost their lives.

Physically she'd recovered from being shot at close range, the bullet having passed through her body and ending up in the wall behind her. But, Celia knew she would never forget the sound of her own voice, when hours later, she'd asked the recovery nurse what had happened and knew by the woman's expression that many people had died. She didn't learn the names of the victims until she'd been taken to a private room and her family members had begun arriving en masse. It was her brother Diego who'd finally told her that Dr. Yale Trevor-Jones and Dr. Colton Riley had died that night. Rival gangs had turned Miami Hospital's E.R. into a killing field. Her patient and three other gang members had also died.

Pulling her knees to her chest, Celia rested her forehead on her knees and waited for her heartbeat to return to normal. She'd taken a medical leave of absence in addition to grief counseling to cope with the death of the man she'd planned to marry—Yale Trevor-Jones— but she still was unable to exorcise the horror caused by Miami's gang fighting over a very lucrative drug operation.

Images of the days and nights she'd shared with Yale flooded her mind. When she'd met him for the first time she realized immediately that he was different from any of the men in her past. They'd shared the same passion for medicine, the same zeal for helping those without resources in underserved communities. Yale could have joined the family practice begun by his grandfather, treating the children of an affluent Connecticut suburb, but instead he had chosen to work in a city hospital.

What had made the loss so devastating for Celia was that she and Yale had planned to open a free clinic in a low-income Miami neighborhood. They'd purchased an abandoned building and had planned to meet with a contractor to renovate the space to include waiting and examining rooms and a place where children could play while waiting to be seen. Yale's specialty was pediatrics and hers was internal medicine. Their future plans also included adding a pediatric dentist and an ob-gyn.

She slowly looked up when she heard the telephone ring shattering the silence in the large bedroom. Celia knew she had to get away from Miami, even if only for a month or two. Waking up to tropical temperatures, palm trees, the ocean views, the sounds of Spanish interspersed with English and luxury yachts moored along the Intracoastal was a constant reminder of the days and nights she'd lain in Yale's arms while they'd planned their future.

She reached for the cordless phone without bothering to look at the display. "Hello."

"*¿Cómo estás,* Cee Cee?"

A hint of a smile parted her lips when she heard her older brother Diego's greeting. There was no doubt he was in a good mood. Employees of ColeDiz International, Ltd. were thrilled now that its CEO, Diego Cole-Thomas, had married and become a father. He now greeted them with smiles and effusive handshakes. Before he'd met Vivienne Neal, most people, including family members, found Diego Cole-Thomas cold and intimidating.

"Good morning, Diego."

"Have you looked at the clock, Celia?"

Sitting upright, Celia took a quick glance at the clock on the bedside table. She groaned inwardly. It was after three in the afternoon. "I suppose I should've said good afternoon."

"Are you still in bed?"

Her brother's voice had changed, layered with concern that put her on the defensive. "I didn't know I needed your permission as to when I should and should not go to bed." Her retort was followed by a long silence, and Celia knew Diego was struggling to control his temper.

"You don't need my permission to do anything, Celia. It's just that I'm concerned about you spending so much time by yourself."

Tears filled her eyes, but she blinked them back. "I'm sorry I snapped at you, Diego," she said before exhaling an audible breath. "I feel better when I'm alone because I don't have to pretend all is well when it isn't. Most times I'm okay, but it's when I dream about what happened that I find myself getting depressed."

"Are you depressed now?"

She smiled. "I'm fighting it."

"May I make a suggestion without you biting my head off?"

"Yes. And even if I disagree with you I promise not to bite your head off."

"I spoke to Nick earlier this morning, and he wants you to stay at the horse farm until you're called to testify."

Celia rolled her eyes upward. "Nick knows how I feel about horses. I don't like them and they don't like me."

"It's not about horses, Cee Cee. It's about a change of scenery."

She smiled again. "You must be clairvoyant, big brother, because I was just thinking about leaving Miami for a few months to get my head together."

"Where are you going?"

"North Carolina."

"No, Celia. If you go there you'll be more isolated than in that mausoleum of a house you wander around in."

"Will it make you feel better if I take a lover for the summer to keep me company?"

"That's not funny, Celia."

"Make up your mind, Diego," she countered. "I know you've been talking to everyone because you believe I'm either crazy or going crazy. I'm neither. What I am is mourning the loss of the man I loved, the man who was to become my husband and the father of my children. He was murdered right in front of my eyes, and my only consolation was that I didn't watch him die. I am going away, and hopefully when I come back I'll be able to start over."

There was another brief silence. "Will I see you before you leave?"

"Of course," Celia said.

She would stay in Florida long enough to see her brother, sister-in-law and nephew, and to spend time with her parents and grandparents before driving up to North Carolina. Perhaps on her return trip she would stop at her younger brother's horse farm in western Virginia.

Two minutes later, she ended the call, swung her legs over the side of the bed and walked to the en suite bathroom. She'd committed to leaving Miami, and hopefully upon her return she would be able to get her life back on track.

FBI Academy—Quantico, Virginia

Gavin Faulkner reached up in an attempt to loosen the tie under his shirt collar. He stopped and then remembered why he'd worn it. Earlier that morning, he'd gotten a call from his supervisor that he was to meet him at 0900 hours. Bradley MacArthur ended the terse message with a direct order that he wear a suit and tie.

As a special agent working undercover, there were few occasions when he had to wear what he'd referred to as an authorized noose. He much preferred jeans, boots, tees and a pullover sweater. The temperature had to drop several degrees before he deigned to wear a coat or jacket.

"Agent Faulkner, you may go in now."

Gavin, rising to his feet, stared at the dour-faced woman guarding her boss's door like a rottweiler about to pounce on an unsuspecting intruder. "Thank you, Ms. Rossen." He gave her his best toothpaste-ad grin. He knew he'd shocked her because she stared silently at him, her mouth agape.

Ms. Claire Rossen didn't like him, and the feeling was mutual. The first time he'd been summoned to meet directly with Mac, she'd neglected to inform her boss that the newly appointed undercover special agent had arrived on time when she directed Gavin into his supervisor's office twenty minutes later.

He'd endured the tongue-lashing about the importance of punctuality, and then calmly asked Mac why he wanted to see him. The question had quickly diffused the career agent's harangue, and within seconds the two men regarded each other with respect. He smiled at Ms.

Rossen as he stepped into the sun-filled office. Much to his surprise, she returned his smile.

"Good luck, Gavin."

It was the first time Claire had addressed him by his first name. His smile was still in place when he recognized the men sitting at a conference table in a corner of the large office. "Good morning, gentlemen," Gavin said, greeting and shaking hands with associate directors of the FBI, DEA, ATF and the U.S. Marshals Service. A shudder of excitement rushed through his body when he realized he was to become a participant in a joint Department of Justice operation.

Bradley gestured to an empty chair. "Please sit there, Agent Faulkner." Gavin sat. It was the only place at the table with a file folder. "Before you examine the contents of the folder in front of you, I want you to know that your name was at the top of the list for this operation."

Thick, black, silky eyebrows lifted a fraction when Gavin met the resolute stares of the men looking back at him. "Am I correct to assume that I was the only name on the list?" The ATF and DEA officials exchanged barely perceptible smiles.

"Yes," the assistant Bureau director acknowledged. "Raymond Prentice, aka Ray Peterson, and sometimes known as Roy Perkins has just earned the number-one spot on the Bureau's Most Wanted List."

A lump formed in Gavin's throat, and he closed his eyes for several seconds. His expression was unreadable when he finally opened them. "What happened?"

Bradley laced his fingers together atop the table. "We got word from the inside that his cover was compromised following the kidnapping of the owner of a gun shop near Waynesville, North Carolina."

"What happened?" Gavin repeated, glaring at his supervisor.

"The plan was to leave no witnesses, but Ray wounded the store owner, who was able to give the police a description of his kidnappers. Ray managed to slip away from the group, and is hiding out in the mountains near the Tennessee border. Right now he doesn't trust anyone and that includes his government. Gavin, we need you to bring him in."

"What if he doesn't want to come in?"

"It will be up to you to convince him to come in," said the nattily dressed ATF supervisor.

"Who's his contact on the inside?" Gavin said anxiously, asking yet another question.

The head of DEA field offices cleared his throat. "She's the girlfriend of one of the men responsible for getting guns across the border to Mexican drug traffickers. She said there's a contract out on Ray to bring him in dead or alive."

"How do you gentlemen want him? Dead or alive?"

The ATF director angled his head. "We'd like to bring him alive, but without compromising the most important DoJ joint task force operation we've put together in years. We've got direct orders from the Oval Office to stop the flow of drugs and killings along the U.S.-Mexican border."

Gavin clenched his teeth and a muscle twitched noticeably in his lean jaw. "What you're telling me is that you're willing to offer up Raymond Prentice as a sacrificial lamb in order to save your mission."

A bright red flush crept up Bradley MacArthur's face to the hairline of the mane of shockingly white hair, which had begun turning gray in his early twenties.

"Special Agent Faulkner, I shouldn't have to remind you of the oath each and every one of us took when we joined the Justice Department. If need be, I'd sacrifice my first born if it meant stopping the flow of drugs and putting those responsible for murder and trafficking behind bars for the rest of their natural lives."

Gavin nodded. "I suppose that answers my question. When do I start and where am I going?" His voice was even, shaded in neutral tones that belied the inner torment of assuming the responsibility of rescuing or killing his own brother—Raymond Prentice.

Bradley unlaced his fingers as he stared at his agent. "We know this is not going to be easy for you. But the fact is you're the best man for this mission. You'll only have twenty-four hours to familiarize yourself with the operation before you head out to North Carolina."

Resting a hand on the file folder stamped OPERA-TION: Top Gun, Gavin gave each man a long, penetrating look. "This is going to be my last field assignment."

"What is it you want?" asked the ATF supervisor.

Silence filled the room as Gavin and the fastidious bureaucrat engaged in a stare down. "I want your job," he said with a sardonic smile. Pushing back his chair, he stood, gathered the folder and inclined his head. "It's been a pleasure." Turning on his heels, he walked across the room, feeling the heat from the glares at his back as the four men exchanged glances.

The ATF director recovered quickly. "Why, that ballsy bastard," he whispered under his breath. "There's no way in hell he'll ever get my job."

Bradley MacArthur's bushy brows lifted a fraction. "He may not be after your job."

"But…but you heard what he said, Mac."

"I heard him, Walter. However, it may be in your best interest to play nice with Faulkner, because he just may be your boss in the very near future. The man is one of the best the Bureau has seen in decades. As a former decorated Army Ranger and with several post-graduate degrees to his credit, Special Agent Faulkner could have any of our jobs at a moment's notice."

Gavin closed the door behind him as he winked at Claire Rossen. He walked past her desk to a room where he could sit and read the file on Raymond Prentice. He was serious when he had said he wanted out of the field. In three years he would turn forty, and by that time he knew he would be more inclined to sit behind a desk. What he didn't want to think about was not finding his brother before the gun traffickers did.

Chapter 2

Celia inhaled a lungful of crisp mountain air wafting through the open windows of her late-model Toyota Highlander hybrid. The exterior temperature on the rear-view mirror read seventy-two degrees, sixteen degrees cooler than what it would've been if she'd remained in Miami. It was late May, and south Florida afternoon temperatures were already in the mid-nineties.

She'd left Palm Beach later than she'd planned, and hadn't been able to make up the time because of a storm front that had stalled over the Southeast. There were times when the rain had come down so heavily, traffic along the interstate had been reduced to a crawl. However, the rain had stopped entirely by the time she reached Asheville, North Carolina's city limits. The blue-gray haze hovering above the Great Smoky Mountains never failed to make her smile.

Why have I stayed away so long? she thought. The house with three bedrooms, two and a half baths built on more than two acres of lush land with panoramic mountain views had been her first big-ticket purchase once she had gained control of her trust. She'd fallen in love with the region while attending Meharry Medical College in Nashville, Tennessee, and each time she returned it was to wind down from the nonstop pace as an emergency-room critical care physician.

She was luckier than most of the students at medical school. She hadn't been burdened with six-figure student loans because of her family's wealth. Her great-grandfather, Samuel Claridge Cole, had established ColeDiz International, Ltd. in 1925 and it was now the biggest family-owned agribusiness in the United States.

Celia was always very low-key when it came to her wealth. She'd shared an apartment with another student in college and in medical school, and had driven an affordable car until she'd earned her medical degree. She knew she'd shocked her mother when she revealed that she did her own laundry instead of sending it out and had learned to cook rather than eat in restaurants or order takeout.

Celia and her two brothers had grown up in a household with a live-in housekeeping staff, a full-time chef, drivers and a grounds crew. When her college roommate—who had come from a poor Detroit neighborhood and was on full academic scholarship—called her spoiled and pampered, Celia took offense and refused to talk to her for a week. The stalemate ended when she asked her roommate to show her how to do laundry. Learning how to separate whites and colors segued into shopping for groceries and eventually cooking lessons.

After four years, Celia and Rania Norris were not only roommates and friends, but sorority sisters.

Even her fiancé had been completely in the dark when it came to her wealth until she'd purchased an oceanfront mansion from her cousin. Nathaniel Thomas-Mitchell had designed the prize-winning showcase house as a wedding gift for his bride. But after the drowning death of their two-year-old daughter, Nathaniel and Kendra divorced. Eventually they relocated to Chicago, reconciled and remarried. Celia had bought the six-bedroom, seven-bath house, hoping she and Yale would raise their children there, and then grow old together.

She and Yale had had their first serious argument because he'd felt she hadn't trusted him, and that she'd thought if he'd known of her wealth he would have proposed marriage because of her money. He'd admitted that he would marry her even if she were a pauper. Fortunately, she wasn't destitute.

She was only a few miles from downtown Waynesville when she decided to stop at a supermarket in a shopping center. Not only did she need to fill the pantry and refrigerator, but she also needed cleaning products. It had been more than a year since she'd been at the house and she hated to imagine what would greet her when she arrived. There was no doubt that the house would be filled with dust and cobwebs, but hopefully nothing more. When she'd locked up the house last summer, she had emptied and cleaned the refrigerator, then unplugged it. She hadn't had to concern herself with break-ins because she'd installed a security system that was linked directly to the sheriff's office and fire department. Her nearest neighbor e-mailed her once a week to give her updates on the property.

Maneuvering into a parking space near the entrance to the supermarket, Celia cut off the engine and got out of her SUV. Reaching for a shopping cart, she walked into the market and was met with a rush of cool air from the air-conditioning.

Gavin stood in the supermarket produce aisle, checking the fresh herbs and vegetables in his shopping cart with what was listed on a recipe card for the Thai salad he'd planned to prepare for dinner. The recipe called for two different types of cabbage, but with more than half a dozen varieties on display, he was a little confused.

He'd just moved into a nearby cabin, compliments of the government, and had spent the past two days settling in. Gavin did not mind eating out, but he'd recently begun preparing his own meals in an attempt to eat healthier.

"Excuse me, miss, but can you please tell me the difference in these cabbages?"

Celia stopped filling a plastic bag with peaches. She stared at the tall, solidly built man with stubble on his lean brown jaw. His large dark eyes and strong masculine features made for a strikingly attractive image. He was casually dressed in a white tee, jeans, boots and a well-worn black baseball cap.

"It all depends on what you want to prepare," she said.

Gavin went completely still when the woman with a profusion of black curls grazing the nape of her neck turned to face him. Her small round face reminded him of a doll with her large dark eyes, pert nose and a temptingly curved mouth. He knew it was impolite to stare, but he couldn't pull his gaze away from her flawless face, which was the color of brown velvet. Even her voice matched her face. It was low and very sexy.

He blinked. "What did you say?"

Celia smiled, dimples dotting her cheeks like thumb-prints. "I said it all depends on what you want to make."

"Slaw—it's a spicy Thai slaw." Gavin couldn't believe he was stammering like an awkward adolescent.

"Perhaps you should try the Savoy or Napa cabbage." Leaning over, she tried reading what was written on Gavin's index card. "What does your recipe call for?"

Gavin gave her a sheepish grin, revealing a mouth filled with straight white teeth. "I guess I forgot to write down the type of cabbage."

"You can't go wrong with the Savoy or Napa."

"You must be a fabulous cook."

Her eyebrows flickered. "Why would you say that?"

"You know right off the top of your head which type of cabbage I should use."

Celia wanted to tell him that if it hadn't been for Rania she wouldn't have been able to boil an egg. "It's just common sense. Asian dishes call for Asian ingredients."

"Sometimes common sense isn't that common," he quipped. "Do you shop here often?"

Eyes narrowing in suspicion, Celia asked, "Not really. Why?" Whenever she'd come to Waynesville for more than a week, she would visit the supermarket to restock her pantry. However, if she'd planned to stay for an extended weekend, then she shopped at the smaller downtown markets and variety stores.

"I need soba noodles, and I'd hoped you would know which aisle they were in."

"If they do carry them, then you'll probably find them in the aisle with the other imported products."

Gavin shook his head. "Why didn't I think of that?"

Celia wanted to tell the gorgeous stranger that either

he truly lacked common sense *or* he'd embarked on a cooking project that exceeded his culinary expertise. "Good luck with your spicy Thai slaw."

"Thank *you* for your invaluable assistance."

Turning back to her shopping cart, she glanced at its contents. She'd selected seasonal fruits, fresh herbs and vegetables. All she needed was dairy and then she would head home.

She pushed her cart away from the produce section slowly, glancing over her shoulder at the delicious-looking man. Her pulse quickened when she saw him standing motionless, staring at her. Raising her hand, she waved, and then turned down another aisle.

Twenty minutes later, she pushed her cart out to the parking lot and transferred her groceries from the cart to the cargo area of the vehicle. As soon as she sat behind the wheel, her eyelids felt heavy. She'd been on the road more than twelve hours. Her plan to clean the house would have to wait. After all, she had tomorrow and the day after tomorrow and the rest of the summer to do all she needed to do before returning to Miami. She hoped when she did return to Miami that she wouldn't be the same woman who'd left.

Celia unlocked the door to the house she regarded as her sanctuary, a place to heal. What she didn't want to do was relive the last time she'd come with Yale. Miraculously, they had been able to coordinate four days of vacation and they'd traveled to North Carolina to unwind. Four days stretched into six when a freak snowstorm blanketed the Blue Ridge and Great Smoky Mountains, and they were trapped inside until the roads were cleared. It would be the last time she and Yale would spend time together in what he'd always referred to as "the mountains."

She deactivated the security system and walked in, wrinkling her nose when she encountered a buildup of heat and muskiness. Within minutes she flicked on lights and opened windows. Clean mountain air swept into the rooms through the screens, quickly dispelling the stale odor. The imprint from the bottom of her running shoes was clearly outlined in the layer of dust covering the wood floors. Yale had chided her for covering the furniture with dustcovers, but the diligence then now saved her hours of housework.

Her intent to clean the house tomorrow had changed when Celia realized the daunting task she couldn't put off until the next day. It took four trips to her car to bring in her luggage and groceries. She discovered a spurt of energy when she cleaned the refrigerator, vacuumed the floors, dusted furniture, cleaned the bathrooms and made her bed.

The sun had set behind the mountains, taking with it the warmth of the day when Celia sat on the wraparound deck outside her second-floor bedroom, sipping from a mug of steaming coffee. She'd showered, changed into a pair of cotton pajamas and then added a thick cotton pullover and socks to ward off the cooler night air.

Without the bright lights from hotels, towering office and high-rise apartment buildings the stars in the night-time sky appeared brighter, closer. Closing her eyes, Celia felt a gentle peace sweep over her body. It was as if she'd come to her own private world where she didn't want for anything. All she had to do was wake up, eat, drink, walk, read, watch television, go to bed and then get up to do it all over again.

Now she understood why people dropped out of society to become recluses. It took too much effort to make it through each day. She'd been trained to save lives. And yet, she'd stood by and watched a boy take the lives of her patient, fiancé and another doctor before he was shot by another boy. What Celia hadn't been able to grasp was that all of the gang members were sixteen and younger. Instead of hanging out at the mall, flirting with girls or tinkering with cars, they'd carried guns not to protect themselves, but to savagely and arbitrarily take the lives of other human beings.

Now, Celia, don't get maudlin. The inner voice, the one she called her voice of reason, pulled her back to center *and* helped her maintain a modicum of stability. She took another deep swallow of coffee and placed the mug on a low table before settling deeper into the cushioned chaise.

She closed her eyes again and moments later succumbed to a dreamless slumber where there were no screams, bullets or tears.

Gavin felt restlessness akin to an itch he wasn't able to scratch. He'd prepared the slaw, and the results were even better than he'd expected. He'd also prepared a three-bean salad, grilled chicken and sweet tea.

Leaving the government-registered SUV parked in the garage, he'd set out on foot to familiarize himself with the surrounding countryside. His brother was out there, hiding in the mountains and/or forest from a group of ruthless men and women who were ordered to kill him on sight.

Gavin hadn't seen or spoken to his brother in more than two years. Raymond Prentice had been so deep undercover that if he hadn't recognized his eyes, Gavin wouldn't have known who he was. Ray could change his appearance by losing or gaining copious amounts of weight. He would shave his head, grow his hair, beard and affect different accents. Although the wounded gun-shop owner had given law enforcement officials an accurate description of Raymond Prentice, the technicians at the Bureau had subtly altered the mug shot to disguise the undercover agent's features.

Born Orlando Wells, he'd become Gavin's foster brother when Gavin's mother took him in after he'd been placed in her care by a fellow social worker. Orlando didn't remember his drug-addicted parents, and at nine hadn't shed a tear when told of their deaths from an overdose of crack cocaine. Malvina Faulkner legally adopted Orlando and after college and a stint as a Navy SEAL, he was recruited by the ATF. Orlando Wells Faulkner had become Raymond Prentice and anyone they wanted him to be.

His younger brother had always been a risk taker, and if Orlando survived this undercover mission, Gavin would do everything within his power to convince him to leave the ATF. Their mother's greatest fear was that after burying her husband, who'd died in the line of duty, she would also bury one or both of her sons. The elder Faulkner, a former Vietnam War Green Beret, joined the Bureau as an undercover agent. He'd infiltrated a radical group in the early 1980s, but lost his life during a confrontation between group members and the police.

Gavin continued walking along the shoulder of a narrow two-lane road. He'd estimated he'd walked half a mile and a total of eight cars had passed going in either direction. The population of Waynesville was about ten thousand, and that meant most long-time residents were familiar with one another. However, during the summer the number of tourists visiting the mountain region swelled the numbers appreciably.

Being on the run during the summer months and attempting to hide out in a tourist area was advantageous for the undercover agent, but would prove to be the opposite for Gavin because it would make his search more difficult.

His orders dictated that he work alone, without the assistance of regional agents or local law enforcement. The members of the joint task force did not want anything or anyone to compromise their attempt to eradicate a gun-trafficking network spanning more than twenty states.

Gavin knew what lay ahead was a daunting task, but he had to cover acres of virgin forests, mountain caves and miles of streams to rescue the FBI's Most Wanted before the gun traffickers found him.

Chapter 3

Gavin decelerated when he spotted a dark shape in the middle of the road. He'd spent most of the morning driving along Route 441, which led into the Great Smoky Mountains National Park. He'd walked the trails, searching for Orlando Faulkner. After more than six hours, he'd decided to head back to Waynesville.

He'd gotten up before sunrise to plan his strategy. He'd gone over a map detailing western North Carolina, highlighting the many cities he'd planned to visit ranging as far east as Black Mountain. His travels would take him south to Hendersonville and Flat Rock, then northwest to Asheville and as far west as the Great Smoky Mountains, and if necessary, into Tennessee.

Slowing and pulling off onto the shoulder, he got out of the truck, his right hand pressed to the automatic tucked into his waistband under his T-shirt. Going to one knee, he saw a small dog. Each time it attempted to move, it let out a small whimper.

He rested a hand lightly on the canine's back. "What happened to you, buddy?" Gavin's head popped up when he heard the sound of tires on the roadway. A car was coming closer. Standing, he waved his arms over his head, motioning for the motorist to stop. Fortunately, there was still enough daylight for whoever was driving the vehicle to see him.

Celia saw the figure of a man standing in the middle of the road, waving frantically. She pushed a button on the steering wheel, raising the driver's-side window. Slowing, she stopped within feet of the man she recognized as the one who'd asked her about cabbages two days before.

She lowered the window with his approach. "What's the matter?"

Gavin smiled, despite the seriousness of the situation. He'd grown up around pets, but it was dogs that were his personal favorite. Orlando liked cats because he claimed they were silent and unpredictable. His brother would pretend to be a cat and try and sneak up on Gavin before he detected his presence. Eight out of ten times he was successful.

He leaned into the window. "There's an injured dog in the road."

Celia pushed open the door, but Gavin wouldn't let her get out. "Let go of the door."

He shook his head. "You don't need to see it."

Her eyes grew wider. "Is it dead?"

"No."

"Then, let me see it."

"No," Gavin repeated.

"I'm a doctor," she finally said.

Gavin froze. "You're a vet?"

"No! I'm a medical doctor. Now, get away from the door so I can look at the poor creature."

He took a step back, opening the door and reaching for her hand to assist her. As his gaze swept over the woman who claimed she was a doctor, a slow smile tilted the corners of his mouth. The other day she'd worn a pair of jeans, a baggy T-shirt and running shoes. Today she looked softer, more feminine in a white tank top she'd paired with a pair of black cropped pants and leather sandals. The delicate pink polish on her bare toes matched her fingernails. A black-and-white striped headband held a profusion of curls off her face.

His gaze lingered on her profile when she knelt to examine the whimpering canine. "What's wrong with him?"

Celia glanced up at the man towering over her. "He has a laceration near his belly. And judging from the swelling, it's infected." She stood up. "I need for you to pick him up and place him on the rear seat of my truck, while I call to find a number for the nearest vet."

"I'm going to put him in *my* truck, while you pull yours off the road," Gavin countered.

Celia rolled her eyes at him. "Whatever. Just be careful with him."

"How do you know he's a male?"

"I know he's a *he* because I checked. And, he's also a puppy. He still has his milk teeth." When she'd opened his mouth, two tiny rice-like particles fell into her palm.

She returned to her vehicle, maneuvering it over to the shoulder behind the black GMC Yukon hybrid. Reaching for her BlackBerry, Celia called information, pen and paper ready to jot down the number. Her heart sank when the operator gave her numbers of veterinary hospitals more than twenty miles away. She called each one only to find they were closed. The only one with evening hours was in Asheville.

Getting out, she approached the man wearing a pair of khaki walking shorts, thick white cotton socks, Doc Martens, a black tee and matching baseball cap. She didn't know his name or anything about him, but he was the most virile-looking man she'd ever seen.

"Where am I taking him?" Gavin asked.

"You're going to take him to my house. All of the vets in the area are closed and the nearest one with evening hours is in Asheville."

Gavin shot her a suspicious look. "What are you going to do?"

"Clean his wound. Now, stop jawing and follow me. Please drive slowly. He's already in enough pain without you jostling him further."

"Ma'am, yes, ma'am."

"The name is Celia Cole-Thomas."

"What's your husband going to say when you bring home a strange man and injured dog?"

"I don't have a husband, Mr.—"

Gavin was hard-pressed not to smile. He didn't know why, but he'd hoped the tall, slender woman with the infectious dimpled smile wasn't married. "It's Faulkner. Gavin Faulkner."

"Let's go, Mr. Faulkner. Every minute that puppy doesn't get medical attention gives the infection the advantage."

Celia slipped behind the wheel, maneuvering around the Yukon with North Carolina plates, and drove in the direction of her house. She didn't want to get stopped for speeding although she'd wanted to get home to set up a mock operating room before Gavin Faulkner arrived.

Her parents had given her a genuine alligator medical bag stamped with her monogram the day she'd graduated medical school. She could still recall the joy of filling the bag with bandages, scissors, forceps, scalpels, syringes, gauze and medication she replaced whenever they passed their expiration date.

She parked in the driveway rather than in the two-car garage. Moving quickly, she got out, unlocked the door and disengaged the alarm, while leaving the front door open.

She retrieved her bag, spread a stack of towels on the table in the kitchen's dining area and turned a hanging light fixture to the brightest setting. She'd placed two pairs of latex gloves and the instruments needed to clean and suture the wound in the dog's side on a folded pillowcase when Gavin walked into the kitchen, cradling the puppy to his chest.

"Put him down on his uninjured side," Celia ordered Gavin. "After I wash up I want you to do the same."

His eyebrows lifted a fraction. "Why?"

She gave him a dimpled smile. "You're going to be my assistant."

"Oh, hell, no," Gavin protested.

"Oh, hell, yes, Gavin Faulkner! If you didn't care about this animal you never would've stopped. Now, stop sniveling and do as I tell you."

Gavin glared at Celia. He wasn't sniveling. In fact, he'd never sniveled about anything in his life. He wanted to tell her only girls sniveled but didn't want her to think he was a sexist.

Celia took his silence as acquiescence. "Please watch him while I go and wash up."

Taking off his cap, Gavin tossed it on one of the four chairs at the oaken round table. His gaze shifted between the motionless puppy and Celia's retreating back. He hadn't realized how slim Celia was until he saw her from the back. She was taller and much slimmer than women who usually garnered his attention. At six-four and two hundred twenty pounds, he liked women who were a bit more substantial than the sharp-tongued doctor.

He'd only mentioned the possibility of her being married because of her hyphenated last name. There were many professional women who'd elected to keep their maiden names.

Exchanging places with Celia, Gavin went into the half bath off the kitchen to wash his hands and forearms. He felt like an actor stepping into a fictional role as a surgeon when using a nail brush and antibacterial soap to scrub his fingers. Shaking off the excess water, he returned to the kitchen. Standing only inches from Dr. Celia Cole-Thomas, he smiled down at her head when she dabbed his arms and hands with a towel before holding a pair of latex gloves for him to slip on.

"Damn, Doc, they're too tight."

Celia shot him a frown. "Stop whining, Gavin. They won't be on long enough to cut off your circulation." He tried flexing his fingers. "Stop that or you'll rip them," she added, this time in a softer tone as she slipped her hands into a pair of gloves.

"Why do I have to wear them if you're going to perform the procedure?"

"I'm operating in what is a non-sterile environment.

I'm going to put Terry under, and I'm going to need you to hold him steady."

Gavin gave her a sidelong glance. "When did he become Terry?"

"He's a fox terrier, therefore, he's Terry."

"You can't name someone else's dog, Doc."

"Stop calling me that. And I doubt if he's anyone's pet. He's filthy and undernourished, which means he's probably a stray."

Celia ripped open a package with a sterile syringe and inserted it into a bottle of morphine, filling the syringe with a small amount of clear liquid. "Please hold him, Gavin. He's going to feel a little prick."

Gavin held the puppy's head between his palms. "How do you know how much to give him?"

"It's based on body weight. I doubt if this little guy weighs more than seven pounds. You, on the other hand, would have to be injected with the entire bottle before you'd go out."

His eyes narrowed. "What are you trying to say?"

Celia swabbed an area on the puppy's hip, wiping away dirt and debris. If she'd had the time, or if the wound hadn't been infected, she would have given the dog a bath. She gave Gavin a quick glance. "You're at least six-four or five, and I'm willing to bet you weigh about two-twenty or thirty, and that translates into injecting you with a lot more morphine to put you down than what I'm going to give Terry."

Gavin exhaled an audible breath. "I really don't like the term *put down.*"

Terry let out a small yelp with a prick of the needle. Seconds later he lay completely still. His ribs were clearly visible under a sparse coat of grimy, light-colored wiry fur.

Celia winked at Gavin, her gaze lingering on his cropped black hair. "Not to worry, Mr. Faulkner, I promise not to put you down. You can let go of his head now."

Concentrating intently, she shaved the area around the wound and cleaned the infected flesh. She applied a topical antibiotic then closed the laceration with small, even sutures.

Gavin leaned over to survey her surgical skill. "You do very nice work, Dr. Thomas."

"Thank you. You can take your gloves off now."

"When is he going to wake up?"

"He'll probably sleep for the next two to three hours. I'm going to call the animal hospital in Asheville to let them know I want to bring him tomorrow for an observation. After that, I'm going to try and clean him up."

"I'll do that," Gavin volunteered as he gently lifted the puppy off the table.

Celia gave him a skeptical look. "Are you sure?"

He nodded. "Yes, I'm very sure. Where are you going to wash him?"

"We'll use the mudroom."

She led the way across the kitchen to a side door that led to an unheated mudroom. It was where she stored garden equipment and did her laundry. She filled two plastic basins: one with warm water and a mild shampoo and the other with lukewarm water for rinsing. Reaching for cleaning cloths from a stack in a canvas basket, she spread them out on the utility table attached to a wall.

"Gavin, please try and not wet the sutures."

"I'll be careful," he said as she turned and walked out.

He dipped a cloth into the soapy water, wringing out most of the moisture, then began the task of washing and rinsing the grime covering the puppy's fur. Gavin poured out the water, refilling each bin before he was able to discern the white coat with a faint tan patch of color on the back of the neck, back and above the tiny tail. Wrapping a fluffy towel around the canine, he picked him up and dropped a kiss on the top of his head.

Celia stopped in the doorway to the mudroom, smiling when she saw the tender moment between Gavin and the dog. There was something about him that enthralled her. The longer she remained in his presence, the more she knew it had nothing to do with his face or body.

Even as an adolescent, she'd never been one to find herself attracted to a boy because he was cute. For Celia, it was always deeper than that. With Yale, it had been his passion for medicine, yet with Gavin she hadn't been able to identify what it was. For all she knew he could be married with half a dozen children.

When his head came up, he saw her staring at him. "He smells wonderful."

She smiled. "He looks adorable. I spoke to a veterinarian at the animal hospital, and he's set up an appointment to see Terry at eleven."

"I'll go with you."

Celia shook her head. "Don't bother. I can take him."

"Are you going to be able to hold him while you drive?"

"Maybe I'll ask my neighbor to go with me if she's not busy." Children's book illustrator Hannah Walsh was also a stay-at-home mother. She was now in her last trimester with her second child.

"I'm on vacation which means I have a lot of free time," Gavin countered. He wasn't on vacation, but on assignment. Accompanying Celia to Asheville would fit nicely into his plans. He had to present himself as a tourist or garner unwarranted attention.

Crossing her arms under her breasts, Celia angled her head. "I'm also on vacation. But wouldn't you rather spend your free time vacationing with your family than babysitting an injured puppy?"

She didn't tell Gavin that she'd been on vacation for the past year. Somehow, she couldn't bring herself to return to the hospital and relive the horror of the minute that had changed her and her life forever.

A beat passed. "No."

"Why not, Gavin?"

"Because other than my mother, brother and some cousins, I don't have much of a family. I'm going with you because I'm concerned about my dog."

"*Your* dog? I save his life and you say he's your dog?"

"Why don't we compromise?" Gavin suggested.

"How?"

"Since we're both on vacation, we can share Terry."

"I'll agree. But he stays with me until he's fully recovered."

He extended a hand. "You've got yourself a deal."

It couldn't have worked out better for Gavin than if he'd planned it in advance. Hanging out with Celia Thomas would provide the perfect cover when he became the typical tourist, touring the area and asking questions.

Celia offered Gavin her brilliant dimpled smile when she took his hand. Slowly, seductively, his gaze moved from her parted lips to her throat and still lower to her chest before reversing direction. She tried to ignore the eddying sensations racing along her nerve endings. She didn't know who Gavin Faulkner was, or what he did for a living, yet she'd agreed to share a stray puppy with him.

"Deal."

Gavin released her soft, delicate hand. "I'll come by

and pick you up at ten." Turning on his heels, he made his way out the mudroom.

"Gavin?"

He stopped. "Yes."

"Leave the puppy."

"Oops," he said, hiding a grin. "He's so light I forgot I was holding him." Celia extended her arms and he handed her the sedated dog. Taking a step, he angled his head and brushed his lips over her cheek. "Kiss Terry for me when he wakes up."

Celia experienced a jolt of awareness from the press of his mouth on her face. She followed him as he walked through the kitchen, living room and dining area and to the door. She stood in the doorway, staring into the encroaching darkness as nightfall descended on the mountain like someone pulling down a gossamer, navy-blue curtain. She stood in the same spot, staring at the red taillights of Gavin's vehicle until he disappeared from her line of sight.

Celia found Gavin so compelling, his virility so forceful that he reminded her of what she'd missed—had been missing—for nearly a year.

She wanted a man, but more than that she needed a man to make her feel alive, desirable. She'd joked with her brother about taking a lover for the summer. After meeting Gavin Faulkner, the joke was upgraded to a notion. Besides, she mused, she could do a whole lot worse than the hunky stranger who cooked and had a soft spot for dogs.

Chapter 4

Gavin supported his back against the headboard of the bed in the master bedroom. He'd enjoyed hanging out at this house overlooking a picturesque valley. His temporary residence was a far cry from hotel decor that failed to vary much from one chain to another regardless of the upgrade.

Scrolling through his cell-phone directory, he punched in a secure number, grinning when he heard a familiar voice come through the earpiece. The analyst had the sultriest voice of any woman he'd encountered. Now that he heard it again, there was something in its timbre that reminded him of Celia Thomas's voice. There was just enough of a drawl in Celia's cadence to garner his complete attention whenever she spoke.

"Good evening, Vera. When did you switch to nights?"

"I put in the request several months ago when Peter

was reassigned to forensics. There's no way we can afford to leave two teenage boys unsupervised for long periods of time. The last time Peter and I worked days they almost burned the house down. I know you didn't call to get an overview of my home life, Gavin. What's up?"

"I need you to run a Florida plate for me." He gave Vera Celia's license plate number.

"How much do you want to know about her?"

"Everything from the day she was born."

"Let me call you back, Gavin."

"I'll be here." Pressing a button, he ended the call. Gavin knew he could count on Vera Sanchez to come up with the information he needed on Celia Cole-Thomas. If he was going to connect with her on a more personal level, then he wanted to know what to expect.

She'd told him that she was a doctor—that was verified by her surgical skills. She'd also said that she was on vacation. He wanted to know where she lived in Florida, her family connections, whether she'd been married, had children and if she'd ever been arrested.

Crossing bare feet at the ankles, Gavin stared at the image of the news anchor on the flat-screen television on the opposite wall. He picked up the remote device and began channel surfing. The late-night news was over, so he had his pick of reruns, movies and infomercials.

When he spoke to Mac, he would thank his supervisor for putting him up in a place and permitting him access to cable television. He found a channel airing a movie about Nelson Mandela and the South African prison official who'd befriended him during his twenty-seven year imprisonment for his opposition to apartheid.

Halfway into the film, Gavin's cell phone rang and he was loath to answer it. However, he knew he had to take the call. "Faulkner," he said by way of identifying himself. His cell phone was programmed with voice recognition. If he lost or misplaced his phone and someone attempted to use it, then it would be rendered inoperable within seconds.

"Dr. Celia Cole-Thomas has a very interesting life," Vera began.

Gavin listened, stunned by the information Vera had come up with on the woman. "Thank you, Vera. You're invaluable."

"Always glad to help. Be safe, Gavin."

"Always, Vera, always."

He hung up and closed his eyes. He'd never been shot or wounded when he'd served as an Army Ranger or during his tenure as a special agent with the Bureau. But on the other hand, Celia—who'd taken an oath to protect life—had nearly lost hers during a street-gang shootout in a hospital's E.R., where she'd become an eyewitness to murder.

She'd said that she was on vacation, but what Dr. Thomas hadn't said was that her vacation was also an extended medical leave.

Gavin wondered if the reason she hadn't returned to the hospital was because she'd been traumatized by the murders, or because she was still mourning the shooting death of her fiancé.

Forcing his attention back to the film, he temporarily pushed all thoughts of the woman with the dimpled smile and sexy voice to the recesses of his mind.

Celia heard whining and opened her eyes. She sat up and scrambled off the bed. Terry was sitting up in the makeshift bed she'd fashioned from a wicker laundry basket and a pillow. After making certain he'd recovered from the effects of the sedative, she'd driven to a twenty-four-hour Walmart to pick up puppy food and supplies.

Kneeling, she picked up the puppy. He'd soiled the wee-wee pad. "Good morning, baby boy," she crooned softly. "How are you feeling?" Celia was greeted with a yawn. "Are you still sleepy from the drug?" Terry had become her first non-human patient.

Cradling Terry to her chest, she walked to the French doors, punched in the code on the security keypad on the wall and opened the doors leading out to the deck. She placed Terry on the flagstone surface and returned to the bedroom.

Celia made a mental list of the items she had to purchase from a pet store: bed, crate, lead and harness. She wouldn't trust the terrier to have the run of the house until he was housebroken.

She wasn't certain whether Terry would eat, but she knew he had to get some nutrition or he wouldn't survive. She removed the pad, returned him to the basket, carrying it down the staircase and placing it in a corner between the kitchen and pantry. The puppy's nose twitched as he surveyed his surroundings.

Sitting on the floor, she attempted to hand-feed the puppy when he sniffed the bowl containing a small amount of dry food. He'd walked away, taking furtive steps. It took Celia forty minutes to coax the dog to eat five pieces of kibble. She was more successful getting him to drink water before settling him on her lap where he curled himself into a ball.

She traced the tan spots with her fingertips. "Don't get too used to me feeding you, little prince. Once you're healed, either you'll eat by yourself or you'll go hungry." Terry opened his eyes, staring at her as if he understood what she'd said. Celia sat holding the puppy until it fell asleep, then placed it in the basket and went upstairs to ready herself before Gavin arrived.

Celia patted the moisture from her body with a thick, thirsty towel, and then went through her morning ritual of applying a moisturizer to her face and perfumed cream to her body. She'd just slipped into her underwear when the telephone rang. It was a rare occasion when the house phone rang. Her family and close friends usually called her cell.

Smiling, she lifted the receiver from its cradle when she saw the caller ID. "Good morning, Hannah."

"Good morning, Celia. I'm sorry to call so early, but I forgot to ask you yesterday if you were going to Florida for the Memorial Day weekend."

Celia sat on a chair in the bedroom's dressing area. She'd stopped the day before to visit the woman who'd welcomed her with a pan of scrumptious lasagna and an apple pie the day she'd taken possession of the house.

Hannah Walsh, who'd been a newlywed, had just celebrated the publication of the first book she'd illustrated, and Celia made certain to buy copies for every one of her young cousins. Hannah had taught daycare, and her husband worked night security at a department store while attending classes to earn a criminal justice degree. Five years later, Daniel became a North Carolina state trooper and a father for the first time within the same week.

"No. I've decided to hang out here for a while. I'm not certain when I'm going back."

"If that's the case, then I want to invite you over for a Saturday afternoon barbecue. Please tell me you'll come."

"Of course I'll come. Do you want me to bring anything?"

"No. We have everything. I just want to warn you that Daniel has invited some of his single buddies and now that they know you're available, you may get more attention than you want."

Celia smothered a groan. She was more than familiar with Daniel Walsh's buddies. They were overly friendly, good-natured and quite vociferous after imbibing one too many beers. She didn't know if Gavin had plans for the weekend, but if she invited him to go with her, then he would become her buffer.

"Would you mind if I bring a guest?"

"Of course I don't mind. The more the merrier. I'm going to have as much fun as I can before the baby comes. Having to care for a newborn while dealing with a two-year-old and balancing a career will definitely test my patience *and* my sanity."

"You'll do just fine, Hannah, only because you're the most organized person I've ever met."

"Don't you mean obsessive-compulsive?"

"That, too," Celia teased. "What time should I come?"

"I'm telling everyone to come around two."

"I'll see you Saturday at two." She hung up and glanced at the clock on the fireplace mantel. It was nine-forty. She had to get dressed and be ready to leave by ten.

"Is there something wrong, Gavin?"

Gavin blinked as if coming out of a trance. Celia Cole-Thomas was a chameleon. Each time he saw her she looked different. This morning, she'd brushed her hair off her face and secured it in a twist on the nape of her long, slender neck. A white linen blouse, black tailored slacks and a pair of ballet-type patent leather flats bespoke simple elegance. The pearl studs in her ears matched the single strand around her neck, while a light cover of makeup accentuated her large eyes and lush mouth.

"No," he admitted. "You look—wonderful." He'd said wonderful when he'd wanted to tell Celia that she looked beautiful. He took a step, pressing a kiss to her cheek. "And you smell delicious."

A flush heated her face. Celia wanted to tell Gavin he looked and smelled delicious, too. The aftershave on his clean-shaven jaw was the perfect complement for his body's natural masculine scent.

"Thank you. Please come in."

Gavin stepped into the entryway, his penetrating gaze cataloguing the furnishings. The night before, he'd been too involved with helping Celia with Terry to take note of anything.

"How's Terry?" he asked, following Celia into the living room of the split-level house. The fireplace was the room's focal point, competing only with the arch in the ceiling paneled with fir and illuminated with concealed strip lighting. The walls, covered with a coffee-colored fabric, complemented varying shades of cream and tan suede and leather on a club chair, love seat and sofa.

Celia smiled at Gavin over her shoulder. "Come and see for yourself."

Slowing, he glanced around the dining area, mapped out by a border of cherry inlay in the oak flooring.

Sunlight coming in through oak-framed French doors spilled over the gleaming waxed floor. A bouquet of yellow and white spring blooms on a cherrywood table added a homey touch.

An island separated the open kitchen—with stainless-steel appliances—and the dining room; the ceiling styles in the two spaces were as varied and intricate as the one in the living room. The ceiling was flat over the kitchen with recessed lighting, while it was pitched over the dining area. Glass inserts in the kitchen cabinets came to the same roof-like peak as the cathedral ceiling over the dining table.

The abundance of wood imbued a sense of warmth and hominess. A cushioned sitting area—reminiscent of a window seat—under a row of windows was the perfect spot to sit, read or survey the activity in the kitchen and dining area at the same time.

"Do you own this house, or are you renting it?" Gavin had asked a question to which he knew the answer.

"I own it."

"How long have you lived here?" He'd asked yet another question to which he knew the answer.

Celia stopped, turned and stared up the man who made her feel something she didn't want to feel: desire. Although she'd found herself in love with Yale and planned to marry him, he never evoked the all-consuming desire she felt whenever she and Gavin Faulkner occupied the same space.

The tall man standing in the middle of her kitchen wearing jeans, a navy blue golf shirt with a familiar designer's logo over his heart and a pair of low-heeled boots gave off waves of sensuality that threatened to smother her with its intensity. He'd removed the stubble, and the strong line of his lean jaw made him even more attractive.

"I don't live here year-round."

"You live in Florida." The query was a statement. "Your truck has Florida plates," Gavin explained when her eyes grew wider.

"Miami," Celia confirmed. She'd given Miami the Spanish inflection, it sounding like *Me-a-me.*

Gavin smiled. "You speak Spanish?"

Celia's smile matched his. "*Sí.* I have Cuban roots that go back to my great-grandmother."

"Every time I go to Miami I put on at least five pounds because I can't stop eating the food," he admitted.

"Maybe I'm biased, but I believe Caribbean cuisine is superior to any other in the world."

Gavin's expression changed, vertical lines appearing between his eyes when he gave her a level frown. "I wouldn't exactly say that," he countered.

"Tell me what's better than Caribbean cuisine, Gavin?"

He registered the slight reproach in her tone. "Southern cooking. Have you ever had North Carolina-style barbecue pulled pork?"

"No. But I bet it's not as good as—"

"Don't say it, Celia," he said, holding up a hand and interrupting her. "We'll have a cook-off, and you can prepare your best Cuban dish while I'll make the pulled pork."

Celia's eyes narrowed as she considered his challenge. "Bring it, brother."

Gavin winked. "You just don't know what you're in for, beautiful. I hope you're not a sore loser."

Celia returned the wink. "I wouldn't know because I've never lost a challenge. Speaking of barbecue, my neighbor invited me to her house on Saturday to celebrate the holiday. If you're not doing anything, I'd like you to come with me."

Crossing muscular arms over his chest, Gavin angled his head. "Are you asking me out on a date?"

Celia bit her lip, dimples deepening with the gesture as a flush suffused her face. Her embarrassment was short-lived. "What's the matter? You've never been asked out by a woman?"

"I've been propositioned a few times, but I've never been asked out."

"Well, don't look for me to proposition you, Mr. Faulkner. If you're not coming with me, then please let me know so—"

"The answer is yes, Miss Thomas." Gavin agreeing to go with Celia had nothing to do with his mission. He'd agreed because he wanted to spend time with her. Accompanying her would also permit him to pick up bits of gossip from the area residents. "May I ask one question?"

"Sure."

"Why did you ask me and not some other guy?"

There came another pause as Celia pondered his query. "I asked you because I don't want to be bothered with some *other* guy."

Gavin's expressive eyebrows lifted a fraction. "So, you want to *use* me to run interference?"

"Yes."

He shook his head. "Damn, Doc, you really know how to bruise a dude's ego."

Celia rolled her eyes upward. "My heart bleeds for you, Gavin. I'm willing to bet a year's salary that every second there are at least a hundred *dudes* somewhere in the world using women for their own selfish reasons."

Gavin sobered. "I've never used a woman."

"Maybe not you, but I've been a victim on a few occasions."

"Do you like…men?" he asked hesitantly.

"Of course I like men. I was engaged…" Celia's words trailed off before she could tell Gavin about the ordeal that left her with visible *and* invisible scars.

"What happened, Celia?"

She shook her head. "I don't want to talk about it."

"You don't want to or you can't?"

"Both," she confirmed. "Not right now." She glanced at her watch. "I think we'd better get going or Terry's going to be late for his appointment."

Terry began whining when he saw her, his tail moving like a pendulum. "Look at you, baby boy." Leaning over, she picked him up. "You're almost good as new." Turning him around, she stared at his side. "I take that back."

Gavin moved closer. "What's the matter?"

"He's biting the stitches. He's going to need one of those plastic collars." Celia wrapped Terry in a towel, handed him off to Gavin while she locked up the house.

"I'll drive," Gavin said, opening the passenger-side door to his vehicle. He handed her the puppy. Placing his hands around her waist, he lifted her and Terry effortlessly and settled her on the seat.

"Show-off," Celia teased.

Gavin ignored the taunt. Picking her up was like lifting a child. His fingers had spanned her waist with room to spare. Either Celia Cole-Thomas was naturally thin or anorexic. He'd hoped it was the former.

Rounding the vehicle, he slid in beside her and started the engine. "Give me the address to the hospital and I'll program it into the GPS." There were less than thirty miles between Waynesville and Asheville, and barring traffic delays they would arrive within half an hour.

Belted in, Celia settled back to enjoy the passing landscape. She didn't want to think about the man sitting less than a foot away. She'd asked a man, a stranger, to accompany her to a friend's get-together. What made it so incredible was that she knew nothing about him beyond his name. If they were to present themselves as a couple, then she needed to know more.

"What do you do for a living?"

"I'm in personal security." The lie rolled off Gavin's tongue as smoothly as honey. It was a lie he'd told so often that he could repeat it even if he'd been injected with a truth serum.

Celia turned to stare at his strong profile. "What's the difference between regular security and personal security?"

"People hire me to protect their person."

"Rich people?" she asked.

Gavin nodded. "Have you seen the film *Man on Fire* with Denzel Washington?"

"Yes."

"Well, I'm Jon Creasy without being the hard-drinking, burned-out CIA operative."

Celia sat up straighter. "Are you armed now?"

Gavin stared out behind the lenses of his sunglasses. He knew he had to tell Celia the truth because he was mandated to carry a firearm while working a case.

"Yes." He gave her a quick glance. "Does that bother you?"

A nervous smile trembled around her mouth. "No. My brothers, uncles and most of my male cousins learned to handle a gun in their teens."

Staring into a firearm pointed at her and then watching Yale fall with blood soaking the shirt of his scrubs bothered her; seeing her patient shot at point-blank range bothered her and continued to bother whenever she relived the scene in her dreams.

"Have you ever fired a gun?"

Celia focused her gaze on the road. "Yes. It was at a firing range. My father claimed I needed to learn to handle a firearm because I'd never know when I'd have to defend myself. What he didn't know and still doesn't know is that I favor legislation for gun control."

"I take it you don't believe in the Second Amendment."

"I believe in law-abiding citizens' right to own weapons, but should criminals have the same right?"

"Criminals don't care about the law one way or the other, Celia. They live by their own code, and at times administer their own form of justice."

You're preaching to the choir, Gavin, Celia mused. "Who do you work for?" she asked, deftly changing the topic of conversation.

"My cousins. The main office is in Charlotte." Gavin's cousins did own and operate a security company in Charlotte, and at any given time would verify that he worked for them.

"Who have you protected?"

"I can't tell you names because we're bound by a confidentiality ruling that we would never divulge the identities of our clients. What I will tell you is that I've guarded the children of actors, sports figures, entertainers and an occasional business mogul."

"Why did you choose such a dangerous profession?"

Gavin signaled, maneuvering off Route 74 toward Interstate 40 and Asheville. "It was either security or law enforcement. I make a lot more money providing personal security, my assignments are flexible and I get to travel all over the world on someone else's expense. That's something I'd never be able to do as a police officer. Why did you decide to go into medicine?" he asked, smoothly directing the focus away from him.

Celia's head came around and she stared at him. "Why don't you want to talk about yourself?"

Gavin's fingers tightened on the steering wheel. "I just answered all of your questions, Celia."

"Not all of them."

He gave her a sidelong glance. "What else do you *need* to know?"

"Were you ever married?"

"No," he answered honestly.

"How old are you, Gavin?"

He chuckled softly. "Now, if I'd asked you your age you would've told me to mind my own damn business."

"No, I wouldn't."

"Okay. How old are you, Celia?"

"I'll turn thirty-four in August."

Gavin's gaze shifted to the lighted GPS screen. They were less than ten miles from the animal hospital. "I thought you were younger. I'm thirty-seven."

"Do you like women?"

His deathlike grip on the wheel tightened. "Hell, yeah, I like women. Why would you ask me that?"

"Unmarried at thirty-seven. I was just checking." Celia averted her head so he wouldn't see her smile.

Gavin relaxed his grip, realizing Celia was just testing him when he saw her shoulders move. So, he mused, the doctor did have a sense of humor. She'd been sharp-tongued and all business when she'd shouted orders at him the night before.

"You think I'm gay?"

"No, Gavin. The thought never crossed my mind."

"And if I was?"

"I'd still want you to be my date for Saturday. Someone's sexual proclivity has no bearing on me. Once consenting adults close the door to the bedroom they can do whatever they want."

Gavin's opinion of Celia went up appreciably. She was pretty, smart and open-minded. His role as an undercover agent left little or no time for a normal relationship with a woman. The few long-term relationships he'd had usually ended when he wasn't willing to take it to a level that included marriage and children. He'd submitted a request for a desk position, and if or when it was approved he would consider marrying and starting a family.

"Do you like men?" he asked.

The seconds ticked as Celia stared through the windshield. "Yes, I do. Why?"

Resting his right arm over the back of her seat, Gavin ran his fingers over the nape of her neck. "Just checking."

He wasn't disappointed when she turned to smile at him, neither aware of the invisible web of awareness making them willing captives.

Chapter 5

Reaching for Celia's hand, Gavin held it protectively in his strong grasp as he led her across the animal hospital's parking lot. Her brow had knitted in consternation when the veterinarian who'd examined Terry recommended keeping the terrier for at least three days. He'd complimented Celia's surgical skills and reassured her that Terry's chances of survival were very good. The canine's treatment plan included pain management and IV feeding.

Leaning down from his superior height, Gavin pressed his mouth to her ear. "I thought we were going to share Terry."

Celia shivered slightly from his moist breath. "We are."

"That's not possible when you registered him as Terry Thomas, not Terry Thomas-Faulkner."

She didn't know whether to sucker punch Gavin or

laugh for his teasing her. She did the latter. "You know you're a little crazy."

"I'm serious, Celia."

"What are you going to do with a dog when you're off protecting the world's powerful elite?"

"The same could be said for you when you're practicing medicine."

"But I'm not practicing medicine. I'm on leave, and *if* or when I return I'll have someone take care of him."

Slowing his stride to accommodate Celia's shorter legs, Gavin dropped her hand and wrapped an arm around her waist. He felt a modicum of guilt because he knew facts about Celia she'd probably forgotten or wasn't aware of.

He wondered whether she knew that her late fiancé had fathered a son at seventeen. The baby's mother had given him up for adoption. Trevor-Jones had another secret. Although he'd been caught cheating in high school, his family's name, money and clout got the charge expunged from his permanent records.

Gavin didn't know whether Celia's decision not to practice medicine was because she was still grieving the loss of her fiancé or because she'd feared a repeat of an episode that almost cost her her own life.

"Why aren't you practicing?" She stopped abruptly, causing him to stumble but he quickly regained his balance.

Celia stared up at Gavin. Wearing flats put her at a distinct disadvantage. Standing close to five-ten in her bare feet, whenever she wore heels not many men towered over her.

"I don't want to talk about it."

"I'm sorry for prying." Gavin actually hadn't expected her to disclose any facts about her personal life.

"It's not about prying, but me not wanting to, as they say, spill my guts to a stranger."

Putting both his arms around her waist, Gavin pulled Celia to his chest. "After a couple of dates we should stop being strangers."

She lifted her chin. "Who said anything about a couple of dates? After Saturday's cookout we may never see each other again."

"How soon you forget, lady doctor. You promised to share Terry with me and there's still our cook-off challenge."

Lids lowering, lashes brushing the tops of her cheeks, Celia was able to conceal the rush of excitement eddying through her body. She'd boldly asked Gavin to go to Hannah's with her, something she'd never done with any other man, but she didn't want to be presumptuous and assume he wanted to see her again. After all, he'd come to the mountains on vacation, not to become involved with a woman.

"How long is your vacation?"

Gavin pressed a kiss to Celia's forehead when what he'd wanted was to taste her mouth. Her mouth and voice were the personification of sensuality.

"It's as long as I want it to be," he said after a comfortable pause. "I'm leasing a time-share. I plan to stay through the Labor Day weekend."

Her eyes caught and held his amused gaze. "You're kidding, aren't you?"

Attractive lines fanned out around Gavin's eyes when he smiled. "No, I'm not. I just finished a job where I spent two months traveling with a businessman and his family throughout Europe and Asia. Once I returned to the States it took a week to balance my body's circadian rhythm and even longer to readjust my taste buds. Speaking of taste buds," he said without pausing to take a breath, "how about sharing lunch with me?"

Her smile was as intimate as a kiss. "I'd love to share lunch with you."

Tightening his hold on her slender body, Gavin tucked Celia into the hard planes of his physique. Holding her, inhaling her feminine scent made him aware that she wasn't skinny, but slender. Her womanly curves fit perfectly within the contours of his length.

"What do you feel like eating?"

Celia closed her eyes, melting against the man who reminded her why she'd been born female. A rush of craving, longing and trembling she'd never known held her in a vise-like grip, refusing to release her.

He looks so good.

He smells so good.

He feels so good.

And I need him to make me feel good—to help me to heal inside and out.

Hot tears pricked the backs of Celia's eyelids with the silent entreaty. She'd spent the past year wallowing in fear and grief. As a doctor she'd come face-to-face with life and death on what had become a daily basis. She'd called the time of death on patients ranging from newborns to centenarians, and it was never easy. She was a scientist *and* a realist. It was inevitable that life was always followed by death.

What she never would've anticipated was that her own life could've possibly been ended by a teenage boy who had resorted to murder because of a frivolous boast.

Gavin eased back, staring at the woman in his embrace. "Are you all right, baby?" The endearment had slipped out unbidden.

Celia nodded, smiling. "I'm real good," she admitted. And she was. Being cradled in Gavin's arms made her feel as if she'd been frozen, locked away in a state of suspended animation for the past year, and now she was finally thawing out. "There's a restaurant called Carmel's on Page and Battery Park. They have good food and alfresco dining."

"Let's do it. You're going to have to show me how to get there."

Glancing at his watch, Gavin noted the time. It was almost one. He'd suggested lunch because he'd only drunk two cups of coffee earlier that morning. Most of his time was spent on the computer, reading updates from a secure government site in order to gather information as to the whereabouts of Raymond Prentice.

It was as if his brother had literally dropped off the planet. Meanwhile, the band of gun thieves had successfully pulled off two more robberies—one in Arkansas and the other in Oklahoma. What Gavin found puzzling was the speed at which they'd traveled from one state to another. They'd robbed a shop in Jonesboro, Arkansas and three hours later they hit another dealer near Lawton, Oklahoma, only miles from the Fort Sill Military Reservation.

An ATF memo indicated the gang's major focus was on U.S. law enforcement dealers. Another memorandum was circulated to dealers, warning them to be vigilant and to alert their local law enforcement of individuals who appeared to be window-shopping instead of purchasing firearms.

The latest information from the inside informant was

that a member of the group, a former Army sniper, was left behind to search out and execute Raymond Prentice. Gavin knew it would be a race against time to find his brother before the sniper.

Celia and Gavin decided to wait for a table outside the restaurant because they wanted to take in the sights of downtown Asheville while enjoying the balmy spring weather. Once they were seated she ordered smoked turkey breast, Swiss cheese and a cranberry-horseradish mayonnaise on sourdough bread.

Gavin had selected a crab cake sandwich with ré-moulade sauce, romaine, tomato and red onion on a Kaiser roll. He'd also ordered a half carafe of white wine to accompany their lunch, and after a glass, Celia felt completely relaxed.

"I can't remember ever drinking wine with a sand-wich," she said, smiling.

Gavin stared across the table at his dining partner. There was something about her bearing and body language that called to mind the graceful movements of a prima ballerina.

"Haven't you had wine with bread, cheese and salad?"

Celia nodded. "Yes."

"We ordered dishes with lettuce, tomato, cheese and bread, so drinking wine is permissible."

"Do you like traveling?"

Her question was so unexpected that it gave Gavin pause. "Yes and no."

Propping her elbow on the table, Celia rested her chin on her fist. "Why yes and no?"

His lids came down, hiding his innermost thoughts from her. He didn't like lying to Celia, but he couldn't afford to be forthcoming because it would reveal his identity and his mission.

"It's always nice to visit a country where I'd never been. The downside is I find myself getting homesick." He glanced up at her. "And I get homesick for the worst things."

"Like what?"

"Hamburgers, franks, deep-dish pizza and Southern fried chicken."

Celia's eyebrows lifted. "What about North Carolina pulled pork?"

"That, too," he crooned as a dreamy expression came over his face. "Have you done a lot of traveling?"

"I used to when I was a young girl. My dad would take me with him on business trips to Belize, Mexico, Jamaica and Puerto Rico. Once I entered high school, academics became a priority for me. I knew I wanted to become a doctor, so all of my spare time was spent studying. I have a few doctors in the family, so they would give me study tips for the MCAT. Thanks to them I scored in the top one percent."

"Where did you go to medical school? No, I take that back. What schools did you apply to that accepted you?"

Lowering her arm, Celia dabbed her mouth with a napkin. "I applied to all the Ivy League schools. The others were Johns Hopkins, Howard and Meharry. I was accepted into most of them, but decided on Meharry."

"Why Meharry?" Gavin asked.

A mysterious smile softened her parted lips. "I fell in love with this part of the country. The first time I drove through the Great Smoky Mountains I felt as if I'd stepped back in time, and I made a promise to myself that once I became a doctor I would buy property here."

"Do you keep all of your promises?" he teased.

"Maybe not to myself, but if I promise someone else something, I do everything within my power to keep it."

Leaning over the table, Gavin gave Celia a long, penetrating stare. "Will you promise…"

"Promise what, Gavin?"

A deafening silence swallowed them in a cocoon of anticipation where they were able to shut out everything and everyone around them. The seconds ticked as a slow smile parted Gavin's firm lips. "I want you to promise me that we'll be civil when it comes to Terry."

Slumping back in her chair, Celia's expression registered disbelief. She'd thought what he'd wanted to propose had something to do with them, not the dog. Perhaps, deep down inside she wanted it to be different—that she'd met Gavin under another set of circumstances.

She also wasn't oblivious to the admiring glances women diners directed at Gavin. Celia wanted to tell them they could look, but he was going home with her. Her fingers tightened around the stem of her wineglass. Now, where had that thought come from? She, who'd professed not to have a jealous bone in her body, was suddenly struck by the green-eyed monster.

"I promise." She placed her hand over her wineglass when Gavin attempted to refill it. "Please. No more."

His hand halted. "You only had one glass."

"One glass is my limit."

Gavin leaned over the table. "What happens after the second glass?"

Celia also leaned closer. "I lose my inhibitions."

"No!"

"Yes-s-s," she slurred. "My tongue doesn't work well after one glass."

Reaching over the table, Gavin took her hands in his. "I promise not to take advantage of you if you do drink that second glass."

I wouldn't care if you did, she mused. Easing her right hand from his loose grip, Celia traced the rim of the wineglass with her forefinger. "I trust you to keep your word," she lied.

Gavin's gaze moved from Celia's face to her chest. He could discern the lace on her bra under her blouse. The flesh between his thighs stirred when he recalled the press of her firm breasts against his chest. He wanted Celia Cole-Thomas in his bed, he between her legs and his hardened flesh buried so deep inside her they wouldn't know where one began and the other ended.

"Are you an only child?" He had to say something, anything to take his mind off the solid bulge in his jeans.

Celia smiled. "No. I'm the dreaded middle child. I have an older and younger brother."

"Being the only girl should've made it easier for you."

"Wrong, Gavin. Being the only girl isn't what it's cracked up to be when you're a Cole."

Gavin forced back a smile. He hadn't realized how much he wanted Celia to open up to him. "Is there something special about being a Cole?"

"Very, very special. Have you ever heard of ColeDiz International, Limited?"

A beat passed as he pretended to search his memory. "No. Why?"

"ColeDiz is the biggest family-owned agribusiness in the United States."

"Will I be able to look it up on the Internet?"

Celia nodded. "You can, but chances are you won't find much information because it's privately owned.

There was a time when most of the top positions were relegated only to those with Cole blood, but my father changed that. Now, only the CEO is mandated to be a direct descendant of Samuel Claridge Cole."

"Who is Samuel?"

"He *was* my great-grandfather. The male members of the family are encouraged to join the family business, while the girls can choose any profession."

"Who's the CEO?"

"My older brother, Diego."

For a moment, Gavin studied Celia intently. "Is your younger brother involved in the family business?"

She shook her head. "Nicky wants nothing to do with growing and exporting coffee, bananas and cotton. He bought a horse farm in Virginia, and spent millions on horseflesh to improve the bloodlines. He struck gold last year when one of his Thoroughbreds came in first in the International Gold Cup race. My brother did something I thought was very strange. He announced that he was retiring New Freedom and putting him out to stud."

Gavin touched a napkin to the corners of his mouth. "That's a smart move. He can offset his expenses with what he can collect in stud fees."

"That's what he said."

"It looks as if your younger brother has found his niche. I…" Whatever Gavin was going to say was pre-empted when his cell phone rang. Removing it from his waistband, he stared at the caller's name. Pushing back his chair, he came to his feet. "Excuse me, but I have to take this call.

"Faulkner," he said softly, identifying himself as he walked over to where he couldn't be overheard. Gavin felt a knot in the pit of his stomach. "Did you find Ray?"

"No. I don't know how he did it, but he got word to the North Carolina field office that he's not coming in until he feels it's safe to surface. And, he's only going to turn himself in to you."

"Weren't you able to trace the call?"

"Yeah. It originated somewhere near the Cascades."

"How did he get to Oregon?"

"That's the million-dollar question. By the time we'd dispatched agents from Portland, Salem and Eugene, there was no trace of him. We don't know how long it's going to take him to crisscross the country undetected, but if we have to wait six months, then so be it."

"The next time he contacts anyone, tell him to call me."

"That's not going to happen, Faulkner. One thing the Bureau doesn't want is for anyone to make the connection between the two of you. Stay put and Prentice will contact you."

Without warning, the line went dead. Instead of going out to look for Raymond Prentice, he would wait for him to come to him.

His jaw tightened when he clenched his teeth. He was hoping his brother didn't view his predicament as a recon mission, playing cat and mouse with a group of ruthless men who viewed him as a traitor. However, Ray Prentice had an advantage the others didn't: Navy SEAL training.

Securing the cell phone to his waistband, Gavin returned to sit opposite Celia. Smiling, he stared at her as if seeing her for the first time. Celia Cole-Thomas was sexy, and he suspected she was totally unaware of how sexy she was. Wisps of black hair had escaped the twist on the nape of her neck. His gaze lingered on her full lower lip before moving up to the large dark eyes that reminded him of a velvet midnight sky.

He'd been ordered to wait in Waynesville for the man who topped the FBI Most Wanted list to contact him, and interacting with the beautiful doctor was certain to make his stay quite enjoyable.

"What are you smiling about?"

Her dulcet voice caressed his ear. "I just got some good news," he half lied. "My next assignment has been postponed to the end of the summer, and that means I get to have an extended vacation to hang out with Terry and Terry's mama just a wee bit longer."

"Why do I get the impression that you're a wee bit smug about slacking off?"

"And you're not, Dr. Thomas? I mean slacking off?"

Sudden anger lit Celia's eyes. She'd told Gavin that she didn't want to talk about why she wasn't practicing, but he'd insisted when he'd refused to disclose the names of the celebrities and high-profile personalities he'd protected.

Raising her hand, she signaled for their waiter. "I'll take the check, please."

Rising slightly, Gavin reached into the pocket of his jeans for a money clip. "I'm paying." The two words were barely off his tongue when Celia gave the waiter a large bill.

"Keep the change."

The young man was all smiles. "Thank you, Miss."

Gavin stood up, reaching for her arm, but she was too quick, pulling away and walking to where he'd parked his truck. He managed to catch up with her at the corner. This time when he reached for her arm, he tightened his grip, not permitting her to escape him.

"If you ever do that again I'll…"

Celia rounded on him. "You'll do what, Gavin?"

They'd engaged in a stare down that would only end in a stalemate.

"I'll think of something by the time I get you home."

"Bully tactics don't work with me. Remember, I grew up with two brothers and I can roll with the best of them."

Escorting her across the street, Gavin clamped his teeth together to keep from saying something that would jeopardize his fragile friendship with a woman who unknowingly had seduced him by their occupying the same space.

She hadn't indicated she was remotely interested in him, yet he felt something intangible that made him want to get to know her in the most intimate way conceivable.

He'd been forthcoming when he told Celia he liked women. He enjoyed their company and he enjoyed sleeping with them. However, he didn't sleep with every woman he dated because he hadn't wanted to use them just for sex. With those he hadn't slept with he'd managed to maintain an ongoing friendship.

His feelings for Celia bordered on ambivalence. He liked her, yet didn't want to like her too much, because when he returned to his apartment in northern Virginia to await his next assignment, he didn't want to have to wrestle with emotional baggage.

The return trip to Waynesville was accomplished in complete silence—Celia staring out the side window while Gavin concentrated on the road ahead of him. He maneuvered off the county road and onto the local one leading to Celia's house.

He didn't turn off the engine when he got out and came around to assist her. His hands went around her waist and he lifted her off the seat, holding her aloft.

Two pairs of dark eyes fused, warring, neither wanting to give the other quarter.

"Put me down," Celia ordered through clenched teeth.

Pulling her closer, Gavin complied, their bodies pressed together. Then, without warning, his head came down and he slanted his mouth over hers. He knew he'd shocked Celia when her lips parted, giving him the access needed to take full possession of her mouth.

His tongue dueled with hers until he caught the tip between his teeth, sucking softly. She stopped struggling and melted against him when he released her tongue and simulated making love to her. His right hand came down and cupped her hips so she could feel the hardness straining against his fly.

Celia felt pinpoints of heat prick her face, breasts and the area between her legs. Curving her arms under Gavin's shoulders, she held on to him as if she feared being swept away in a maelstrom of longing where she would never surface again.

Gavin took a step, pressing Celia against the bumper of the truck. Banked passion flared to life as he ground his crotch against hers. Mouths joined, he lifted her to sit on the bumper, he moving to stand between her knees. He'd fulfilled two of his wishes. He'd tasted her mouth, was between her legs, but hadn't joined his body to hers.

Celia had felt dead, empty inside until now. She wanted and needed Gavin to make love to her but common sense returned to shake her into an awareness of what Gavin was doing and what she was permitting him to do.

"No, Gavin. We can't."

Celia's entreaty penetrated the thick fog of passion cloaking Gavin's mind. His head came up, and he stared down into twin pools of black-filled shock rather than fear. He couldn't believe he'd been ready to make love to Celia on the top of a truck like an animal in heat!

He took a backward step without releasing her. His fingers tightened slightly as he eased her off the bumper until her feet touched macadam.

He was annoyed with Celia for making it look as if he were a kept man, but even more angry with himself because he'd lost control. "Don't ever insult me again by reaching into your purse or I'll kiss you again, and it won't be where no one will see us."

Celia blinked as if coming out of a trance. The laughter that began in her chest spilled over as her shoulders shook. "Do you actually believe you were punishing me because you kissed me without asking permission? You give yourself a little too much credit in the lovemaking department," she taunted. "I *let* you kiss me, Gavin."

Gavin thrust his face to within inches of hers, staring at her thoroughly kissed mouth. "You let me kiss you. But the all-important question is will you *let* me make love to you?"

Celia experienced a sense of freedom with Gavin she'd never felt with Yale. Although ten years her senior, Yale had not been very adventurous. Their lovemaking was satisfying because she always took the initiative to make it that way. If she'd left it up to Yale he would've made love to her only to procreate. She wasn't what she would call horny, but sexually deprived. She'd missed foreplay, after-play and cuddling.

"I don't know." Celia didn't know because she'd never been one to engage in gratuitous sex, and that's what it would become if she allowed Gavin to share her bed.

Leaning in closer, Gavin kissed the end of her nose. He'd felt himself a winner only because she hadn't said no. "It's all right, baby. I will never pressure you to do anything you don't want to do."

Celia winked at him. "And I promise not to pressure you into doing something you don't want to do." She kissed his cheek. "Go home, Gavin, so I can plan for our cook-off challenge."

A network of lines fanned out around Gavin's eyes when he smiled at the woman who made him feel things he didn't want to feel, made him want to do things he shouldn't do. "Is it going down at my place or yours?"

"My place, of course."

"Do you have a grill?" Celia nodded.

"I'll see you tomorrow around ten."

"Why so early?" Celia asked.

"It's going to take at least eight hours to cook my pork." Gavin reached for Celia's handbag off the console between the seats, handing it to her. "I'll wait until you're inside before I leave."

He watched her walk and waited for her to open and close the door before driving away. His plan to punish her for what he considered the ultimate insult whenever he took a woman out to eat had backfired.

Gavin knew he had to be careful—very, very careful when interacting with Celia Cole-Thomas or he would find himself in too deep.

Chapter 6

Celia stood with her back pressed against the door as the sound of the truck's engine faded in the distance. Her knees were shaking so hard she found it difficult to keep her balance.

She'd pretended not to be affected by Gavin's love-making when what she'd wanted was to mate with him—on the hood of a vehicle and out in the open where anyone could see them.

Sliding down to the floor, Celia pulled her knees to her chest and lowered her head. If she'd followed her therapist's advice, she knew she wouldn't be going through the emotional turmoil that made her do and say things that made her question her sanity.

But, she hadn't been completely honest with the therapist or herself—until now. She'd told the psychiatrist about how she'd believed she'd died, but her colleagues had brought her back to life, how the night-mares kept her awake at night and that she sat up until sunrise before attempting to go back to sleep.

A wry smile twisted her mouth at the same time a single tear trickled down her cheek. What Celia hadn't disclosed to her therapist or anyone else was that she'd blamed herself for Yale's death. He hadn't been sched-uled to work that day, but he'd switched shifts with another doctor because he'd wanted to talk to her about her pronouncement that although she wasn't ending their engagement, she'd moved out because she needed to put some space between them.

She and Yale hadn't set a date, and his constant ha-ranguing that he didn't want to wait until he was fifty to father a child had begun to annoy Celia. Whenever she reminded him of their commitment to opening the free clinic, he'd drop the topic for several weeks and then bring it up again.

Yet that last time, Yale had done something that was totally out of character for him. He'd begun crying. It was the tears and the pleading that made her agree to meet him when her shift ended. What she hadn't expected was for him to work the E.R. on his day off.

Celia had mentally beaten herself up over and over. The "what ifs" had attacked her relentlessly. What if she hadn't dated a man who was ten years older than she and too controlling? What if she hadn't agreed to move in with him when she'd had her own apartment? What if she hadn't agreed to marry him when all of her instincts told her he was so wrong for her free-spirit personality?

She knew her parents weren't happy when she'd moved in with Yale, but she was an adult and there wasn't much they could say. It hadn't been the same with her brothers. Both Diego and Nicholas complained about her *shacking up* with a man when she could afford to live on her own. Celia eventually resolved the problem when she purchased her cousin's oceanfront mansion.

Buying the property signaled a turning point in her relationship with Yale. He'd become more controlling and at times had been downright mean-spirited. Living apart from her fiancé gave her the opportunity to see another side of the man with whom she'd pledged her future. She'd loved Yale, but she hadn't been in love with him.

Now, there was her dilemma of Gavin Faulkner. The powerfully built personal bodyguard was a constant reminder of what she'd never had *and* what had been missing in her life—passion.

Swiping at her tears with her fingertips while pushing to her feet, Celia knew wallowing in self-pity wasn't going to solve any of her problems. She knew it would take time for her to come to terms with her feelings of guilt, but she didn't have a lot of time when it came to Gavin Faulkner. He was going to spend the summer in the mountains, and that meant they would be seeing each other because of their promise to share Terry.

Will it make you feel better if I take a lover for the summer to keep me company?

The question Celia had asked her brother came back in vivid clarity. She knew it wouldn't make Diego feel better, but she knew unequivocally it would make her feel much, much better than she did now.

Thinking about Gavin reminded her that she had to call the local butcher to order a boneless pork loin for her *puerco asado* cook-off challenge. Her sorority sister had turned her on to Southern cooking and her grandmother had helped her to perfect the Caribbean dishes that had been passed down through countless generations.

Retreating to the bathroom off the kitchen, Celia washed her face, touched up her makeup and took the pins out of her hair. Using a brush, she fluffed up her curls, then left to drive into town to buy what she needed to put together an authentic Cuban dish that was certain to tantalize the most discerning palate.

Celia woke to the sound of rain tapping rhythmically against the windows. Moaning softly, she turned her face into the pillow in an attempt to go back to sleep, but popped up when she remembered that Gavin was coming over.

He'd said he was going to cook his pork on a grill. That wasn't going to be possible because there was no way he could grill in the rain. "Yes!" she whispered. He would be forced to forfeit the challenge because of a rainout. Meanwhile, she only needed the oven in which to roast her pork dish.

Swinging her legs over the side of the bed, Celia walked into the en suite bath and filled the garden tub with warm water before adding a generous amount of perfumed bath salts. The night before she'd made a marinade for the boneless pork loin the butcher had trimmed and tied together as per her instructions. The aroma from the garlic and dried oregano she'd ground into paste had permeated the kitchen. She'd rubbed the paste into the meat she'd scored with the tip of a knife, then added salt and pepper. A marinade of fresh lime, orange juice and a dry red wine was poured over it, and then she covered the pan with plastic wrap. Celia had refrigerated the meat, turning it every couple of hours so it could meld with the spices.

A clock on the bathroom fireplace mantel chimed eight times. Reaching for a bath sponge, Celia squeezed a generous dollop of scented body wash on to the sponge and began washing her body. Gavin said he would come at ten, and she wanted to complete all her tasks beforehand.

Dressed in jeans, a long-sleeved pullover and running shoes, Celia cleaned up the bathroom, made her bed and had positioned a number of lemon-scented votive candles throughout the first floor to offset the lingering smell of the marinade, chiding herself for not using the exhaust fan the night before. When she'd taken the pork out of the refrigerator and uncovered it, the mouth-watering aromas wafted throughout the kitchen like a release of compressed air.

She'd slipped a single-cup disk into the coffeemaker when her cell phone and doorbell rang simultaneously. Reaching for her cell phone, she punched the talk button as she walked to the door. "Hello."

"Hello, Celia. This is your *abuela*."

She smiled. It wasn't often that Nancy Cole-Thomas called. Her grandmother expected her grandchildren to call her on a regular basis, not the other way around.

"How are you, *abuela?*" she asked.

"That's what I should be asking you, *nieta*. Didn't you promise to call me once you got to that godforsaken place where if someone attacked you no one could hear you scream, let alone find you for months?"

Peering through the security eye, Celia saw the distorted image of Gavin staring at her. She unlocked the door. "Come in."

"Who are you talking to, Celia?"

"I'm sorry, Grandma, I was just telling my friend to come inside."

"Don't you dare call me Grandma!"

Celia motioned to Gavin to take his aluminum-covered pan to the kitchen. "I'm sorry, *abuela.*"

Nancy Cole-Thomas had insisted her grandchildren learn Spanish because their mother hadn't spoken a word of the language. She'd also insisted they call her *abuela* instead of grandma, grandmother or nana. Nancy had never approved of her son marrying Nichola Bennett, and forty years later the two women barely tolerated each other.

"How are you doing, Celia?" Nancy's voice was softer, gentler.

"I'm doing well."

"Are you eating?"

Celia closed and locked the door behind Gavin, her gaze lingering on his back when he walked past her. He'd paused to wipe his shoes on the mat she'd put down to absorb dirt and moisture.

"Yes, I'm eating. Today I'm making *puerco asado* with white rice and an avocado and mango salad."

"Don't forget to make some *mojo criollo.*"

Celia's smile was dazzling. "Thank you for reminding me."

Nancy's chuckle came through the earpiece. "What's roast pork without a potent Creole garlic sauce?"

"You're right, *abuela.*" Her grandmother had just given her the pièce de résistance to win the pork challenge.

"I know you have company, so I'm not going to keep you. But, I do want you to call me to let me know you're okay. After all, you're my only granddaughter and I love you, Celia."

"I know," Celia said softly. "And I love you, too. I'll call you next week."

She ended the call and then turned to find Gavin. He was standing a few feet away. Why, she thought, hadn't she heard his approach? He hadn't shaved and the stubble shadowing his jaw made him appear dangerous. He was dressed entirely in black—baseball cap, jeans, cotton pullover and a pair of Timberland boots.

"Please don't sneak up on me like that."

"I'm sorry, but I didn't want to disturb your telephone conversation. I have to go back to the truck to get the wood chips and a few other things."

Celia rested her hands at her waist. "How are you going to grill in the rain, Gavin?"

He flashed a white-tooth grin. "I'm not. You have a double oven, so you can use one and I'll use the other." Taking a step, he lowered his head and brushed his mouth over hers. "I know what you were thinking, beautiful. You thought I was going to have to forfeit because of the weather. Think again, because yours truly is a pork meister and neither rain, sleet nor snow will keep me from making the best North Carolina-style barbecue pulled-pork sandwiches this side of the Piedmont."

Inhaling his mint-scented, moist breath, Celia pressed her mouth to his. "Is there a difference between eastern and western North Carolina pulled pork?"

Gavin went completely still. He knew if he touched Celia, that he would forget his promise not to do anything she hadn't wanted to do. Kissing her the day before had conjured up salacious thoughts that had kept him from a restful night's sleep. Each time he drifted off to sleep he woke up with an erection that made him feel as if he were coming out of his skin. Rolling over and sleeping on his belly only served as a temporary respite. He knew his craving for Celia wouldn't be assuaged until they made love.

"There's a big difference. Along the coast the sauce is a basic vinegar and red pepper, while up here in the mountains it is tomato-based and thicker."

Peering up at Gavin through her lashes, Celia tried to quell the shivers making it virtually impossible for her to draw a normal breath. The heat from his body, the potent scent of his cologne had ensnared her in a sensual web of longing that made her want to beg him to make love to her.

"Which sauce are you going to make?"

Gavin stared at the rapidly beating pulse in Celia's throat. He knew what she was feeling because he was experiencing the same—a sexual tension that bordered on hysteria. He exhaled an audible breath. His first mistake had been to approach her at the supermarket, the second was bringing the injured dog to her home and the third and final mistake was issuing a challenge in which he was certain he would get to see her again.

"Both. That way you can let me know which you like best."

Celia lowered her hands. "I just thought of something, Gavin. Don't we need a third party to judge whose pork is better?"

"No. I'll let you know if your pork is better than mine."

She flashed a sensual pout. "How can you be certain I'll be as impartial?"

A hint of a smile played at the corners of his mouth. "You're a doctor, Celia."

"What does that have to do with anything?"

"Every doctor I've ever met I found to be very

ethical. You're probably no different." Gavin winked at
her. "I'll be right back."

"Have you had breakfast?" she asked as he headed
for the door.

"No."

"It's going to be a while before we sit down to our
pork-fest, so I'll see what I can come up with to tide us
over."

"I like pancakes and waffles," Gavin said before
opening the door and walking out into the rain.

Celia wondered if he'd remembered seeing a box of
pancake mix in her shopping cart the day they'd met in
the supermarket, or he'd assumed she would have some
on hand. She also liked pancakes and waffles, but
instead of slathering them with butter and syrup she preferred topping them with fresh fruit in their own juices.

She'd returned to the kitchen and gathered what she
needed to prepare breakfast by the time Gavin walked
in, setting a large box filled with a variety of foodstuffs
on the floor. He'd removed his boots.

Staring mutely, she saw a package of hamburger
buns, a jar of dill pickles, bottles of spices, ketchup,
honey, vinegar and a large bag of wood chips.

Gavin saw the direction of her stunned gaze. "This
is for real, Celia."

"I suppose I'm really going to have to bring my A
game."

"Bring it or go home, baby," he taunted.

Crossing her arms under her breasts, she angled her
head. "Oh, it's like that?"

Gavin assumed a similar pose. "It's like that. And I'm
not going to soften the blow because you're a girl."

"What if I resort to tears?"

"Forget it, baby girl."

"What if I…" Her words trailed off when Celia realized what she was about to propose.

"What if you what?" Gavin asked.

"Forget it, Gavin."

He dropped his arms. "Oh, no, sweetheart. You have to finish what you started to say." Celia compressed her lips tightly, dimples deepening in her flawless cheeks. Smiling, Gavin raised his eyebrows as realization dawned. "I will concede right now if you'll allow me to seduce you."

Celia's jaw dropped. He'd read her mind. "That's not fair!"

"Why isn't it fair, Celia?"

"I win and you get the spoils."

"No, baby. We would both win, because I'd make certain you would enjoy making love to me as I would enjoy making love with you."

Her eyebrows lifted. "So, it would be a win-win competition."

"I'd like to believe it would be."

Pulling back her shoulders, Celia felt emotionally stronger than she had in a very long time. She was no longer the little girl who had to fight to prove her worth in a family where males dominated. She'd come to terms with being labeled a nerd because she preferred studying to hanging out with the boys who'd shown an interest in her.

She was beyond the taunting of the girls at her college when they'd discovered she sent her laundry out instead of doing it herself. And she'd realized her life-long dream to become a doctor the day she walked across the stage to receive her medical degree.

It had taken a kiss from a man—the one standing in her kitchen—to shock her into an awareness that she'd accepted less than she'd expected or deserved from a man she'd planned to spend her life with.

"I know it's going to happen," Celia said in a quiet voice. "When or where is something I don't think either of us can answer right now."

Gavin ran his fingers through the soft curls framing her face. "We've got time."

Celia rested her forehead on his shoulder. They had the summer, and when it ended she knew she wouldn't be the same woman she'd been last week, this week or even tomorrow.

Celia and Gavin worked side by side in the kitchen as if they'd choreographed their movements. She felt like an actor in a film production where food had become a character. She thought of movies like *Soul Food, Like Water for Chocolate, Tortilla Soup* and her personal favorite—*What's Cooking?*

She sliced peaches, honeydew and cantaloupe for a fruit cup and pureed berries in a food processor as toppings for the waffles, while Gavin had begun the task of filling a pan with apple-infused wood chips, which he'd soaked in water. Within half an hour the kitchen was filled with the aroma of seasoned pork and fruity wood. Celia estimated her roast pork loin would cook in three hours, whereas it would take almost twice that long for Gavin's.

Celia was surprised that she and Gavin were bonding over food, when it had been medicine with her and Yale. Perhaps, she mused, there was some truth in the adage about not bringing one's work home. Medicine was the only thing she and Yale had in common.

* * *

Light from the hanging fixture over the kitchen glinted off Gavin's black cropped hair as he sat opposite Celia, staring intently at her mouth whenever she opened it to take a forkful of food. He was enthralled with her delicate grace. Everything about her exuded elegance, from the way she held her silverware to her ramrod-straight posture.

He drained a goblet of chilled freshly squeezed orange juice. "Where did you learn to cook like this?" The buttermilk waffles topped with fruit were delicious.

"My college roommate taught me," Celia admitted. "Before I met her I didn't know how to turn on a stove."

Gavin gave her an incredulous look. "Who cooked for you?"

"My mother employed a full-time chef, because she'd never learned to cook. It's been a bone of contention between her and my grandmother for years."

Celia entertained Gavin with stories of the pranks she'd played on her parents, with the assistance of several of her cousins, how she'd come of age while in college and the physical and mental sacrifice she'd endured to become a physician.

She gave Gavin a dimpled smile. "There you have it. The life and times of Celia Cole-Thomas."

"Were you named for Celia Cruz?"

"Yes," she confirmed. "How did you know?"

Gavin winked at her. "Lucky guess."

Some sixth sense told Celia it was not a lucky guess, that Gavin Faulkner wasn't what he'd presented to her. He claimed to be a personal bodyguard, admitted to carrying a firearm, although he'd managed to conceal it from her; he'd traveled widely and was on a first-name basis with wealthy people who'd sworn him to secrecy.

"I don't believe you, Gavin." She'd spoken her thoughts aloud.

His expression stilled, becoming impassive. "Why wouldn't you believe me, Celia? You claim to have Cuban roots and Celia Cruz was Cuban, so I'd assumed you were named for the Queen of Salsa. Now, if I told you that I liked you the way a man likes a woman would you believe me?"

There was an open invitation in the depths of his dark eyes that wrung a smile from Celia. "Yes."

"Why is that?"

"I felt your erection when you kissed me."

"Are you always so candid?"

"You had a hard-on, Gavin. There aren't too many more ways to say it unless you want a clinical description."

Gavin held up a hand. "No, please don't."

"Did I embarrass you?" she asked, teasing him.

"I don't embarrass easily," he countered.

"We'll see."

"What's that supposed to mean?"

"My, my, my," she crooned. "Don't tell me you're getting defensive."

"There's nothing to defend, Celia."

"Are you going to deny my brother hired you to protect me?"

"What are you talking about?"

"Did Diego pay you to look after me?"

A beat passed as Gavin's internal radar went into overdrive. Celia believed her brother had hired him to protect her. "You believe your brother hired me to protect you from *what*, Celia?"

She rolled her eyes and exhaled a breath. "Diego has been hovering over me like a mother hen since I'd agreed to testify at the trial of a gang member who'd shot up the hospital where I worked."

He folded his arms over his chest. "What happened?" he asked, not confirming or denying he'd come to the mountains to protect her.

Celia told Gavin everything about the shooting in shockingly vivid detail. She also revealed that she was to be the state's only witness for the young man charged with multiple counts of capital murder, manslaughter, attempted murder and depraved indifference. Although he'd sustained a gunshot wound to the head, the fifteen-year-old, who was to be tried as an adult, had spent more than eight months in a coma. His parents wanted doctors to take him off life support but a court order overruled their request. He eventually came out of the coma and was declared fit to stand trial.

"Although I didn't see his face, I could identify him by his tattoo."

"What about his tattoo, Celia?"

"He belongs to a street gang that has the same tattoo of a dagger dripping blood on the backs of their left hands. But to differentiate one from the other, each member adds their own unique signature under the three red drops of blood."

Lowering his arms, Gavin stood up and sat down next to Celia. Vera had given him sketchy details about the E.R. shooting. What she hadn't told him was that Celia was to become the prosecutor's lead witness.

"What was his signature tat, baby?"

A wry smile twisted her mouth. The image of the tattoo was imprinted on her brain for an eternity. "It was a snarling pit bull standing in a pool of blood."

Gavin swallowed a savage expletive. "Is there a date set for the trial to begin?"

Celia shook her head. "I was told it wouldn't happen until the end of the summer. The prosecutors want an airtight case before going to trial."

"Is the little shit out on bail?"

Despite the gravity of the conversation, Celia smiled at Gavin's reference to the young psychopath. "No. The judge set the bail so high his family would have to rob Fort Knox to come up with enough cash to bail him out."

"What makes you think I'm here at the behest of your brother to protect you, Celia?"

Turning her head, Celia met Gavin's resolute stare. "After I was released from the hospital, Diego hired a security company to guard my house 24/7. He's fearful that I'll become a victim of gang retaliation because I was able to identify one of the shooters. He sent his personal driver to drive me wherever I had to go, and he convinced my brother Nicholas to have me spend time at the horse farm when he knows I don't like horses."

Gavin pressed his mouth to the column of her scented neck. "I don't know either of your brothers, Celia, but if they feel you need protection, then I'm volunteering for the role."

"You're kidding, aren't you?"

"Do I look like I'm kidding?"

Her eyes moved slowly over his face, looking for a hint of guile. "I don't know, Gavin," she said after a pregnant pause. "I don't know because I don't know you."

A grin of supreme male satisfaction parted his lips. "But you will get to know me," he crooned. "You'll get to know everything you *need* to know."

"What if I pay you for your services?"

"No, you won't," he protested. "I don't want or need your money."

"What *do* you want, Gavin?"

Tracing the outline of her ear with his finger, Gavin replaced it with his mouth. "I want you, Celia." His gaze dropped to her mouth.

She shivered from the warm breath wafting in her ear. "Are you certain you don't want me to pay you?"

"I'm very, very certain."

"Why won't you take money from me, Gavin?"

"Because then I'd become your employee, and I've made it a practice never to mix business with pleasure."

"Are you saying you want me to pleasure you, Mr. Faulkner?"

Gavin was frustrated. Why, he thought, was she making it so difficult for him to get close to her? She'd told him about the shootout at the E.R., but hadn't mentioned that one of the fatally injured doctors had been her fiancé, which led him to believe that she was still mourning a dead man.

"No. I'm not offering to protect you in exchange for sex."

"Are you always so ethical?"

"What's it going to be, Celia? Will you permit me to take care of you?"

Celia pondered his query. No man, other than her father, brothers and male cousins had ever offered to *take care* of her. The men in her family did it out of familial obligation because of the Cole dogma that the women rule and the men serve. The women were responsible for setting up and running their households, nurturing their children, while their men protected their families and perpetuated the family fortune.

"Yes," she said.

Cradling her face between his hands, Gavin angled his head and sealed their agreement with a tender kiss. The intense craving to sleep with Celia had eased with her acquiescence.

He was going to enjoy romancing the sexy doctor while waiting for his brother to surface.

Chapter 7

Shifting his chair, Gavin eased Celia over to straddle his lap. "What do you want, Celia?"

She rested her forehead against his, their mouths inches apart. "Right now, I don't know what I want. If you'd asked me what I need, then I'd tell you that I need you. I lost my fiancé in the shootout and I've spent the past year going through a tumult of emotions: grief, guilt, fear and outrage."

Gavin kissed her forehead. "Why would you feel guilty, baby? Was it because you survived when the other two doctors died?"

Celia swallowed the lump in her throat, making it difficult for her to speak. "One of those doctors was my fiancé. Yale wasn't scheduled to work that night, but we'd had an explosive argument the day before. He'd changed his schedule because he wanted to talk to me once my shift ended."

"Couldn't he have set up another time for the two of you to talk?"

A wry smile twisted Celia's mouth before she buried her face between Gavin's neck and shoulder. "If you'd known Yale, then you'd know he wasn't one to let things sit and simmer."

Gavin rubbed her back as one would a fretful child. "If you don't mind my asking, what had you argued about?"

"I'd bought a house from my cousin and hadn't told him about it."

"Was there something wrong with the house?"

Easing back, Celia stared at the man holding her protectively in his embrace. "There was nothing wrong with the house. Nathaniel, who's an architect, designed the house as a wedding gift for his bride. After they were divorced, I'd asked Nathaniel to sell it to me. The design has won a number of awards and it sits on prime Miami Beach real estate."

"It must be quite the showplace." Gavin's voice was shaded in neutral tones.

"It's magnificent, Gavin. But, Yale considered it an act of betrayal."

"Why?"

Celia paused, her gaze downcast as she recalled the acerbic words her late fiancé had flung at her. It had taken a full minute for her to react to his bitter tirade. She told Gavin about the clinic she and Yale had planned to open. "Yale used his inheritance to buy the building, and what he hadn't known was that I was going to underwrite the cost of renovating the property and the medical equipment. After he'd discovered what I'd paid for the house he went ballistic, accusing me of not loving or trusting him enough to tell him how much money I had."

"You weren't married to him, so your net worth was none of his concern."

"When I told him that, it just made him more incensed. I moved out of the apartment and into the house because I got tired of the sniping and hostile glares. I told Yale that I wasn't ending the engagement but needed to put some space between us. Living and working with someone 24/7 can put strain on a relationship."

Cradling her head in his hands, Gavin kissed the end of her nose. "I wouldn't know about that because I've never had a relationship with someone with whom I worked." Even when he'd gone undercover with a female agent, Gavin had made certain not to become emotionally involved with her.

"I think Yale's ego was somewhat bruised. He hadn't expected me to move out."

Gavin kissed Celia again, this time on her mouth. "You can't blame yourself for someone else's actions. It was his choice to change his shift. It was beyond your control."

Looping her arms around Gavin's neck, Celia rested her head on his shoulder. "That's what I keep telling myself."

"Believe it, Celia."

She wanted to believe it but when she least expected, doubt would creep in, shaking her confidence. Celia sat up straight, going completely still when she felt Gavin's hand searching under the hem of her pullover.

"What are you doing?"

"I want to see what he did to you."

It was a full minute before Celia realized he was talking about the shooter. "No, Gavin. I won't let anyone see it."

He chuckled softly. "I'm not anyone, sweetheart. Remember, I'm your personal *bodyguard*."

"You're really taking this bodyguard stuff to heart, aren't you?"

Combing his fingers through her hair, Gavin held the mop of black curls off Celia's small, round face. "You just don't know how serious I am, Celia Cole-Thomas," he whispered, placing feathery kisses over her forehead, each eye, nose and mouth. He didn't kiss her mouth; he caressed it with his lips.

Warming shivers swept over Celia; she was melting into Gavin's warmth and strength. He'd appointed himself her personal bodyguard and she would let him protect her from fears and dangers—known and unknown.

Shifting slightly, she pulled up the right side of the pullover, baring her back. "I'm scarred, Gavin."

Gavin lowered his hands and tugged at the hem of her shirt, pulling it up and over her head. His gaze lingered on the soft swell of firm brown breasts rising and falling above the lace of a silk bra the same hue as Celia's complexion. "You're not scarred, Celia. You're beautiful."

"And you're one smooth liar, Gavin Faulkner."

Without warning, his expression changed, becoming hard, derisive. "Did you call your late fiancé a liar when he said you were beautiful?"

"You heartless SOB!"

Celia's right hand swung up in an arc, stopping in midair when Gavin's fingers snaked around her wrist. Her free hand came up and within seconds she found herself prisoner to Gavin's superior strength. He hadn't hurt her, but she was unable to escape the fingers doubling as manacles.

"And you're a selfish, spoiled brat, Celia," Gavin countered. "You've come to the middle of nowhere to wallow in grief when you should be rejoicing that your life was spared, that your parents didn't have to bury a child like so many parents are doing nowadays because of senseless gang violence. You feel guilty because the man you'd planned to marry felt the need to try and control not only your life, but also his own and in the end he lost everything.

"Then, there's the fear. You fear letting go of your past so you can embrace your future. Have you thought maybe there's a reason why you didn't die with the others? That perhaps you were spared because as a healer there is someone out there waiting for you to help save their life? You talk about outrage. Just who are you angry with?"

"The little *shit* who has such a wanton disrespect for life that he thought nothing of shooting up an emergency room!"

Gavin smiled for the first time since he'd begun his angry outburst. "Now you're talking, baby. Hold on to that rage because it will be your testimony that will ensure that little punk will never see the light of day for the rest of his life."

"I intend to do that. And for you edification—I'm neither spoiled nor a brat."

"I'm sorry," he apologized.

Celia lowered her gaze. "I'll have to think about accepting your apology."

"What's there to think about, Celia?" Gavin cupped her chin, raising her face to meet his eyes. "Maybe I should've called you a sexy nerd."

She flashed a dimpled smile. "At one time I *was* a nerd."

"What about now?"

Her smile grew wider. "I'm a free spirit in training." A moment passed. "Apology accepted. And I'm sorry I called you heartless."

"I think the slur was a *heartless SOB*."

"That, too," she added.

"Are you really sorry?"

"Yes, I am."

"Show me, Celia." His voice had lowered at the same time he stared at her chest.

Looping her arms under his shoulders, Celia pressed her breasts to his chest and brushed her mouth over his. She placed gentle kisses at the corners, then pulled his upper lip between her teeth before giving the lower one equal attention.

Gavin claimed the sexiest mouth of any man she'd ever seen. His top lip was firm, but it was the lower, slightly petulant and incredibly sexy lip that drew her rapt attention. Their tongues met, parried, engaging in a dance of desire. Celia's tongue simulated her making love to Gavin, her hips following suit.

His hands sliding down her denim-covered thighs, Gavin anchored his hands under Celia's knees as he rose to meet her thrusting hips. He'd hardened so quickly he feared passing out. He couldn't believe he was sitting on a chair in Celia's kitchen and she was giving him a lap dance.

Gavin closed his eyes rather than stare at the rush of excitement darkening Celia's face, her moist parted lips, heaving breasts, fluttering lashes and warmth and sensual scent of her perfumed body. She quickened her movements, both gasping at the same time to tamp down on the rising ecstasy threatening to erupt. He opened his eyes, going completely still when he heard it. Celia also froze. She'd heard it, too. Someone had rung the doorbell.

"Are you expecting anyone?" Gavin didn't recognize his own voice.

Celia shook her head. "No. My neighbor always calls before coming over." The doorbell chimed again. "I better go and answer it."

Gavin held on to her upper arm when she scrambled off his lap. "You're not going anywhere until you put your shirt on." He stood up. "I'll answer the door."

"No, Gavin!"

He turned to glare at her. "Have you forgotten I've promised to protect you? Now, please get dressed before whoever is on the other side of that door will draw their own conclusions as to what we've been doing." Turning on his heels, Gavin walked across the kitchen.

"We weren't having sex," Celia called out to his broad back.

"You're right about that," he confirmed, not breaking stride. "We were making love."

Gavin continued to tell himself that what he and Celia had shared was lovemaking when they weren't in love with each other. He liked her, wanted to sleep with her, but falling in love with her was not an option.

He peered through the security eye to see a man staring back at him. "Who is it?"

"Nicholas Cole-Thomas. Is my sister here?"

He opened the door. Even if the tall man hadn't identified himself, Gavin would've recognized him as Celia's brother. They had the same coloring, hair texture and delicate features. He peered over Nicholas's shoulder to find a late-model Lincoln sedan parked behind the Yukon.

"Please come in."

"Nicky! What on earth are you doing here?"

Gavin turned to see Celia standing in the middle of the living room, both hands resting at her waist. She'd put back on her top. She looked like a woman who'd just been made love to, and he wondered if her brother would notice the heightened color in her cheeks or her lush mouth.

Nicholas took off a yellow slicker, hanging it on a coatrack in the corner of the entry. Bending over, he removed his boots, leaving them on the mat with Gavin's. Minute lines fanned out around a pair of large black eyes that had spent too much time squinting in the sun. "I wanted to surprise you."

Arms outstretched, Celia closed the distance between her and her younger brother. "Well, you did." She kissed his smooth cheek when he lifted her off her feet. "What are you doing so far from home?"

Nicholas, mindful of the injury that had almost cost his sister her life, cradled her gently to his chest. "I was in Louisville on business, but decided to make a detour on the way back to the farm." He pressed his mouth to Celia's ear. "Who's the linebacker?" he whispered for her ears only.

Celia pushed against Nicholas's shoulder. "Please put me down." Reaching for his hand, she smiled at Gavin. "Nicholas, this is my friend, Gavin Faulkner. Gavin, Nicholas." The two men shook hands while exchanging perfunctory greetings. "Nicky is the brother who owns a horse farm in Virginia."

Gavin took in everything about the younger man in one sweeping glance. He was several inches taller than six-feet and lean with curly black hair, dark skin and equally dark penetrating eyes that missed nothing. Gavin could almost hear him thinking—*who the hell are you, and what are you doing with my sister?*

"Thoroughbreds?" he asked. Nicholas nodded. "Beautiful animals."

"Yes, they are," Nicholas confirmed.

Celia noticed the strained tension between the two men. Looping her arm through her brother's, she rested her head against his shoulder. "Gavin and I just finished eating. Can I get you something?" What she couldn't reveal to Nicholas was he'd interrupted her giving Gavin a lap dance.

"I'll have *café con leche*, thank you." Nicholas hadn't taken his gaze off Gavin. "How do you know my sister?"

Gavin forced back a smile. It'd taken Nicholas Cole-Thomas less than two minutes after being introduced to ask the question. "You'll have to ask her."

Nicholas's eyebrows shot up. "Cee Cee?"

"Nicky! Must you always be so gauche?"

"Just answer the question." Nicholas's southern drawl had become more pronounced as he struggled to control his temper. "I decide to drop in to visit my sister, only to find her with a man who—"

"He's my bodyguard," Celia said, interrupting him. "He's here to make certain I'm protected until I return to Miami."

Nicholas's gaze shifted from his sister to Gavin, and then back again. "You hired him?"

Celia released her brother's arm and walked over to stand next to Gavin. "Yes, I did. I realized what you and Diego were up to when he said you wanted me to stay at the farm." Her eyes narrowed. "You know I'm afraid of horses, Nicky, so why would you suggest I come to a horse farm? Once I decided to leave Miami I contacted an agency that provides personal protection. Gavin was available, so you can tell the others that I'm quite safe."

"If you want to have me checked out, then I'll give you the name and number of the company who contracts my services," Gavin volunteered.

The skin over Nicholas's high cheekbones tightened when he clenched his teeth. "I'll be certain to have you checked out. Where did you get your training?"

Folding muscular arms over his chest, Gavin gave the brash young man a sardonic smile. "Ranger School."

Nicholas smiled for the first time. "You were military?"

Gavin returned the smile. "75th Ranger Regiment," he said proudly. "What about you?"

"I broke family tradition when I went to the Naval Academy. After graduation, I had to decide whether to go to flight school or spend time on the water."

"I'm willing to bet you chose the water."

"That's right!" Nicholas confirmed with a wide grin. "However, I wound up under the water instead of on a battleship or carrier. Spending months at a time on the bottom of the ocean tested my sanity and resolve."

Celia exhaled a breath. If Gavin and Nicholas were both ex-military, then she knew they would go on for hours. "Why don't the two of you go and hang out on the back porch? Nicky, I'll bring you your coffee. By the way, are you in a rush to get back home?"

Nicholas angled his head. "What's up, Cee Cee?"

A soft smile touched her mouth. "I'd like you to judge a food competition."

The former Naval officer-turned-horse-breeder's gaze shifted from his sister to the man she'd hired to protect her. "What am I judging?"

Gavin inclined his head in deference to Celia. "Tell him, Cee Cee."

Celia glared at Gavin. Her brothers knew she detested the annoying nickname. She explained the details of the competition, with pork as the main ingredient. "You will have the responsibility of judging which dish you like best."

"I can tell you now that I'm partial to roast *and* pulled pork, so I'm not going to be much of a judge." Nicholas sniffed the air. "I can tell you now that whatever is cooking smells incredible."

Gavin flashed a Cheshire-cat grin. "That's my pulled pork."

"You're all right, Brother Faulkner," Nicholas crooned.

"Why, thank you, Brother Thomas," Gavin said, winking at Celia. "Do you need help in the kitchen, Celia?"

She glared at him. "No, *brother.*" Turning on her heels, she retreated to the kitchen while her brother and *bodyguard* walked in the direction of the enclosed back porch.

She'd lived in the house a year before deciding to enclose the porch so she'd be able to utilize the space year-round. A contractor had installed pocket doors and built-in bookcases along one wall. There was also a retractable awning which shielded the porch from the intense summer when converted to a loggia for outdoor dining.

Celia looked forward to beginning and ending her days on the porch with stunning vistas of mountains, verdant valleys and waterfalls as a panoramic backdrop. Although she'd hiked a few trails in the Great Smoky Mountains National Park, she could never convince Yale to join her. He'd said his fair coloring was a deterrent to prolonged outdoor activity. She intended to ask for-

mer Army Ranger Gavin Faulkner to go hiking, fishing
and white-water rafting with her, and if he refused, then
Celia would never let him live it down.

Picking up the remote, Gavin turned on the large, flat-
screen television mounted on a far wall, tuned to ESPN
and raised the volume. It was his turn to put Nicholas
Cole-Thomas on the defensive when he asked, "Did you
stop by just to visit your sister, or is she in real danger?"

Nicholas took a sip from a mug filled with warm
milk, coffee and sugar, peering at Gavin Faulkner over
the rim. "Someone broke into her home despite it being
wired. By the time the police got there they were gone.
Footage from surveillance video showed a landscaping
truck in the driveway. When the police enhanced the
image they discovered the plate was stolen and the company doesn't exist."

"Does she live in a gated community?" Gavin asked.

Nicholas took another sip of the coffee-infused sweet-
ened beverage. He'd come to western North Carolina to
try to convince his sister to return to Virginia with him
until it was time for her to testify. He was prepared for a
volatile confrontation, and had been given a direct order
from his father not to leave North Carolina without her.

When the police contacted Timothy Cole-Thomas to
inform him that his daughter's house had been burglar-
ized, it was the only time in his life that Nicholas heard
his father spew expletives he hadn't known existed.
Once Timothy regained his composure, he ordered his
son to go and bring his daughter back or he'd have her
abducted and forcibly returned to Florida.

"No," Nicholas replied. "But there is a private road
leading to the house."

Gavin rested his elbows on his knees. "How close is her nearest neighbor?"

"The houses are set on half-acre lots, facing the ocean. My dad installed more cameras and armed guards monitor the property around the clock."

"Who knows Celia's staying here?"

"Just the family."

"How about her coworkers?"

Nicholas shook his head. "I wouldn't know. She's been away from the hospital since last July, so I'm not aware if she's been in contact with anyone there. Maybe that's something you can ask her."

Gavin laced his fingers together. "Are you going to tell her about the break-in?"

"I was before you told me she'd hired you to protect her."

"I'm not going to let anything or anyone harm her," Gavin stated solemnly.

Nicholas forced a smile he didn't feel. "I believe you. I lied to Celia when I told her I was in Kentucky on business. My father's orders are to close up this place and take her to Virginia. Cole-Thom Farms is a fortress. Every inch of the property is wired and patrolled. No one can enter or leave without detection, and signs are posted around the perimeter stating: Trespassers Will Be Shot on Sight and If Still Alive, Then Prosecuted."

Gavin suddenly had a newfound respect for Celia's brother. Under Nicholas Cole-Thomas's almost too-pretty masculine face was a man who would go to great lengths to protect his sister. He'd promised Celia he would protect her without regard to why he was in western North Carolina, and had given her brother the same assurance.

He'd received orders to hold his position and wait for Raymond Prentice to contact him; however, Gavin had no idea whether the undercover special agent would contact him the next day, week or month. "I've agreed to protect Celia because a client postponed an overseas business trip until late summer," he lied smoothly. "But if his plans change and he decides to leave sooner, then I'll arrange for a replacement." He made a mental note to call his cousins to have a protection expert on standby.

Nicholas placed the mug on a side table. "I'd like to ask a favor of you."

"What is it?"

"Can you bring her to the farm? She doesn't have to know she's not coming back here."

Vertical lines appeared between Gavin's eyes. "Why the subterfuge? Why can't I just tell her where she's going?"

Stretching long legs out in front of him, Nicholas crossed his feet at the ankles. "My sister was thrown and kicked by a horse—no, I take that back. She was kicked by a pony, so she has an aversion to beings of the equine persuasion regardless of their size. So, to suggest she come and spend any extended time with me is not going to sit too well with her. I've had to remind my parents that Celia is an adult and therefore she can't be forced to do anything she doesn't want to do. All I can do is talk to her, and hopefully she'll understand where the family is coming from."

Gavin pulled his lip between his teeth as he pondered an alternative to get Celia to Virginia if or when his orders changed. "How long are you staying in North Carolina?"

"I'd like to be home before tomorrow evening. Why?"

"Leave everything to me," he whispered like a coconspirator.

"What are you two whispering about?"

Nicholas and Gavin turned to find Celia standing in the doorway to the porch. "Nothing," they said in unison, while coming to their feet.

Celia rolled her eyes. "Please sit down. It may sound rather clichéd, but you two look like a couple of kids caught with your hands in the cookie jar." She walked in, and sat on an off-white love seat with colorful floral throw pillows. "How long can you hang out with me?" Celia asked her brother.

He ran a hand over his curly hair. "I can spend the night."

Kicking off her shoes, Celia pulled her legs up under her body. "I'd hoped you'd stay longer. We don't get to see each other that often."

"It's not as if I haven't invited you to come and hang out with me, Cee Cee."

Gavin gave Nicholas a surreptitious glance. "I've never been to a horse farm."

"Why don't you come with my sister?" Nicholas asked, quickly picking up on Gavin's cue.

Gavin raised his eyebrows questioningly at Celia. "How about it?"

"I'm afraid of horses," she mumbled, pushing out her lower lip.

Pushing to his feet, Gavin sat next to her. He rested a hand over her sock-covered feet. "It's not about riding, Celia. I just want the experience of seeing a horse farm up close and personal."

"Do you ride?"

Gavin gave her a tender smile. "No." He didn't want

to tell her that he'd taken pony rides as a boy at county fairs. Pony and roller-coaster rides, along with the shooting gallery, were his favorite attractions.

Celia's gaze shifted from Gavin to her brother, then back again. "If we go, then what are we going to do with Terry?"

"Who's Terry?" Nicholas asked.

"He's my—he's *our* dog," she said, quickly correcting herself.

Nicholas waved a hand. "Bring the dog with you. He should get along well with the other dogs at the farm."

"How many dogs do you have, Nicky?"

He turned his head so his sister would see his smirk. It was a known fact that Celia had a soft spot for dogs. "Four. We have a bitch that should whelp her first litter in another week."

Exhaling an audible breath while closing her eyes, Celia wondered if going to Virginia and seeing horses up close would help her get over her fear of them. She was only five when she'd fallen off a pony. While she'd lain on the ground he'd stepped on her head, leaving her traumatized. She'd lost count of the number of times Nicky had asked her to come visit him at the horse farm, and after a while he'd just stopped. She knew he'd taken a huge risk when he'd invested so much of his money in a failing farm, and within a couple of years managed to realize a profit for the first time. Nicky had always supported her while she'd never supported him.

"Okay." She opened her eyes, seeing the shock freezing her brother's face. "I'll come. But don't expect me to go anywhere around your horses."

Nicholas flashed a wide white-tooth grin. "If you

don't want to see horses, then you don't have to. Why don't you guys come next weekend?"

"What's happening next weekend?" Celia asked.

"There's an open house at a neighboring farm. Blackstone Farms is one of a few owned and operated African-American horse farms in Virginia. Sheldon Blackstone, who has gone into semiretirement, came to see me a week after I took possession and told me if I needed a mentor then he was the one. I've never questioned anything he said, and the result was a thirty-to-one long shot that came in first at the International Gold Cup."

Celia gave Gavin a sidelong glance. "What do you think?"

He smiled. "It sounds like fun."

"It will be," Nicholas confirmed. "Dress is casual, so you won't have the excuse that you have nothing to wear," he said, smiling.

Unfolding her legs, Celia stood up, both men rising with her. "I think it's time I put my pork in the oven. The refrigerator and pantry are full, so if you want anything to eat or drink before dinner, then you're on your own, because I have to work on a few needlecraft projects for a friend's baby."

Gavin, waiting until Celia walked back inside, leaned over and bumped fists with Nicholas. "If the horses don't spook your sister, then you shouldn't have a problem having her stay with you when the time comes for me to leave."

Nicholas shook his head in amazement. "Either the shootout at the E.R. has mellowed her or you have some helluva mojo, Gavin."

"What are you talking about?"

"Don't get your nose out of joint. One thing Celia

never has been and that's passive. She's stubborn, opinionated and a scrapper. Guys who liked her were always afraid to approach her because she has a 'screw-you' face that kept them at a distance. Somehow she interacts differently with you. I don't know if it's because she views you as her protector or if you're able to crack her tough exterior."

"It could be both, Nicholas."

Chapter 8

Celia, sitting across the dining room table from Nicholas and Gavin, bit into the roll filled with melt-in-the-mouth shredded pork drizzled with a peppery vinegar barbecue sauce and topped with coleslaw. Gavin had added thinly sliced dill pickles and extra sauce on the plate.

She sighed and closed her eyes. "Incredible."

Gavin winked at Celia. "You're an incredible cook, Celia." She'd created a roast pork dish, served with flavorful white rice, black beans, an avocado salad and *mojo criollo*—a potent garlic sauce.

Nicholas speared a forkful of shredded pork that had fallen out of his roll. "While you two are wasting time engaging in a mutual admiration, I intend to get my eat on." His eyes grew wider. "Damn, Gavin! You are good. How you would like to come and work for me at Cole-Thom Farms? I'll pay you whatever you want."

Gavin swallowed a mouthful of black beans. "Doing what?"

"You could take over as the farm's chef."

"Sorry. I like my current job, and my cooking repertoire isn't that versatile."

He'd liked working undercover for the Bureau because he liked being challenged, enjoyed taking risks. But, as he grew older, taking risks was no longer a priority. Staying alive was. Gavin had promised his mother he would apply for a field office position. He knew she would never recover if she lost both her sons in the line of duty. She'd sacrificed enough when agents came to the door with the news that her husband had given his life for the Bureau and his country.

During a one-on-one meeting with Bradley MacArthur, Gavin had requested permission to speak off the record. It was the first time he'd bared his soul to his supervisor. He'd revealed the pain of growing up without his father, his mother's tears whenever she would've celebrated her wedding anniversary if her husband had still been alive, and her fear of losing not one, but her two sons in the line of duty. He'd been forthcoming when he told Mac he loved working as a special agent, but wasn't certain how much longer he would remain with the Bureau if he wasn't assigned a supervisory field office position. Mac promised to see what he could do.

Gavin had served notice when he told the men representing a joint task force operation that bringing in Raymond Prentice was going to be his last field assignment. If the other men hadn't believed him, he knew Mac did.

"What's wrong with the chef you have, Nicky?" Celia asked.

"He's okay, but the man's afraid to cook outside the box."

Celia touched her mouth with a napkin. "He probably needs to take a few continuing education courses. Even though my college roommate taught me to cook it was *abuela* who taught me to raise the bar and not to be afraid of using different spices."

"Too bad our mother didn't listen to her," Nicholas mumbled under his breath.

"Nicholas!" Celia chided softly. "Not in front of company."

"Which is he, Celia? Company, or your bodyguard?"

"I am her bodyguard." Gavin had answered for Celia, resenting the younger man's inference. He'd recalled her talking about being the dreaded middle child, and there was no doubt she was forced to be a scrapper in order to stand up to two overprotective brothers.

Nicholas stared at his sister, and then his gaze shifted to the man on his left. "Maybe it would be better if you didn't tell people you were Cee Cee's bodyguard."

A thick silence filled the dining room as the three occupants stared at one another. "How do you want me to introduce Gavin, Nicky?" Celia's voice had taken on a coaxing quality.

"If you say he's your boyfriend or companion then no one will ask questions."

Celia was totally confused by Nicholas's behavior. Something nagged her as she tried assembling hints and innuendos like a puzzle to make a recognizable picture. Her brother claimed to have stopped by on a whim, he'd invited her and Gavin to visit his farm the following weekend and now he wanted Gavin to pretend he was her lover.

"Why do I have to convince people that Gavin and I are lovers, Nicky?"

Nicholas's impassive expression did not change with her query. "Have you forgotten that you are the only witness in a trial that is certain to attract not only local but national attention?"

"I have no intention of hiding—"

"He's right, Celia," Gavin interrupted. "You'll make it more difficult for me if you don't keep a low profile."

Celia wavered, trying to comprehend what she was hearing from her brother and Gavin. "So, you want me to pretend that you and I have hooked up?"

He cocked his head. "I wouldn't say hooked up. It would be more like *involved*."

"How involved, Gavin?"

"Very involved."

Celia couldn't believe she was having this conversation—and in front of her brother, no less. Her gaze lowered. She stared across the table at Gavin through her lashes. If Nicholas hadn't rung the bell there was no doubt she and her self-appointed bodyguard would've become more than involved. He probably would have ended up in her bed and inside her.

Since she had become involved with Gavin Faulkner she was constantly bombarded with the realization that she was a woman, a very passionate woman who had yet to experience the full range of her sexuality. Celia knew she was able to excite Gavin as much as he excited her.

She didn't want involvement as much as she *needed* it. She'd pledged her future to a man who was ambivalent about sex. It hadn't mattered to Yale if they didn't make love for weeks. At first, she believed it had something to do with his age. But she knew a lot of men in their forties who were still very sexually active. She had great-uncles who'd fathered children in their forties.

Was she physically attracted to Gavin?

The answer was unequivocally yes.

Did she want to become physically involved with Gavin?

The answer was still yes.

Did she want to fall in love with him?

Celia knew without a doubt that she didn't. If the circumstance for her to take a lover for the summer presented itself, then she would, and when it ended she knew she would be mature enough to walk away with incredible memories from the liaison.

The tense lines bracketing her mouth disappeared when she smiled. "You're right," she conceded to no one in particular. "Whenever Gavin and I are out together in public he can be my escort, boyfriend, companion or lover." She winked at Gavin. "The choice is yours, darling."

He inclined his head in a mock bow. "Thank you, baby."

Nicholas picked up a glass of sweet tea. "That was easy," he murmured before taking a deep swallow.

Dinner became a leisurely affair, lasting more than two hours. Gavin and Nicholas talked about everything: the military, politics, sports and the state of the economy. Celia had served sweet tea and pinot noir to accompany the meal, and while she drank the tea, Nicholas and Gavin drank wine. She'd surprised the two men when she retreated to the kitchen to bring out a tray with *flan de coco,* a light and airy coconut flan, and strong, dark, aromatic coffee in demitasse cups.

Gavin rose quickly to take the tray from her. "Why didn't you ask me to help you?" he asked close to her ear.

She flashed an attractive smile, bringing his gaze to linger on her mouth. "Now, that would've spoiled the surprise. I didn't know who'd want lemon peel, but it's there for whoever wants it." Traditionally for Cubans if dark coffee was served at the end of a meal, espresso style, it was never accompanied by lemon peel.

Nicholas, having finished his dessert and coffee, patted his flat belly. "I've overindulged on everything and that includes food and wine. I'm definitely going to turn in early tonight." He raised his half-filled wineglass. "The winner of the pork challenge is…" His words trailed off as he appeared deep in thought. "It's a tie!" Gavin and Celia threw their napkins at him, and Nicholas doubled over laughing. Pushing back his chair, he stood. "I'm going out to my car to get my bag. I don't know about you two, but this farm boy is early to bed, early to rise."

Waiting until her brother left the house, Celia turned to Gavin. "We have a dilemma," she whispered. "How are you going to perform the duties of a bodyguard—"

"Don't worry," he said softly. "I'll help you clean up the kitchen. After Nicholas goes to bed I'll go back to my place, get my things and then I'll come back here. The moment I leave I want you to activate the alarm. You're going to have to give me the code so I can get back in."

Celia nodded like a bobblehead doll. She couldn't believe a man she hadn't known a week, a man who turned her on with a single glance, was going to move into her house for the summer. If she'd planned to seduce him, she wouldn't have been able to come up with a less plausible scheme.

"Okay, Gavin."

"Don't look so worried, Doc. We're going to have a lot of fun hanging out together this summer."

That's what had Celia worried. They would have fun, and then what? At the end of the summer they'd go their separate ways to live their separate lives? Gavin would go back to protecting the rich and famous and once the trial concluded, she would go back to practicing medicine. What they would share for the summer would be placed in a box, covered, tied with a neat little bow and placed on a shelf never to be opened again.

Once she'd recovered from the anesthesia and had remained awake long enough to recall how close she'd come to losing her life in the very hospital where she'd worked, Celia promised herself she would treasure each and every sunrise and sunset because her life had been spared when so many others had lost theirs.

Leaning to her right, she brushed her mouth over Gavin's. "I'm looking forward to it."

Gavin stared at the lush lips belonging to the woman with the dimpled smile. Everything about her pulled him in until he felt trapped in a force field from which he didn't want to escape. No matter how he felt and was beginning to feel for Celia he knew their liaison would come to an end.

He'd offered to protect Celia before Nicholas informed him about the break-in at her house. What had been imagined was now real and *he* was faced with a dilemma. Could he protect Dr. Celia Cole-Thomas and complete his assignment?

Gavin maneuvered into the driveway to the two-bedroom time-share and parked. Reaching for his Black-Berry, he punched the speed dial for Bradley MacArthur.

"Faulkner," he said, identifying himself when hearing his supervisor's greeting.

"How are you, mountain man?"

Gavin smiled. It wasn't often Bradley exhibited a modicum of humor. "I'm good, Mac. I'm going to need your approval to change the base of operation."

"Talk to me, Faulkner."

He told him everything from meeting Dr. Celia Cole-Thomas, his accompanying her to a neighbor's Memorial Day celebration, the unannounced visit from her brother and Nicholas's invitation to spend a weekend at his horse farm in western Virginia.

"Don't hang up, Agent Faulkner. I want to check out something."

Gavin shook his head. Bradley MacArthur had morphed back into his role as an associate Bureau director. Mac must have placed his cell phone down next to a computer because he could hear the rapid tapping of keys.

"Approval granted," Bradley said in a strong voice. "Dr. Cole-Thomas is known and respected in and around Waynesville. You connecting with her will help you blend in and increase the odds of Prentice contacting you. Just be certain to let me know of any changes."

"Thanks, Mac."

"Just bring our man in, Faulkner."

"You…" Gavin couldn't finish his sentence because his supervisor ended the call. It no longer mattered.

He exited the truck and walked into the small house that was to have been his temporary domicile for the summer. Bradley MacArthur's willingness to approve him moving into Dr. Celia Cole-Thomas's vacation retreat nagged at Gavin. Was there a connection to the shootout in the hospital E.R. and other open cases in the Bureau files? He'd wanted to ask—before Mac had summarily hung up on him—if the gun used in the shooting was stolen, and if it was one in a cache linked to the brazen gang crisscrossing the country and targeting gun dealers.

He made quick work of packing his clothes and netbook and of cleaning out the refrigerator. He'd purchased enough food to last only a couple of days, so there wasn't much to throw away. Gavin stripped his bed, putting the linen in an army duffel bag along with the clothes he'd taken from the laundry-room hamper. From now on he would do his laundry at Celia's house. He carried his possessions out to the truck, returned to the cottage to make certain he hadn't left anything, turned off the lights, set the silent alarm, closed the door and pocketed the keycard. The sound of the door closing echoed loudly in the stillness of the night.

When he drove away, Gavin felt as if he had closed the door on one phase of life, only to begin another. There was still the question of the whereabouts of his brother. If or when would he make contact? And if he found his brother, would that be the end of his relationship with Celia?

Celia sat up straighter, her heart pounding in her chest when she heard the distinctive sound of the door being opened. Seconds later it went silent before another buzz indicated Gavin had deactivated and reset the security system.

After Nicholas had gone upstairs to bed, she'd retreated to the back porch to watch television. Forty minutes into the Lifetime movie, she found herself dozing off. There had been a time before she'd been shot that she'd been able to work thirty-six hours before feeling fatigued. Now if she sat still more than half an hour she found herself dozing off.

"Hey, Doc, where do you want me to put my things?"

Celia turned off the television and slipped off the chaise. There was enough light from the lowest setting on a table lamp to make out the outline of Gavin's broad shoulders spanning the doorway.

Walking on bare feet, she closed the distance between them. "Follow me," she ordered quietly.

Gavin complied, staring at the outline of Celia's hips in a pair of fitted jeans. She had just enough curves not to be mistaken for a boy from the back. He usually liked women with a more substantial booty, but he couldn't complain about Celia's chest. She had more than a mouthful or handful—and he had very large hands.

He stopped at the staircase and picked up two bags: a calfskin carry-on and the other a matching Pullman; both were stamped with his initials. The carry-on held his computer, handcuffs, bulletproof vest and several clips of ammunition. Whenever he traveled by commercial aircraft, he had to be cleared before boarding the plane with the firearm and ammunition.

Celia flipped a light switch, and light flooded the way up the staircase and hallway leading to the bedrooms. She stopped at the first room on the right. "This will be your bedroom." Stepping aside, she let Gavin walk in. She'd turned down the bed, left a supply of towels on the table in a corner of the spacious bedroom. A light fixture, similar to those over paintings in museums or galleries, bathed the bed in a soft warm glow.

Gavin's jaw dropped when he surveyed the bedroom Celia had offered him. Crown molding affixed to the ceiling over the bed replaced a fabric canopy, and the off-white panels surrounding the California-king bed matched the wood on the moldings. Moving closer, he peered at the framed oils on the walls. They were Impressionist paintings depicting scenes of nighttime Paris, Venice and Rome. There was a sitting area with a love seat, table and a media center with a flat-screen television, audio equipment and built-in shelves with books and magazines.

"This is nice," he said. "I'm going to enjoy sleeping here."

Crossing her arms under her breasts, Celia leaned against the door frame. "Your bathroom is across the hall."

Gavin smiled at her over his shoulder. "Where's yours?"

"It's in my bedroom."

"Where's your bedroom?"

She angled her head. "It's at the end of the hall on the left."

"So, you put baby brother in between us as a buffer," he teased.

Celia straightened, giving Gavin a long, penetrating look. "Even if Nicky wasn't staying over, nothing's going to happen."

"Not tonight, Celia."

She held her breath until she felt her lungs laboring for air. When she exhaled, breath came out in an audible swoosh. "Are you *that* certain something is going to happen?" Her voice was barely a whisper. Gavin turned to face her. He appeared taller, larger in the muted light.

"If Nicholas hadn't rung the bell earlier this morning something would have happened, Celia. Where did you think it was going to lead?"

"I would've stopped before we'd gone any further," Celia stated confidently.

"You may have been able to stop, but I wouldn't only because I didn't want to. You can't get me that aroused, then expect me to take care of myself the way I did when I was a teenage boy." Gavin leaned in closer. "If you don't want to go all the way, then don't tease me, baby."

Celia's lips parted in surprise. She hadn't expected him to be so blunt. "Point taken, Gavin."

Forcing a smile she didn't feel, she turned and walked down the hallway to her bedroom. She'd lied to Gavin and she'd lied to herself. She wouldn't have stopped him only because she'd wanted it to go on until its conclusion. Nicholas's unexpected arrival had stopped something that had been about to get out of hand. If her brother hadn't come, there was no doubt she would've wound up in bed with a man she'd met four days before in the produce department of a supermarket.

She walked into her bedroom and closed the door behind her. Flopping down on a club chair in the dressing area, Celia closed her eyes. The events of the day came flooding back like frames of film. The images slowed, then paused when she recalled the erotic sensations taking her beyond herself when she'd straddled Gavin's lap.

A shudder passed through Celia as her heart thumped wildly under her breasts, and it took Herculean strength not to retrace her steps and beg Gavin Faulkner to make love to her. She sat, eyes closed, hands fisted until her traitorous body returned to normal. Then she left the dressing room and made her way into the bathroom and took a shower.

When she finally got into bed and pulled the sheet

and lightweight blanket over her body, Celia tried thinking of anything but the man occupying her guest room who was a constant reminder of what she'd been missing…passion.

Chapter 9

Celia felt the heat from Gavin's body when he came up behind her. He smelled of peppermint mouthwash and sandalwood. Smiling, she returned Nicholas's wave when he stuck his hand out the driver's side window. She'd gotten up early to prepare a light repast for her brother before he set out to drive to Staunton, Virginia.

"I like your brother."

Her smile was still in place when she shifted to face Gavin. He'd rolled back the cuffs on a chambray shirt to reveal strong wrists. "He likes you, too. Nicholas can be somewhat standoffish at times. Why didn't you come down to see him off?"

Gavin's gaze lingered on the damp curls grazing Celia's neck before moving down to a white tank top and body-hugging faded jeans. It was the first time she'd exposed so much skin. A sheen of moisture glistened on her bared flesh from the near-one-hundred-degree humidity.

"I didn't want to intrude on your time with him just in case you wanted to discuss personal family business."

"All Nicky talks about are his horses."

"Men and their toys," Gavin drawled.

"Thoroughbreds are very expensive toys."

"So are cars, boats and sporting events," he countered.

"And don't forget women."

Resting his hands on Celia's shoulders, Gavin turned her to face him, unable to read the expression in the eyes that reminded him of the espresso he'd drunk last night. "Was your fiancé unfaithful?"

Celia's lips twisted in what passed for a wry smile. "No. Yale was the last man to creep. He fell asleep as soon as his head hit the pillow. I was talking about other men."

"Men you'd slept with?"

"Men I shouldn't have slept with." Looping her arms around Gavin's waist, Celia rested her cheek on his chest. "Do you regret losing your virginity to the first girl you slept with?"

Gavin nearly choked when he inhaled and swallowed at the same time. "What?"

Easing back, she saw his stunned expression. "Just answer the question, Gavin."

Gavin did not want to believe some of the things that came out of Celia's sexy mouth. She was the most outspoken woman he'd ever had the pleasure of meeting. "Of course I don't regret it."

"Was she a special girlfriend?"

"No. She was someone I'd met at a party. I was a high school senior and she a college freshman. She was smart, pretty and I let her know with very few words what I wanted. Her parents were away visiting relatives, so we went to her house and I spent the night."

"Did you ever see her again?"

Lowering his head, Gavin pressed a kiss to Celia's damp hair. "Nope."

"Didn't that bother you?"

"Why would it have bothered me, Celia? I wanted the experience of sleeping with a woman for the first time and she was willing to oblige me. It had nothing to do with love. It was all about lust."

"That's what my first serious boyfriend said after I found out that he was sleeping with me and at least four other women at the same time. He said he believed in lust, not love. In other words, I'd become a receptacle for his lust."

"He sounds like a real idiot," Gavin whispered. "Better you found out what he was all about before you ended up married to him."

Celia smiled. "The names I called him weren't quite that nice."

Gavin pulled her closer. "When it comes to sex, men view it differently than women do. For some men it's base reaction—a physical release, while for most women emotion is involved. Guys call it sex and women lovemaking."

"And for you, it's lovemaking," she said, repeating what he'd confirmed after her aborted lap dance.

"I'd like to think it is. Enough sex talk, Celia, because right now my imagination is going into overdrive." He wagged a finger at her. "And no more lap dances."

A wide grin split Celia's face, her dimples deepening. "Don't tell me it was too much for you," she teased.

Gavin didn't know whether to laugh or sweep her up

and carry her upstairs to his bedroom. Once there, he would do what he'd wanted to do the moment he'd kissed her. There was something about Celia Thomas that was so inherently sexy that she took his breath away.

She'd disclosed that her first boyfriend had cheated on her and she'd offset this when she'd agreed to marry a man whose low sex drive kept him from creeping around with other women. Dr. Yale Trevor-Jones may have been ten years Celia's senior, but that should not have precluded him from enjoying a healthy sex life—unless he had underlying physical problems that contributed to him not making love to his fiancée.

Celia was a woman a man would make love to—every day and every night!

The thought flooded Gavin's mind when he remembered her response to his kissing her for the first time, and then yesterday in the kitchen when she'd straddled his lap. It was obvious she was a passionate woman, but he couldn't understand why she'd chosen to marry a man who preferred sleeping to making love to his woman. And if they had married, how long would it have been before she would turn elsewhere for physical gratification?

"It wasn't too much," he stated with no expression on his face. "It wasn't enough." His eyebrows lifted with her soft gasp. "Because you didn't get to finish what you'd begun. The next time you decide to grind on my lap, be prepared to go all the way, baby. Now, what's on today's agenda?"

Celia gasped again. This time she couldn't believe Gavin had segued from talking about her grinding with him to asking what she'd planned for the day. "I'm going to call the animal hospital and check up on Terry, weed my flower garden, put up several loads of laundry, and then go to the pet store to buy a bed, a chew toy, harness, leash and travel crate. I also plan to stop by the nursery to pick up a few tomato plants."

"Can I help you with anything around the house?"

"Yes, Gavin."

He smiled. "What is it?"

"Stay out of my way, dah-lin."

Throwing back his head, Gavin laughed loudly. "You really sound like a down-South girl."

Celia wrinkled her nose. "That's because I am from down south. You say you're from Charlotte, but you don't sound as if you were raised in the south."

Gavin sobered. He'd lost whatever southern drawl he'd had after working with a speech coach. "I never said I was from Charlotte. I said my cousins' security company is based in Charlotte."

"Where did you grow up?"

"Silver Spring, Maryland." Cradling her face in his hands, Gavin kissed the end of her nose. "Enough questions. After you finish your household chores and errands, I'm going to take you out to dinner. Maybe I'll be able to find a place that offers live entertainment and dancing."

Holding on to his wrists, Celia went on tiptoe. "You dance?"

"Yes, I dance."

"Do you samba?"

"No. Where did you learn to samba?" Gavin asked.

"I have relatives in Bahia."

"Bahia, Brazil?"

Celia nodded. "Yes. The first time they invited me down for Carnivale I lost my mind. I partied non-stop, around the clock for days."

Sliding a hand down the length of Celia's arm, Gavin laced their fingers together. "Did you wear one of those skimpy costumes that leaves nothing to the imagination?"

"I plead the Fifth."

"Hey-y-y, Doc. You got funky, didn't you?"

She lifted a shoulder. "It *was* a little risqué."

"That's something I'd like to see."

"Maybe next year if you're not off protecting someone and I get off from the hospital, you can come with me."

The instant the invitation rolled off her tongue, Celia realized she was being premature. Her future was vague at best, because she didn't know where she was going to be the next day. There was still the upcoming trial, the aftermath and the question as to whether she would return to the hospital or focus all her energies on setting up the clinic.

"I'm sorry, Gavin."

"For what?"

"For being presumptuous. I shouldn't have extended an invitation when I don't know where I'm going to be next year."

Gavin saw a modicum of vulnerability in Celia for the first time. He wondered if Nicholas had mentioned the break-in at her Miami Beach home. "You don't plan on returning to Florida?"

"I plan to go back, but…"

"But what, Celia?"

She waved her free hand. "Nothing. I'd better get started on the garden before it rains." The mountains were nearly obliterated by the smoke-like fog. An average rainfall of eighty-five inches qualified the upper elevation and higher peaks of the Smoky Mountain as a temperate rain forest. "I left the fixings for an omelet in the refrigerator for you."

A rumble of thunder echoed in the distance. Gavin looked skyward. Angry black clouds hung over the mountains like a shroud. "You're going to have to put off working in the garden. It's about to storm."

"I'm going to see how much I can get done before the skies open up."

Short of forcibly restraining Celia, Gavin knew she intended to work in the garden despite the impending thunderstorm. Meteorologists had predicted rain for the next two days, then clearing and sunny weather for the holiday weekend.

"Have you eaten?" he asked, following her into the house, closing and locking the door behind them.

"I'm good," Celia said over her shoulder.

Quickening his pace, Gavin fell into step with Celia. "What does that mean?"

"I ate."

He gave her a sidelong glance. "What did you eat?"

She cut her eyes at him. "You're supposed to protect me, not monitor what I eat."

"If you don't eat, then there will be nothing left of you to protect."

"What are you trying to say, Gavin?"

"You're nothing but skin and bones, and I happen to like my women just a wee bit thicker than you are."

"It doesn't matter, because I'm not your woman," Celia countered, smiling.

Looping an arm around her waist, Gavin pulled her to his length. "You think not?"

Raising her chin, she smiled up at him. "I know not."

Gavin's expression changed as if someone had lowered a shade, concealing his innermost feelings. It was obvious Celia had no inkling of the dangers facing her. Someone had broken into her home, hoping to find her there, while Bradley MacArthur hadn't hesitated to approve his request to move out of the time-share and into Celia Cole-Thomas's vacation home. It was not what Mac said but what he didn't or wouldn't say that led Gavin to believe the shooting at the hospital was somehow linked to OPERATION: Top Gun.

He knew the shootout was gang- and drug-related. However, it was the weapon of choice used in the wanton murders that left members of law enforcement slack-jawed. Aside from having the same gang ink, each member carried a Desert Eagle. Unparalleled in handguns, the fifty-caliber chrome-tinted firearm was designed to reduce a target to a bleeding pulp. Celia was more than lucky to be alive. She was blessed, because the bullet had missed her vital organs.

It was as if the gun thieves had a shopping list that included the Desert Eagle, M4A1, AK47, M16A2, and the M249 SAW with a 200-round belt. The thieves also scooped up night-vision goggles and M84s. An M84 thrown into a room rendered occupants totally deaf and blind within seconds before reconnaissance rush in to subdue or eliminate their target. Another lethal weapon had appeared on the shopping list: a scythe with a nineteen-inch blade. Those who purchased the stolen weapons were either stockpiling them or preparing for war. The Department of Justice had confirmed that some of the weapons were used by several Mexican drug cartels in the deaths of police officers, civilians and gangsters.

"I promised you and your brother that I would protect you. That translates into you belonging to me for the summer and, therefore, *my* woman. When I ask you to do something don't hesitate or question me. To do so could possibly put not only your life but also mine in jeopardy." The tense lines around his mouth grew tighter. "I don't tell you how to practice medicine, so don't interfere with what I have to do to keep both of us safe."

Squaring her shoulders, Celia pulled herself up to her full height. "Nice speech, Gavin, but what does it have to do with my weight?"

"You need to eat, Celia," he countered sternly.

"But, I do eat."

"Sure, you eat. You pick at your food like a finicky child, leaving half of it on your plate. It's sinful the way you waste food. You may have been born with a platinum spoon in your mouth, but I grew up with kids who if they didn't take advantage of school breakfast and lunch, then they didn't eat. I didn't grow up wealthy, but there was never a question of not having enough to eat."

Celia felt properly chastised. Gavin was right. Each time they'd shared a meal she'd left food on her plate. Food that had to be thrown away, or could've been eaten by someone with little or no resources.

"Okay, Gavin," she conceded.

His eyebrows lifted questioningly. "Okay what?"

"I will eat breakfast with you."

Gavin felt a small measure of victory. If he were completely honest with Celia then he would've told her that he liked her body, but if she were to become malnourished he would be forced to call her brother and have him arrange for her to recuperate at the horse farm.

He affected a mock bow, the gesture fluid and graceful for a man his size. *"Gracias, Señorita Tomás."*

"Hey, you," Celia crooned, "I didn't know you spoke Spanish."

"I don't. I probably don't know more than ten words."

"Well, *m'ijo,* by the end of the summer you'll know more than ten words."

Resting his forehead on Celia's, Gavin pressed a kiss on the bridge of her nose. "Are you going to give me an exam?"

"*Sí, m'ijo.* And it won't be a number or letter grade. The final grade will be a Pass/Fail."

He smiled. "That's fair enough." He led her into the kitchen. "Sit down and I'll cook."

"I want a one-egg omelet," Celia announced as she sat on a high stool at the cooking island.

Gavin rolled his eyes upward. "There's no such thing as a one-egg omelet. Either it's two or three."

"Okay. Make it two."

Gavin lay on a recliner on the patio, watching Celia as she sat on a low stool pulling weeds from an over-grown flower garden. Thunder rumbled in the distance like the roar of an angry bear. There were intermittent flashes of lightning, but no rain.

She'd eaten more for breakfast than she had at dinner. Then, she hadn't had more than a few forkfuls of beans, rice, roast and pulled pork. She'd drunk coffee, but hadn't eaten the flan. He'd watched her pick at her plate, believing she was a picky eater when the thought came to him that she may possibly be bulimic. However, she'd proven him wrong when she ate all of her omelet, a slice of raisin toast, sliced fruit and two cups of coffee. Celia hadn't gone to the bathroom but to the mudroom to put on a pair of rubber boots and gardening tools.

There was another flash of lightning that lit up the entire sky. Gavin was on his feet. There had been enough light to see the shadowy outline of a dog. Reaching for the automatic tucked into the ankle holster, he rose to his feet and slowly made his way off the patio to the perimeter of the garden. Celia shifted the stool and the canine took two tentative steps. A roll of thunder shook the ground, followed by lightning that illuminated the countryside.

It'd only taken a glance for Gavin to recognize the shape crouched less than ten feet from where Celia sat as a coyote. "Don't move, baby," he warned quietly.

Celia glanced up, her eyes widening when she saw the gun pointed at her. The tears filling her eyes blurred her vision. Trance-like, she removed her gardening gloves. "Gavin, no." Her voice was a trembling whisper.

He took a step. "Don't talk and please, baby, don't move."

Raising his hand, his gaze never leaving the animal, he fired a warning shot within inches of the animal's ear, the sound reverberating like an echo. The smell of cordite hung heavily in the air as the coyote turned, ran and disappeared in the undergrowth of a copse of trees. Pushing the firearm into the waistband behind his back, Gavin approached Celia, who hadn't moved. When he reached out to touch her she began screaming, the ear-piercing shrieks lingering and carrying across the gorges and valleys like the wind.

Celia felt a fear she'd never experienced before, not even when she'd stared into the bore of the large handgun held by a boy who would eradicate two lives as naturally as exhaling. She hadn't believed he would shoot her or Yale because she knew they weren't his target. But after he'd fired the first shot it was as if he couldn't stop.

She couldn't believe she'd invited a man into her home, a man she trusted and he wanted to kill her. It was better if she'd died in the cubicle in the E.R. than in a house in the mountains where her nearest neighbor couldn't hear her even if she'd screamed at the top of her lungs. Her grandmother was right. If Gavin killed her, then it would be days, if not weeks before someone came looking for her body. Perhaps it was a good thing that she'd promised Nicholas she would come to Virginia the following weekend. If she didn't show up at least he'd know where to come looking for her.

Gavin took a step backward when Celia came at him, her fingers clawing at his face. He parried her flagging arms, and then grabbed her wrists, holding them at her sides while she screamed like someone possessed.

"Stop it, Celia!" He smothered a groan when her knee came up and made contact with his groin. Tightening his hold, he swung her up until she lay across his shoulder. He held her legs while she pounded his back, the blows bouncing off like hail hitting a roadway. Gavin carried her back into the house and dropped her on the chaise like a limp bedroll. He didn't give her a chance to move when his body covered hers.

Celia couldn't move and she couldn't breathe with the pressure of Gavin's body making her his prisoner. "Let me up."

"Not until you calm down."

"Calm down? How the hell am I supposed to be calm when you tried to kill me?"

Gavin stared at the high color in Celia's cheeks. It was the first time he noticed a sprinkling of freckles over the bridge of her nose that even the hot Florida sun hadn't been able to conceal. "If I'd wanted to kill you, baby, you wouldn't be talking right now."

Still struggling, Celia attempted to free herself. "Why, then, did you shoot at me?"

He smiled. "I wanted to scare off a coyote that was stalking you."

"You killed a coyote?"

"No, Celia. I frightened off a coyote. But, if he had attacked you, then I definitely would've had to kill it."

"Why didn't you shout at it instead of firing your gun?"

Gavin sobered. "What if it would've attacked you instead of running away? Then I'd have to take you to the hospital to be tested for rabies, and as a doctor you know what that entails." His eyes narrowed. "Why did you think I was trying to kill you, Celia?"

She closed her eyes. "I don't know, Gavin. When I heard the shot all I thought about were the few seconds when I saw two people shot before I felt the fire in my side." Celia opened her eyes to see Gavin staring at her as if she were a complete stranger. "Just for a nanosecond I believed you were a hit man. That someone had paid you to eliminate a witness."

"You're kidding, aren't you?"

"No, I'm not. You have to be aware of the number of witnesses that are murdered every year to keep them from testifying."

"You're wrong about me, baby. If I'd wanted to kill you I would've done it already. I could've put a bullet in your head when you stopped to help Terry, and then gotten back into my vehicle and drove away. There would've been nothing to link me to your death. No fingerprints and no DNA."

Celia nodded. She knew Gavin was right, but seeing the gun in his hand was like an instant replay of the moment when her life was in the hands of a crazed teenager bent on revenge and retaliation. "I'm sorry, Gavin. Seeing you with that gun was like déjà vu."

Supporting his weight on his elbows, Gavin cradled her head between his hands. "I promised to take care of you, not hurt you," he said softly and close to her parted lips.

A shiver of wanting raced through Celia's body. She knew what she proposed to ask the man molded to the length of her body bordered on brazenness but she was past caring.

"You can take care of me by making love to me."

Gavin went completely still as if he'd been shot, not wanting to believe what he'd just heard. He tried analyzing Celia's request, then chided himself for it. She'd thought she was going to die and his making love to her would confirm that she was still alive, breathing and feeling sensations that symbolized the perpetuation of life.

"Are you certain, Celia?"

A smile flitted across her full mouth. "As certain as I am that you'll protect me."

Needing no further prompting, he moved off the chaise, swinging her into his arms. He smiled when she put her arms around his neck as he walked off the porch, down a hallway to the staircase leading to the second story.

Gavin wanted to make love to Celia so he could eradicate the memory of the man she'd promised to marry. Dr. Yale Trevor-Jones was gone and he would take his place. Not as her fiancé, but as her lover and protector. He carried her up the staircase, walking into his bedroom and closing the door even though they were the only ones in the house. He wanted the bedroom to

become a sanctuary where they would shut out the past
and begin anew. When he made love to her he wanted
to forget every woman from his past and make Celia
forget every other man.

Celia had begged Gavin to make love to her because
she felt empty inside. It had nothing to do with bearing
a child. It was the lack of sexual fulfillment. She hadn't
realized the inadequacies of her first lover until she'd
left him. Not only was he unworthy of her virginity, but
his selfishness was apparent when he failed to make
certain she climaxed before he did.

Chapter 10

Gavin placed Celia on the bed as if she were a fragile piece of crystal. He turned on the lamp on the bedside table. Going to his knees, he removed her boots and socks, his gaze never leaving hers. He searched her face, looking for indecision, but saw strength, determination instead. She'd asked him to make love to her and he would, because it was something he'd wanted to do the instant she'd turned to look at him in the supermarket.

Even without knowing her name or whether she was married or involved with someone, he'd wanted to make love to her, and that had been a first for him. He'd believed he would never see her again, but fate had intervened when he'd flagged down her SUV before she caused further injury to the puppy that had crawled on to the roadway.

By the time he'd celebrated his thirty-fifth birthday,

Gavin had long tired of the lies and head games when it came to interacting with women. Some he would see once or twice, and the few who'd managed to hold his interest for more than a week or two he continued to date. Celia was different. He hadn't known her a week, yet it felt as if they had been together for months. Sharing dinner with her and her brother was easygoing and enjoyable. It had been a long time since he'd felt a part of a family unit because of his brother's undercover stints. Wheras he would take a break between assignments, it hadn't been that way with Orlando. It was as if the ex-Navy SEAL ATF agent had to prove his worth over and over because of his drug-addicted parents.

Placing a hand over Celia's flat belly, Gavin leaned over and brushed his mouth over hers. "Are you certain this is what you want?"

Her lips parted in a demure smile. "Yes, Gavin, it is what I want." Her dulcet voice had dropped an octave, becoming almost a whisper.

He wanted to tell her it would change everything between them. Once they joined their bodies it would change him *and* change her. "Do I need to protect you?"

It took a while for Celia to realize Gavin was asking her whether she was using a contraceptive. She'd had her gynecologist remove the intrauterine device before she was discharged from the hospital. If she were to embark on a summer liaison with Gavin, she didn't want the result to be an unplanned pregnancy. It'd always been her wish to marry, and then start a family.

"Yes, please."

Gavin kissed her again. "Don't run away, baby."

He left the bed and made his way to the walk-in closet and opened the door. He placed the automatic and ankle holster on a shelf, then reached for a toiletry bag, opened it and took out several condoms. Celia's eyes appeared abnormally large when he returned to the bed and placed a condom on the pillow beside her head. It was as if seeing the small packet made what they were about to do real. It was one thing to talk about making love and another to actually engage in the very intimate act where they'd cease to exist as separate entities.

Gavin couldn't understand what made Celia Cole-Thomas so different from the other women he'd slept with. At first, he'd believed he was attracted to her delicate beauty and intelligence. Then it was her strength, but after seeing her reaction to his discharging a shot, he knew it was her vulnerability. Under the tough-girl, scrappy exterior was a woman who'd stared death in the face and survived. And despite the dangers facing her, she was willing to enter a courtroom to testify as to what she'd witnessed to send a murderer to prison for the rest of his natural life, or to death row.

His hands were steady when he unsnapped the waistband on her jeans and eased them off her hips and down her legs. "Very cute." Celia wore a pair of candy-striped, red-and-white silk bikini panties. His expressive eyebrows lifted. "I love peppermint." Before Celia could react, Gavin had pressed his face to her groin and blew his hot breath against the triangle of silk. "You smell delicious."

Heat *and* shame burned Celia's face. She'd never had the experience of a man putting his face between her legs. Even when she'd overheard her female friends and colleagues talk about what went on in their bedrooms, she was never one to contribute to the discussion when it came to oral sex. The first time she'd asked Yale if he'd ever gone down on a woman, he'd stared at her as if she'd been suddenly diagnosed with leprosy or another deadly communicable disease. It was the first and last time she'd broached the subject with him.

She closed her eyes, letting all of her senses take over. Gavin's touch was gentle as he removed her jeans, tank top, bra and finally her panties. Celia felt rather than saw Gavin move off the bed, and she opened her eyes. He stood tall and powerful, looming over the bed like the bronze statues she'd seen in museums. She inhaled a breath, holding it while he unbuttoned the chambray shirt and shrugged it off his broad shoulders. A slight gasp escaped her when she stared at the unbelievable perfection of his toned, muscled upper body.

Celia was transfixed, unable to pull her gaze away from her soon-to-be lover as he undressed and the throbbing between her legs had become an ache only he could assuage. Everything about Gavin Faulkner was different from her late fiancé, from his coloring to his height and breadth. Her eyes followed his every motion as he leaned over to remove his boots and socks, the muscles in his back rippling sensuously. His jeans came next, followed by a pair of black boxer-briefs. Then she did close her eyes, but curiosity forced her to open them seconds later to stare numbly in awe at the long, thick sex hanging heavily between muscled thighs.

Seeing Gavin fully clothed was a turn-on. But, seeing him completely naked set her nerve endings on fire. Heated blood rushed through Celia's body, making it almost impossible for her to remain immobile. As a doctor she'd lost count of the number of naked men she'd seen, yet looking at Gavin completely nude for the first time negated all of her medical training. He wasn't her patient. He was a man with whom she'd asked to share his body. And what a magnificent body it was.

Rising from the pillow, she extended her hand. "Come sit down and put your back against the headboard."

Gavin complied. "What's up, baby?"

Celia straddled his lap. "I have to deal with some unfinished business."

Anchoring his hands around her waist, he pulled her closer. "Does that unfinished business have anything to do with a lap dance?"

Shocks of arousal swept through her when her breasts touched his smooth, hard chest. "Yes. But if it's too much for you—"

"I didn't say it was too much for me," Gavin said, cutting her off. "I said you can't tease me, then not finish what you've started."

"It wasn't my fault that my brother came unannounced."

Burying his face between her neck and shoulder, he nipped the silky skin. "There's nothing to stop us now."

Celia anchored her arms under Gavin's shoulders. "I suggest you wrap up your package now." She didn't want or need any accidents where sex play ended in her becoming pregnant. Scooting down his thighs, she hovered above his knees.

Throwing back his head, Gavin laughed loudly. He'd predicted they were going to have a lot of fun hanging out together, and Celia had just proven him right. "Yes, Doc." Reaching for the condom, he opened the packet and rolled the latex sheath down the length of his penis. His hands went to Celia's waist as he pulled her closer.

Pressing her mouth to her lover's ear, she pulled the lobe gently between her teeth. "Hang on, *m'ijo*. It's going to be a bumpy ride, but I promise to bring you in for a smooth landing."

Gavin laughed again, the sound drowned out by the roll of thunder, followed by an explosive crash of lightning that lit up the entire bedroom. Rain lashed the windows with a fury that rattled them in their frames. But the power of the storm paled in comparison to the storm Celia had created in his loins.

He closed his eyes rather than stare at the carnal expression on the face of a woman offering him the most exquisite sex he'd ever experienced. Her hips were poetry in motion, moving sensually over his penis in an up-and-down motion before changing to one that rocked from side to side. Unknowingly, she'd seduced him the moment she'd opened her mouth to answer his query about the differences in cabbage. Her smoky voice had pulled him in where he wanted to engage in an extended conversation with a stranger.

The condom Gavin had chosen to wear was so thin that Celia felt as if he were wearing nothing, and she feared climaxing before she could know what it was like to have his prodigious erection inside her. It lay against his belly, pulsing as she slid up and down its length. Her breathing deepened as she struggled to force air into her lungs. A small moan escaped her before she fastened her mouth to his breast, suckling him like a starving infant.

Gavin bellowed. It was too much! If he didn't stop Celia he would ejaculate into the condom, something he loathed. Holding her waist in a punishing grip, he reversed their position and holding his penis, he guided it between her legs. He managed to find the opening to her vagina but was thwarted when he felt resistance. She'd admitted she wasn't a virgin yet her body was tight as one. Taking his time, he pushed gently, while preparing her to take all of him.

Celia felt her celibate flesh stretching to accommodate the length and girth of Gavin's sex. There was pain. Good pain. They sighed in unison when he was fully sheathed inside her. She closed her eyes, smiling. It had taken thirty-three years for her to find her sexual counterpart.

"Did I hurt you?"

Her eyes opened. "No," she answered truthfully.

"Are you sure you're not a virgin?" Gavin whispered in her ear.

A moan of ecstasy slipped through her lips when her whole being was flooded with desire for the man pressing her down to the mattress. Everything about Gavin was intoxicating, from the feel, warmth and smell of his flesh, to the hardness filling her. She never tired of looking at his beautiful masculine face.

"I'm not a virgin, and will you please do something for me?"

"What, baby?"

"Stop talking."

"And do what?" he asked.

"Finish what you've started, *m'ijo.*"

Gavin needed no further prompting. He rolled his hips, swallowing a groan when he felt the walls of her vagina squeeze his penis before releasing it. Celia was on fire, and it was racing out of control and spreading to him. The rising scent of their lovemaking had become an aphrodisiac.

Celia rose to meet his strong thrusts in an uncontrolled passion that stunned her with its intensity. She moaned, cried as erotic pleasure seized her in a vise that refused to let her go. Then, it happened. The flutters in her vagina grew stronger, more frequent and then she felt the familiar sensation at the base of her spine signaling she was going to climax.

"No!" The protest came out between teeth clenched so tightly her jaw ached. She didn't want it to be over. It was much too quick. The orgasms came, tumbling over one another when she gave in to the all-consuming passion that had been building since Gavin Faulkner pressed her against the bumper of his truck and kissed her. He'd awakened a sleeping passion that made her crave him every waking moment. She'd told herself she didn't want or need him but her body said differently.

Celia never acted as brazenly with another man as she had with Gavin. His overt masculinity had become a beacon calling out to her and guiding her home. She could feel the heat from him seep into her as she bared her throat and cried out as her body vibrated with liquid fire that swept her away and she floated into nothingness.

Gavin quickened his thrusts as he surrendered to the sensations taking him beyond himself. He'd tried holding back, but his heart felt as if it was going to explode. Burying his face in the pillow beneath Celia's head, he bellowed out his pleasure as the strong pulsing in his sex ebbed, leaving him feeling as helpless as a newborn.

He was shocked at his response to her lovemaking, and deeply disturbed because he realized making love with Celia was a mistake. When it came time for him to leave her, he knew it wasn't going to be easy—not when he lived under her roof and they'd become lovers.

One thing he was certain of: it would take Herculean strength for him to make a clean break. That would only be possible if he continued to remind himself why he was in North Carolina. Making contact with his brother and getting him back safe was his first and only priority. Orlando Wells Faulkner only had him as his lifeline, while Dr. Celia Cole-Thomas had a wealthy family that would move heaven and earth to keep her safe.

Raising his head, he smiled at Celia smiling back at him. "Thank you, baby."

Her smile grew wider. "You're welcome, *m'ijo.*"

Reluctantly, Gavin pulled out, and left the bed to go to the bathroom to discard the condom. When he returned to the bedroom, Celia had turned off the lamp and covered herself with the sheet and lightweight blanket. He sat down on the side of the bed. "May I join you?"

Her shoulders shook with laughter. "I should be asking you if I can stay. After all, this is your bed."

He pulled back the sheet and stared at the scar where the bullet had passed through her side. Lowering his head, he pressed his mouth to the puckered flesh that was a constant reminder of how close she'd come to losing her life. "Move over, baby."

Celia shifted and Gavin got into bed, pressing his groin to her hips. They lay together like spoons and went to sleep.

Gavin woke and peered at the travel clock on the bedside table. The rain had stopped, but dark clouds made it seem as if it were nightfall instead of late afternoon. He couldn't believe he'd been asleep for hours. The scent of a woman's perfume lingered on the pillow beside his, and then the realization that he was alone in bed galvanized him into action. Scrambling off the bed, he reached for his jeans and slipped them on in one smooth motion. Racing over to the closet, he retrieved the automatic.

Taking long strides, he ran barefoot down the hall to the staircase, taking the stairs two at a time. Celia had turned on lamps and ceiling lights on the first floor to offset the unnatural darkness blanketing the countryside.

He followed the sound of music, coming to a stop where he found the object of his unquenchable desire sitting on the window seat in the alcove off the kitchen. Recessed lighting bathed her in a soft flattering glow as she concentrated on wielding a pair of knitting needles. Gavin watched, transfixed as she pulled up a strand of pistachio-green yarn from a quilted bag, winding it around her forefinger.

It was obvious she'd showered because raven-black curls hung loosely around her face and neck. With her bare legs and feet, oversize tee and shorts, she looked as if she were barely out of her teens. She was singing along with a sensual ballad flowing from concealed speakers. Without warning, her head came up to find him watching her. A shy smile spread across her face.

"The prince awakens from his deep sleep." Celia patted the cushioned seat. "Come sit. I called the animal hospital and we can come and get Terry anytime after ten on Monday."

Concealing the firearm in his waist at the small of his back, Gavin approached her. "That's good. How long have you been awake?"

Her hands stilled. "I just got up about half an hour ago."

"Why didn't you wake me?"

"I tried, but you were snoring so loud I didn't have the heart to disturb you."

"I don't snore," Gavin said in protest.

"How do you know?"

"No one has ever complained that I do," he countered.

Celia stared at the man who'd made the most exquisite love to her. She'd memorized every angle in his face so she would be able to pick him out in a darkened room with a hundred other men. Shuttering her gaze, she forced herself not to look below his neck or she would jump him where he stood. "It could be that I'm a very light sleeper."

"Either that, or it comes with being a doctor."

Her head came up. She nodded. "That, too."

A slight frown settled between Gavin's eyes. "Does this mean we're not going to sleep together?"

Celia's eyes narrowed. "Did I say I didn't want us to sleep together?"

"It's not that, Celia."

"Then what is it, Gavin?"

It was his turn to squint at her. "Are you spoiling for a fight, *m'ija?*" He'd spat out the endearment.

Lowering her head rather than let him see her smirk, Celia pretended to concentrate on the blanket that would match the sweater, cap and booties set she'd completed. "Nope."

"If not, then why the attitude, Celia?"

"I don't have an attitude, Gavin Faulkner. I merely stated a fact. You snore. I know you believe you're Mr. Perfect—"

"Stop it!"

The two words came out with the impact of the crack of a whip, causing Celia to sit up and stare at Gavin as if she'd never seen him before. "Don't ever raise your voice to me again."

"I don't want or need your sarcasm," Gavin shot back, refusing to back down. "If my snoring bothers you, then say what you mean. I'll ask you again, and I expect you to be honest with me. Would you prefer that we sleep in separate bedrooms?"

The seconds ticked as Celia pondered Gavin's query. She'd fallen asleep with his arm thrown over her waist, but when she did wake up hours later it was to find him snoring loudly. She'd tried going back to sleep and couldn't. Her attempt to move him enough to change positions had yielded little success, and she had left the bed rather than wake him.

She shook her head slowly. "No, Gavin. I don't want us to sleep apart. Maybe after a couple of nights I'll get used to you calling hogs."

"I thought I was sawing logs," he teased.

"Hogs or logs, they're all the same."

Gavin didn't want to congratulate himself because he'd won a small victory. After making love with Celia, he didn't want to think of not sharing a bed with her again. Making love and then getting up and leaving her was too impersonal. Even when he'd had a one-night stand, he usually stayed with the woman until the following morning.

"Who taught you to knit?"

Celia smiled, her former annoyance with Gavin forgotten. "My mother. She was into fashion and design before she gave it up to become a full-time mother."

Gavin angled his head. "I've made love to you, yet I know very little about you other than you are a doctor, you have two brothers and you live in Miami."

"I'll tell you whatever you *need* to know about me if you let me take you out to dinner."

"I'll let you select the restaurant, but only if I pay."

She held out her hand. "Deal."

Ignoring her hand, Gavin leaned over and brushed his mouth over hers. "I'm going upstairs to shave and shower."

When he got up to walk away, Celia saw the butt of the gun tucked into his waistband. "I don't want to see it, Gavin."

He stopped, but didn't turn around, knowing she was referring to the handgun. "I won't wear it in the house if you keep the alarm on at all times."

"Okay," she said quickly.

Celia watched him leave, and then realized how fast her heart was beating. She'd grown up around guns all of her life but a single incident had her rethinking her views about even more stringent laws when it came to gun ownership.

Gavin smiled at Celia across the space of a small table for two at a downtown Waynesville family-style restaurant. They'd stopped at a pet store to buy items the puppy would need once he was home. Their original plan to share Terry was null and void now that he and Celia were living together.

For a reason he couldn't fathom, Gavin relished the notion of living with Celia. Not only would she fill in the empty hours that went along with undercover work, but she would also fill in as a social accoutrement. He'd discovered people were more willing to relate to a couple than a lone male.

The rain had stopped but the mercury had dropped more than twenty-two degrees, making it feel more like early fall than late spring. Celia wore an oatmeal cashmere turtleneck wrap sweater with chocolate wool gabardine slacks, while he'd chosen a black wool pullover with matching flannel slacks and imported slip-ons. She reminded him of a high school co-ed with the Burberry plaid headband holding the curls off her forehead.

The restaurant was filled to capacity with teenagers, seniors and couples with children ranging in age from toddlers in booster seats to preteens. A number of muted televisions were positioned around the establishment, while a satellite radio station played music spanning the last five decades. Like the varied menu, there was something for everyone.

Celia had ordered baked chicken, a baked potato and spinach salad. His dinner choice was broiled salmon, wild rice and butternut squash. Their waitress had suggested a pitcher of mulled apple cider, which proved to be the perfect beverage complement for the damp weather.

Celia set down her mug of cider and touched the corners of her mouth with a cloth napkin. "What do you want to know about me?" she asked Gavin.

"Why do you hyphenate your last name?"

Her gaze lingered on the skin pulled taut over the ridge of his high cheekbones. "My grandmother claimed she was a feminist decades before the women's liberation movement when she opted not to drop her maiden name. The news didn't sit well with her fiancé, but after a lengthy discussion with his future father-in-law, he gave in. I'd heard rumors that Samuel Cole bought the house in Palm Beach as a wedding gift after Noah Thomas agreed to the hyphenated surname."

Gavin smiled, his teeth dazzlingly white in his brown face. "Your great-grandfather sounds like quite a colorful character."

Celia shook her head. "He was a rogue. He fought in World War I and when he returned to the States he went to Cuba, hoping to buy a sugarcane plantation."

"Did he know anything about growing sugarcane?"

"Samuel Cole was a farmer, as was his father and brothers. They'd begun growing cotton, then switched to soybeans well before it'd become a practice in this country. He never got to buy the plantation because of anti-American sentiment, but got something better out of the deal. He married the daughter of a Cuban cigar manufacturer.

"Marguerite-Joséfina Isabel Diaz was cosseted, beautiful and quite the wild child. With her waist-length hair and dimpled smile she'd become the toast of Havana. She was attending the *Universidad* when the news that she'd posed for a noted artist wearing nothing more than a dressing gown reached her father. He ordered her home, and was in the process of finalizing an arranged marriage when Samuel offered to marry her."

"Are you certain you're talking about the twentieth century?"

Celia nodded. "You have to understand, I'm talking about pre-revolutionary Cuba where it was all about class. M.J.'s antics, as she insisted everyone call her, were an embarrassment to her upper class father, and he was afraid no self-respecting man would marry his daughter. Samuel married her and brought her back to Florida. She gave him four children, two sons and daughters, and he built her a twenty-four-room mansion in West Palm Beach. He expanded his agribusiness with a banana plantation in Costa Rica, and coffee plantations in Mexico, Puerto Rico and Jamaica. He'd managed to survive the Crash of 1929, and went on to become the first black billionaire in the United States. The total worth of ColeDiz International is a carefully guarded secret, because it is family-owned and privately held."

"Is your great-grandfather still alive?"

"No, but my great-grandmother is. She will turn one hundred six at the end of the year. She's somewhat frail and refuses to speak English. All she talks about is how she misses her Sammy and wants to see him."

"Is she in a nursing home?" Gavin asked.

"Heaven forbid," Celia sputtered. "She lives with her eldest son, who provides her with around-the-clock nursing care."

Leaning back in his chair, Gavin gave Celia a steady look. "So, you're a trust-fund baby."

"Yes. However, that's not something I advertise."

"But you told me."

Her left eyebrow lifted. "That's because I know I can trust you not to tell my business. I checked you out."

It was training and years of undercover work for Gavin not to react to Celia's statement. "When and how?" His voice was low, even and his expression hadn't changed.

"When you left to pick up your clothes, I went online and searched for listings of security companies in Charlotte, North Carolina. It took two calls to make contact with your cousins' firm. They verified that you did work for them, but you were currently on vacation. Don't look so put out, Gavin. After all, you did tell my brother he could have you checked out."

He wanted to tell Celia that his cousins were programmed to say he was on vacation whenever he went undercover. Only his mother, cousins and brother knew that he was a special agent with the FBI.

Leaning forward, Gavin winked at her. "Do you trust me now?"

Celia returned his wink. "I'll have to think about it,"

An Important Message from the Publisher

Dear Reader,

Because you've chosen to read one of our fine novels, I'd like to say "thank you"! And, as a special way to say thank you, I'm offering to send you two more Kimani™ Romance novels and two surprise gifts – absolutely FREE! These books will keep it real with true-to-life African American characters that turn up the heat and sizzle with passion.

Please enjoy the free books and gifts with our compliments...

Glenda Howard

For Kimani Press

Peel off Seal and Place Inside...

THE EDITOR'S "THANK YOU" FREE GIFTS INCLUDE:

▶ Two Kimani™ Romance Novels
▶ Two exciting surprise gifts

YES!

I have placed my Editor's "thank you" Free Gifts seal in the space provided at right. Please send me 2 FREE books, and my 2 FREE Mystery Gifts. I understand that I am under no obligation to purchase anything further, as explained on the back of this card.

```
PLACE
FREE GIFTS
SEAL
HERE
```

About how many NEW paperback fiction books have you purchased in the past 3 months?

❏ 0-2	❏ 3-6	❏ 7 or more
EZQE	EZQQ	EZQ2

168/368 XDL

FIRST NAME	LAST NAME

ADDRESS

APT.#	CITY

STATE/PROV.	ZIP/POSTAL CODE

Thank You!

Offer limited to one per household and not valid to current subscribers of Kimani™ Romance books. **Your Privacy**—Kimani Press is committed to protecting your privacy. Our Privacy Policy is available online at www.KimaniPress.com or upon request from the Reader Service. From time to time we make our lists of customers available to reputable third parties who may have a product or service of interest to you. If you would prefer for us not to share your name and address, please check here ❏.**Help us get it right**—We strive for accurate, respectful and relevant communications. To clarify or modify your communication preferences, visit us at www.ReaderService.com/consumerchoice.

BUSINESS REPLY MAIL
FIRST-CLASS MAIL   PERMIT NO. 717   BUFFALO, NY

POSTAGE WILL BE PAID BY ADDRESSEE

THE READER SERVICE
PO BOX 1867
BUFFALO NY 14240-9952

NO POSTAGE
NECESSARY
IF MAILED
IN THE
UNITED STATES

she teased, astonished at the sense of blissful careless-
ness that made her so reckless. Gavin Faulkner was
good for her, and she knew by summer's end, she would
be more than ready to pick up the pieces of her life.

Chapter 11

Gavin pulled on a pair of gray-and-white-striped pajama pants, tightening the drawstring waist. Celia had invited him to a sleepover. It was to take place in her bedroom. Over dinner, she'd revealed facts and details about her family that would've taken Bureau investigators months to compile.

Gavin felt a measure of guilt that Celia was able to speak freely about family secrets when he had to conceal his true identity. He'd told her what she needed to know about him. He was Gavin Tyrone Faulkner, born and raised in Charlotte, North Carolina and thirty-seven years old. Everything else about him was classified. Picking up the charger to his cell phone, he plugged it into the device at the same time the phone rang.

He punched a button. "Faulkner."

"Are you close to a TV?"

"What's up, Mac?"

"Answer my question, Faulkner."

"Yes, I am. Why?"

"Tune it to CNN."

Still holding the phone to his ear, Gavin walked to the sitting area and flipped on the television, punching in the numbers for the channel. He went completely still when listening to the news journalist give an account of breaking news.

"What does this mean, Mac?" The prosecutor in the Miami hospital-E.R. shooting was missing, and the Bureau was treating it as a kidnapping because of a ransom demand.

"Right now, we're going over all of his former and upcoming cases to see if anyone has threatened him with retaliation."

Folding his long frame into a club chair, Gavin pressed a button on the remote, activating the closed-captioned feature. "What haven't you told me, Mac? Do you think this has anything to do with Celia Cole-Thomas?"

"We can't verify anything right now. But, if there is a connection, then she'll be under the protection of the U.S. Marshals. What I can tell you is that the guns used in the hospital shooting were stolen by the same bunch Raymond Prentice ran with and those gang bangers are working for a Miami drug cartel with a network spanning the length of the east coast."

"Are you saying the shooting is linked to OPERATION: Top Gun?"

"Yes."

The seconds ticked when Gavin paused to collect

his thoughts. "I'd like approval to provide protection for Dr. Thomas."

"You know…"

"Mac, don't say it. I know witness protection falls under the jurisdiction of the Marshals Service, but remember this *is* a joint task force operation."

"You have enough on your plate with Ray Prentice."

"I'll bring Ray in. I will also turn Dr. Thomas over to the marshals once the date is set for the trial."

"What's your stake in this, Faulkner?"

A scowl marred Gavin's attractive features. "What the hell are you talking about?"

"Don't get caught up in something from which you won't be able to extricate yourself," Bradley MacArthur warned. "Do not get involved with *your* witness."

A smile replaced Gavin's frown. He couldn't tell his supervisor that it was too late. He was already involved with Celia. "So, she *is* my witness?"

"Don't expect me to put that in writing."

"Thanks, Mac."

"I also want you to know that I've been working on you getting reassigned to a field office. Any place in particular?"

"I'd like to stay close to home." He liked living in northern Virginia.

"I'll see what I can do. Bring in Prentice and keep the lady safe so she can testify, and you can have your pick of any desk between D.C. and Miami."

"Thanks, Mac."

"Be careful."

Gavin closed his eyes as a chill raced over his body. It was the first time in all the years he'd known Bradley MacArthur that he had warned him to be careful. Was something going on that his supervisor hadn't apprised him of? And why had Mac given in so easily when he'd asked to provide protection for Celia?

"I will." That said, he ended the call and turned off the television.

Witness protection meant everywhere Celia went, he'd go. He also had to tell her about the prosecutor's abduction—that is, if she didn't already know. The thought had just entered his mind when the object of his musings walked into the bedroom. Her eyes appeared unusually large and haunted. The expression on her face said she *did* know.

Gavin forced a smile he didn't feel. What he didn't want to acknowledge was the thread of fear weaving its way into his consciousness. He wasn't afraid for himself; he was afraid for Celia.

"I just turned off the television."

Celia walked into the bedroom, closing the distance between her and the man who'd promised to protect her. While setting up the board for a game of Scrabble with Gavin, she'd turned on the television to an all-news station. When she'd heard the announcement that the Miami-Dade prosecutor had been kidnapped at gunpoint in the driveway to his home, she'd felt faint.

"Do you think this is a random abduction, Gavin?"

Gavin pulled her close, feeling the warmth of her body through a cotton tee and shorts. "I don't know, baby. Not only is Alton Fitch a high-profile prosecutor, but he also comes from a very wealthy family. It could be either a crime of revenge or greed." Cradling her face in his hands, he kissed the end of her nose. "Whatever it is, I don't want you to worry about anything. I'm going to take care of you. And that means everywhere you go, I go." Nodding, Celia closed her eyes. "Who knows you're staying here?"

She opened her eyes. The hardened expression on Gavin's face frightened her, and it was the first time she viewed him as a protection specialist. "I've only told my family."

"Do you mean immediate family, or uncles, aunts and cousins?"

She gave him an incredulous look. "When I say family it means *everyone*."

"Are most of your family in Florida?"

Celia shook her head. "They live all over."

"Where is all over?" Gavin was firing questions at her like an interrogator.

"They live in Virginia, Massachusetts, New Mexico, Mississippi and Brazil. Why do you want to know?"

"If and when anyone contacts you—and that includes family members—do not tell them where you are if they don't already know. How about friends? Do any of them know you have a place here?"

"I have a sorority sister who has visited me here a few times."

"What's her name?" Gavin asked, continuing his questioning.

"What does she have to do with anything, Gavin?"

"Just answer the question."

Celia bit her lip until she felt it throbbing between her teeth. "Her name is Rania Norris. She's married, but she never changed her name."

"Where does she live?"

"Why?"

Gavin's fingers tightened on her jaw. "Answer me,

Celia." The three words were ground out between clenched teeth.

"She lives in a suburb outside Detroit."

"When was the last time you saw or talked to her?"

"We haven't seen each other for almost two years, but we talk every couple of months."

"I don't want you to call her, and if she calls I don't want you to take her call."

"What about my family?"

"The same goes for them."

Celia stared at Gavin as if he'd lost his mind. "No. You can't cut me off from my family."

A slow smile eased the lines of tension ringing Gavin's generous mouth. "I'm not going to cut you off from them. Give me the number to your brother's farm. He will be your sole connection to the rest of your family until the trial."

"Does this mean we're not going to see him next week?"

Nicholas had reassured Gavin that his property was guarded around the clock. It was Celia who'd told him that her brother had invested millions to make his horse farm viable and profitable.

"We're going as planned. You're not going to alter your regular activities. What you're going to do is limit your telephone contacts. There are computer experts that can hack a cell phone as easily as taking a drink of water. We don't know if Fitch's abduction is random, or if his abductors have a particular motive for snatching him."

"Do you think I'm that motive?"

Gavin gave her a reassuring smile. "I doubt it. I just want to tie up some loose ends."

The loose ends were people who knew Dr. Celia

Cole-Thomas was the state of Florida's key witness in a capital murder trial. Vera had given him minute details of the hospital shootout. Although the names of the doctors killed in the rampage were printed in the newspapers, their photographs did not appear at the request of their respective families. Dr. Celia Cole-Thomas's name was never mentioned, and Gavin knew it was because of her family's clout in the state that kept that information out of the press.

"I need you to answer one more question for me."

Celia rolled her eyes. "What is it?"

"This cookout we're going to Saturday."

"What about it, Gavin?"

"Do they know about your late fiancé?"

She nodded. "I told Hannah everything, except that I'm going to be the only witness at a murder trial. The other people in the waiting room were either too frightened or things happened so quickly they weren't sure what they saw."

"Did you tell her anything about me?"

"No, Gavin." There was a hint of laughter in Celia's voice. "What's up?"

"I want you to introduce me as your husband."

Celia chuckled as she replayed his suggestion in her head. "Have you gone and lost your mind?"

"No. And, it's not funny."

"I think it is, Gavin. In fact, I think it's hilarious."

Gavin dropped his hands. "Pretending we're married will be the perfect cover for why I'm living with you. If I hadn't given up my time-share, then I would've remained your boyfriend."

"Can't you get it back?"

"No. And I don't want it back."

Exhaling audibly, Celia tunneled her fingers through her hair. "I've lied more since I've met you than at any other time in my life."

"Don't lay that blame on me, *m'ija*. You were the one who told Nicholas that you'd hired me as your bodyguard."

"That's so he wouldn't get in my face about you. He made my life a living hell when he found out I'd moved in with Yale. There are times when my brother forgets that not only am I older than he is, but that I'm quite capable of living my life without his interference."

"Don't knock it, Celia. There are brothers who could care less not only about their sister but also the woman who gave birth to them."

She waved a hand. "Let's get back to this marriage of convenience, Gavin. It is only for this weekend?"

"Let's play it by ear."

"Marriages of convenience only happen in romance novels."

It was Gavin's turn to roll his eyes upward. "Please don't tell me you read *those*."

"Reading *those* kept me sane while I was convalescing. I had my sister-in-law bring me dozens every week. I read them because I knew they were going to end with a happily ever after and at that time I needed as many ups as I could muster."

Gavin felt as if he'd come down with a case of foot-in-mouth. How easy it was for him to forget how close Celia had come to dying.

He took a step and swept her up in his arms. "Will you forgive me for being so insensitive?"

Wrapping her arms around his neck, Celia kissed Gavin's forehead. "I'll think about it."

"Don't think too long, wifey."

"Call me that again and you'll find yourself sleeping on the sofa."

"I can't fit on the sofa."

"That's the idea, hubby." Celia's gaze met and fused with Gavin's. Her teasing fled quickly. "Do you think we can pull it off?"

"Of course we can, baby."

"Are you willing to wear a wedding band?"

"Of course," Gavin confirmed.

Celia, her mind in tumult, buried her face on Gavin's solid shoulder. They were to pretend they were married while the prosecutor who depended upon her testimony to get a guilty plea had been abducted steps from his front door. She closed her eyes, whispering a silent prayer for his quick and safe return.

"We'll go shopping for rings tomorrow," she whispered in his ear.

Gavin tightened his hold under her legs. "I remember seeing a nice jewelry store in Asheville."

Her head popped up. "There's no need to go all the way to Asheville for rings."

"What if someone in Waynesville recognizes you? How will you explain buying rings when we're supposed to be married?"

"You're right, Gavin."

"Spoken like an obedient, dutiful wife. No! Please stop!" Celia had caught his earlobe between her teeth. "I'm sorry, baby."

She released his lobe. "*Obey* or any derivative of that offensive word will never ever be uttered in my wedding vows. The exception will be if my husband agrees to obey me."

Gavin carried her to the bed, sitting and settling her on his lap. "I was the obedient, dutiful husband-in-training when you asked me to make love to you."

Celia covered her face with her hands. "Don't remind me of that. I've never been that brazen."

Reaching for her hands, he eased her down to the mattress. "I'm not complaining, Celia. In fact, I was honored you asked me and not some other man."

"I like making love with you, Gavin."

He ran a finger down the length of her delicate nose, his mouth replacing his finger as he caressed her lips. "And I love making love to you."

Gavin loved making love to Celia and he'd discovered that he liked her—a little too much for it to be a game. The charade of his being her bodyguard had escalated to a pretend marriage, and none of it had anything to do with why he'd come to the Great Smoky Mountains.

He was a special agent for the Bureau, yet, with his supervisor's approval, was operating more like a *wet boy* doing whatever needed to be done to fulfill his mission. His request to provide witness protection for Celia wasn't unreasonable because he was already living with her and she trusted him. Bradley MacArthur hadn't confirmed or denied—or didn't know—whether Fitch's abduction was connected to the E.R. shootout. Gavin suspected OPERATION: Top Gun had many more layers than what he'd read in the classified file. While ATF, DEA and FBI agents were chasing drug traffickers and gun smugglers, his focus was to bring his brother in alive and protect a witness in a high-profile murder trial.

Celia held her breath when she felt Gavin's hand

moving under the hem of her T-shirt, his finger making tiny circles around her belly button. "I thought we were going to play Scrabble."

Lowering his head, Gavin pressed a kiss to her flat belly. "Do you really want to play?"

She tried sitting up, but he pushed her back down. "Of course I want to play. After all, you were the one talking about your undefeated record."

"I don't want to brag, but I should alert you that I was a finalist for my school district for the Scripps National Spelling Bee."

Celia's jaw dropped. "You were a nerd?"

"What's wrong with being a nerd?"

"I just thought you would've been super jock," she countered.

Gavin leaned closer, their mouths inches apart. "I was a nerd *and* a jock. By the time I was fifteen I stood several inches above six feet. High school coaches wanted me to join the basketball team, but I preferred football. I played defense because it gave me the opportunity to pound the hell out of guys that teased me because I wore glasses and made the honor roll. I worked out as hard as I studied and by the time I graduated, I was six-four and a solid two hundred pounds."

"What happened to the glasses?"

"I had surgery to correct my vision."

Celia forgot about playing Scrabble when Gavin lay beside her. She listened intently when he told her he'd graduated valedictorian and enrolled in Howard University on full academic scholarship. He'd majored in pre-law, but wasn't certain whether he'd wanted to practice law.

Gavin stared at the crown molding over the bed. "I was twenty-one with a college degree and I didn't know what I wanted to do next. Instead of going to law school I joined the army. I'd disappointed my mother because she was bragging to everyone at the social services agency where she worked that her son was going to be a lawyer. What she didn't understand was that I was close to burnout. I didn't want to sit in another lecture hall or open one more textbook."

"So, you became a soldier instead." Celia's voice was soft, soothing.

Smiling, Gavin closed his eyes. "I loved everything they threw at me—the rigorous training and the sleep deprivation. I'd applied to and was accepted into Ranger School. It's an extremely intense sixty-one-day combat leadership course conducted over three separate three-week-long phases.

"That was only the beginning." Gavin opened his eyes to find Celia staring at him. "We had combat water survival and a water confidence test. What I found most difficult was the three-mile terrain run followed by what is called the Malvesti Field Obstacle Course. We had to go into a worm pit, which was a shallow, muddy twenty-five-meter obstacle covered by knee-high barbed wire."

"Did you make it on the first try?"

"No, and I have the scars to prove it. It's not a one-time exercise. The obstacle is usually negotiated several times on one's belly *and* back. The Mountain phase tests the limits of mental and physical strength when we were subjected to severe weather and rugged terrain. I almost lost what little food I had in my stomach when I had to climb, then rappel down a fifty-foot sheer cliff."

Celia rested her palm alongside Gavin's face. "Did you ever think of quitting?"

Gavin placed his hand on hers. "Quitting is not in my psychological makeup. I learned to parachute out of a plane and developed the skills to survive in a rain forest or swamp by learning how to deal with reptiles and how to tell the difference between venomous and non-venomous snakes. There were trained reptile experts that taught us how not to be afraid of them. We were put through mock combat raids and missions where we applied everything we'd learned.

"Once we'd earned enough points to graduate, we spent several days cleaning our weapons and equipment. After we got back to the fort we were given PX privileges. We were allowed to use a telephone, eat civilian food and watch television. During this time we were fed three meals a day. I'd weighed two hundred ten pounds when I enrolled in Ranger School and by the time I graduated, I was down to one-seventy."

Celia gave him a look mirroring disbelief. "You lost forty pounds in two months?"

Gavin nodded as he brushed her hair back over her ear to expose a brilliant diamond stud. "My mother couldn't stop crying when she pinned the black-and-gold Ranger Tab on my left shoulder, and I thought it was because she was happy that I'd made it through. I learned later that she was upset because she thought I was dying. I had to explain that it wasn't uncommon for soldiers to lose twenty to forty pounds."

"How long did it take you to put back on the weight?"

"It took about six months. Some Ranger School graduates had weight problems after they returned to their units. They packed on the pounds because they couldn't stop eating. We'd been deprived of food during training to ensure a survivalist mentality."

Celia realized Gavin had mentioned his mother but not his father. "Did your dad approve of you going into the military?"

"I'm certain he would've if he'd been alive. My father was a Green Beret during the Vietnam War. He went into law enforcement after he was discharged. I was ten when he was killed while on duty."

She went completely still, feeling Gavin's pain as surely as if it were her own. "I'm so sorry."

Gavin shuttered his gaze, concealing the pain he'd never permitted anyone to see. He'd loved and respected his father, but it wasn't until he'd entered adolescence that he felt the void when he couldn't go to his namesake for advice about sex and interpersonal relationships.

Ever since he'd joined the Bureau, Gavin's fear was not for himself but for Malvina Faulkner. What were the odds that she would lose not only her husband but both her sons because of their undercover work with the FBI? And not wanting to test the odds, he knew he had to convince his brother to get out before someone discovered his true identity.

Bradley MacArthur had promised to get him a desk assignment, and if his brother wasn't willing to leave the Bureau, then Gavin would try to get Ray Prentice to apply for a position as an instructor at the Academy.

"What did you do after you left the army?"

He opened his eyes. "I went back to college and got a graduate degree in criminal justice, then went to work for my uncle. After he retired, he turned the company over to his sons."

"Do you like protecting people at the risk of losing your own life?"

Gavin's fingers tightened on her scalp. "It's not about

what I like. It's a job, Celia, one I happen to be very good at. Every job and profession has its risks. A hospital is a place where people come to be healed. The staff is devoted to saving lives, yet within a split second, it can become a killing field."

"You're right, Gavin. Never in my wildest imagination would I have ever conjured up the horror of that day."

Gavin pressed a kiss to her forehead. "Enough talk. Are you ready to get your cute little behind kicked?"

Rolling off the bed, Celia rested her hands on her hips. "Let's do it." She walked out of the bedroom, Gavin following and pulling a T-shirt over his head.

Chapter 12

Celia squinted at the tiles Gavin had placed on the Scrabble board. "Are you certain *Laodicean* is a word?" She'd set up the game on a table on the back porch. The shades were drawn over the pocket doors and Gavin had started a fire in the fireplace to counter the chill invading the space.

"Of course it's a word," he said defensively.

"What does it mean?"

"It's lukewarm or indifference to politics or religion. I like the music," he added in the same breath. "What station is that?"

"It's not the radio. It's my iPod." Celia had loaded her iPod with hundreds of songs from her CD collection. She picked up her cell phone and pressed a button.

Gavin shook his head. "You're too much for the heart, Doc." She'd selected Gloria Estefan's *"Oye Mi Canto"* as a ring tone.

Celia flashed a dimpled smile while adding up Gavin's tiles. "I'm going to give you that one because I'm tired of looking up words." A well-worn dictionary rested on a corner of the table. She picked up several tiles and placed them on the board. "*M-e-p-r-o-b-a-m-a-t-e*. Read it and weep, lover," she taunted.

Crossing muscular arms over his chest, Gavin glared at Celia under lowered lids. "What is *that?*"

"It's a bitter carbamate used as a tranquilizer."

He waved his hands. "Hold up, Doc. No medical terms."

She sucked her teeth. "You can't make up the rules as we go along. That should be established from the onset. Besides, weren't you the spelling-bee prodigy?"

"Oh, it's like that, baby girl?"

"Yes it is, baby boy."

"Okay. I'll concede to you using medical terminology, but if I win can I do what I want to you?"

Leaning over the table, she flashed a sensual smile. "Should I be afraid?"

"You should be very, very afraid."

"Are you going to give me a hint of what you intend to do?"

Gavin wiggled his eyebrows. This Celia he liked. She was soft, teasing. He'd experienced her rage when she thought he'd shot at her, and he saw her professional side when she barked orders like a drill sergeant before she'd operated on Terry.

When they'd lain on the bed together he'd told her things about his past he'd never revealed to any woman—even women with whom he'd had more than a passing relationship. He didn't know what it was about the tall, slender doctor with the mop of raven curls, large dark brown eyes and dimpled smile that had him pretending they were married. He wasn't commitment or marriage phobic, yet he'd never entertained the notion with another woman.

"If you concede now, then I'll show you."

Celia's impassive expression didn't change when her gaze shifted from the board to the man sitting only a few feet across the table from her. "I didn't make it in a male-dominated profession to concede a board game to a man with an overblown ego."

"Is that what you think, Celia? That I have an overblown ego?"

"It's not what I think, Gavin Faulkner. It's what I know."

"I'm not going to apologize because I did well in school."

"And I don't expect you to," she countered. "What if the tables were reversed, Gavin, and I asked you to concede? There is no doubt you would've had a few choice words for me. And I want you to remember one thing."

"What's that, wifey?"

Celia's mouth tightened, struggling not to spew the expletives poised on the tip of her tongue. "Didn't I tell you not to call me that?"

"What's wrong with it?"

"I find it denigrating. It's like a man calling his wife his bitch or old lady."

There were only the sounds of Brandy singing a hauntingly beautiful ballad, the crackle of burning wood, followed by the hiss of falling embers behind the decorative fireplace screen when Celia and Gavin stared at each other. They'd agreed to pretend they were married, but the strange thing was they were verbally sniping at each other as if they were actually married.

Gavin nodded. "I'm sorry. Will you accept my apology?"

Although Celia thought she saw his lips twitch, she decided not to prolong the issue. "Yes. Apology accepted."

She'd always tried to avoid verbal exchanges; she found them unsettling and most times nothing was resolved. It had been that way in her arguments with Yale. It was always his way, or not at all.

"It is my turn?" Gavin asked.

Celia turned the rotating board. "Yes, it is."

Rubbing his hand along his jaw, he studied the tiles on the board, and then glanced at the ones on his rack. He picked up all of his letter tiles. "I believe this is a word you're quite familiar with, darling," he drawled with supreme confidence.

Celia didn't want to believe she'd been bested when she saw the word. "Variloa," she whispered. "It's the virus that causes smallpox." Pushing back her chair, she rounded the table and wrapped her arms around Gavin's neck. "Congratulations." She didn't want to tell him that it was the first time in years she'd lost a game of Scrabble.

Easing her down to his lap, Gavin nuzzled Celia's ear. "Thank you. And I thank you for being a gracious loser."

Pulling back, she studied his face. "Did you think I was going to throw a tantrum?"

"No. But I do know that you're very competitive."

Her eyebrows lifted a fraction. "And you're not, Gavin?"

"Only a little," he grudgingly admitted.

Celia sucked her teeth loudly, a habit her mother detested. She'd lost count of the number of times she'd been punished whenever she'd sucked her teeth or rolled her eyes at Nichola Bennett Thomas. Her mother, who'd been raised by her grandmother after her parents were killed in an automobile accident, was old-fashioned when it came to child rearing. It had become a source of contention between Nichola and her mother-in-law, along with the fact that Nichola was completely inept in the kitchen.

"Liar," she whispered, brushing her mouth over his. A soft gasp escaped her parted lips when Gavin came to his feet. His hands tightened under her knees when he carried her over to the chaise.

He placed her on the leather-covered chair, his body following hers down. "I'm only competitive when it comes to my woman."

Celia tried to make out his features in the semidarkness. There was only the light from the fire and the floor lamp near the table. Her heart beat a rapid tattoo against her ribs. "Am I your woman, Gavin?"

"You doubt me, baby?"

She shook her head. "I don't know." Celia didn't recognize her own voice; it'd dropped an octave.

Increasing the pressure of his groin against hers, Gavin trailed kisses along the column of her neck. "That means I'm going to have to show you. I'm going to make love to you, but I don't want you to touch me."

Celia froze. "That's impossible."

"No, it's not, baby. Now, close your eyes and relax." He wanted to put her through an exercise based on trust, an exercise similar to when a person fell backward hoping someone would catch them before they hit the floor or ground.

"Where do you want me to put my hands?"

"Rest them on the arms of the chair. Take a deep

breath, hold it and then breathe out through your mouth." He smiled when her breasts rose then fell under the T-shirt that was at least several sizes too big for her. Gavin wondered if it had belonged to her late fiancé.

Gavin found it odd that Celia had been engaged to marry Trevor-Jones. She hadn't spoken of an undying love for the man with whom she'd planned to spend the rest of her life. Had she, he wondered, just wanted to be married, or had she accepted his proposal out of a warped sense of obligation? After all, they had been living together.

He and Celia were living together, if only for the summer, *and* he'd convinced her to go along with the subterfuge of their being husband and wife. If he were given a lie detector test then Gavin would be forced to admit that he didn't want to let Celia go, that he wanted to spend all of his waking and sleeping hours with her.

It wasn't just her face, dimpled smile, curly hair, slim curvy body and intelligence, but her spunkiness and frankness that held him enthralled. If she wanted something, she asked for it. If she didn't like something, then she was quick to make it known.

She was the first and only woman with whom he'd played *house,* and he enjoyed cooking, shopping, sharing meals and a bed with Celia. Gavin wasn't certain how long he would live under the same roof with her, but he planned to enjoy it for as long as the opportunity presented itself.

Gavin waited until Celia appeared to be totally relaxed: her breathing was deep, even and her hands lay limply on the cordovan leather arms. Reaching for the chenille throw on the back of the chaise, he angled Celia until she lay on the soft fabric.

"I'm going to turn you over—don't open your eyes, baby," he warned in a soft tone, "and I'd like you to rest your head on your arms."

Celia decided to play along with Gavin. When he'd proposed her permitting him to do whatever he wanted to her if he beat her at Scrabble, she'd searched her mind wondering what he had intended. *So far, so good,* she thought, turning over on her belly.

A soft moan escaped her parted lips when Gavin massaged her calf muscles. His hands moved up to her thighs, then reversed themselves to linger on her feet. She felt as if she'd been drugged. Blood flowed sluggishly in her veins, her limbs felt like lead and she couldn't move if her very life depended upon it. She didn't know what Gavin was doing to her but whatever it was, she wanted it to continue—forever, if possible.

Celia had had massages in the past—Swedish, deep tissue, aromatherapy, hot stone and reflexology. It was as if Gavin had combined them, making her feel as if she were floating outside herself.

"What are you doing to me?" she mumbled. He'd increased the pressure on her inner thighs.

"I'm trying to get you to relax."

"I am relaxed, Gavin."

"No, you're not. There's still some tension in your lower extremities."

There was tension because his hands were doing things to her body that fired her libido. His hands were making love to her. "What are you going to do when I'm totally relaxed?"

Moving up on the chaise, Gavin pressed his mouth to Celia's ear. "As they say in your romance novels, I'm going to have my way with you."

She moaned again. His fingers were now working their magic on her buttocks. She gasped when the area between her legs grew moist. "How do you know what's in a romance novel if you haven't read one?" Celia had to talk, if only to keep her mind off the throbbing at the apex of her thighs.

"My mother has read them for years, and one day I picked up one to see what had her so addicted. I laughed when reading about a man root or throbbing manhood. Why not say penis and be done with it?"

"The books have evolved to where the author can use penis and erection. And some books labeled erotica are actually soft porn."

Images from some porn flicks popped into Gavin's head when he slid a hand under Celia's belly to unbutton her shorts and pull down the zipper. "What do you know about porn, baby?"

"My girlfriends at college used to throw monthly porn parties. Whoever hosted the party always selected the movie and supplied the food and beverages. My roommate and I were pre-med, so we weren't into serial dating. By my sophomore year I'd sworn off men, so we were more than willing to host a monthly porn night. Everyone liked to come to our apartment because of Rania's cooking. I paid for the food, so we were able to step it up when we offered more than chicken wings and cheap wine."

Gavin chuckled, the sound coming from deep in his throat. "You were a bunch of nasty girls."

Celia sucked her teeth loudly. "Surely you jest, Gavin. I'm willing to bet you have a porn collection, along with girlie magazines with naked women with their legs so wide open you could see their—" She swallowed an inaudible gasp when she found herself naked from the waist down. Gavin had removed her shorts and panties in a smooth continuous motion. "What are you doing!?"

Gavin flipped Celia over as if she were a small child, anchoring his hands under her knees and raising her hips until his face was between her legs. He didn't give her time to react when he rested her legs over his shoulders. It was impossible for her to wiggle out of his grasp.

Cradling her hips in one hand, he feasted when his rapacious tongue searched the folds until he found the opening he sought. His mouth was masterful, possessive, his tongue plunging inside the quivering flesh, tasting and branding Celia as his own. He didn't know what it was about her that made him make love to her so intimately, but he couldn't stop himself. It was as if he had to have Celia Cole-Thomas—all of her.

Celia was drowning in a maelstrom of pleasure. Her curiosity about oral sex was dispelled with the slow, deliberate licking and suckling of Gavin's tongue and mouth. She'd waited more than thirty years to experience the full extent of her femininity, but the wait was worth it because of the man with his face between her legs.

I want to lose myself in love.
Let you have me completely.
If I give you all my trust.
Can I just let me go?

The words from Brandy's "Fall" reverberated in her head as Celia tried concentrating on anything but the telling ripples sweeping over her body. She was going to have an orgasm. She didn't want to climax, because then it would be over when she'd wanted it to last, to go on and on and on.

But passion—long-denied—would not be denied. Her body stiffened, her hips rising even higher as a shudder shook her. She relaxed but only to have another orgasm seize her. This one was stronger, longer and Celia threw back her head and screamed. The screams overlapped one another as the orgasms kept coming.

It was as if she'd been in a coma. And in the time where she'd come out of the darkness and into the light, she felt her heart swell with an emotion so strong, so totally foreign that she didn't know who she was.

To those who were familiar with her, she was Celia Cole-Thomas, second child and only daughter of former CEO of ColeDiz International, Ltd. Timothy Cole-Thomas and his wife Nichola Cole-Thomas. At the moment she'd forgotten her name, her profession and why she'd come to North Carolina. Everything ceased to exist except the man who made her feel things she'd only imagined.

It didn't matter that she knew so little about Gavin Faulkner, that he'd told her more about his military experience than he did his family. What mattered was how he made her feel. Perhaps she had to sleep with other men who'd left her less than fulfilled to appreciate the one who did.

Now she understood what her first serious boyfriend meant when he said it wasn't about love, but lust. Closing her eyes, Celia breathed out the last of her passion as her trembling body went still, then limp.

Gavin felt his own desire swell as Celia's ebbed. Bringing her pleasure had aroused him, but he knew nothing would come of it. He'd taken the responsibility of using protection, and he didn't want to complicate their short-lived relationship with a baby. After he brought Ray in, he would go back to Washington and either wait for his next assignment or reassignment. Celia would return to Miami for the trial, and once it was over she would go back to practicing medicine. If luck was with him, then he would hope to have at least three months with her before the curtain came down on their staged performances.

Lowering her legs, he moved up the length of her body, supporting his weight on his elbows. A knowing smile touched his mouth. "How do you feel?"

Celia smiled, but didn't open her eyes. "I'm so relaxed I could fall asleep right here."

"It's too cool to sleep down here tonight."

Celia opened her eyes. "We can get some blankets and sleep on the floor in front of the fire."

"We'll rough it another time, princess."

"Speaking of roughing it," she said. "Will you go hiking and white-water rafting with me if I plan an outing to the Great Smoky Mountains National Park?"

"Sure."

"I…" Gavin froze. The telephone was ringing. He gave Celia a long, penetrating stare before his gaze shifted to the handset on the table next to the chaise. The telephone's display read: Private. "Are you expecting a call?"

Her eyelids fluttered wildly. Celia was just as surprised as Gavin, only because the house phone rarely rang. The last call had been her grandmother. And the lateness of the hour was also unexpected. It was after eleven.

"No, but I better answer it." Leaning to her left, she picked up the receiver. "Hello." Her greeting was shaded in neutral tones.

"Miss Thomas?" asked a man with a soft, drawling

voice that suggested he'd spent most of his life in the South.

"Who's asking?"

"Is this Dr. Celia Cole-Thomas?" he questioned again.

The indescribable lingering joy Celia felt when Gavin made love to her slipped away, leaving her cold and distant. "Look, mister, whoever you are, if you don't identify yourself, then I'm going to hang up."

Gavin recognized the expression of annoyance settle into Celia's features. He'd seen it enough to know it didn't bode well for the person on the other end of the line. He pantomimed and mouthed for her to push the speaker feature, giving her a thumbs-up signal when she did.

"Good night—"

"I'm A.D.A. Elijah Morrow from the Dade County D.A.'s office," he said, identifying himself. "If you're Dr. Thomas, then I'd like to inform you that I've taken over D.A. Alton Fitch's cases. I know it's rather late to be calling, but I was told to follow up on his cases listed as priority."

Celia's eyes were unusually large as she met Gavin's. She knew he was tense because of the twitching muscle in his jaw. "How did you get this number?" She'd asked because Alton Fitch had always called her cell phone, and she searched her memory to recall if she'd ever given him the number to her North Carolina home. Her eyes grew wider when Gavin made a cutting motion across his throat.

"I'm sorry, but you have the wrong party," she said and disconnected the call.

Gavin pried the receiver from her death-like grip and set it in the cradle. "Do you recognize his name?"

Reaching over, Celia picked up her shorts and slipped

into them. "No. I can't remember if I ever gave Mr. Fitch the number to this place."

"How did he contact you?"

"Most times he called my cell. There were a few times when he'd leave voice mail messages on my phone in Miami, but never here." Her lids fluttered again. "If I didn't give him the number, then how did this guy get it, Gavin?"

"If he is who he says he is, then it's very easy for him to get any of your listings. Did you inform the D.A.'s office that you were coming here?"

Celia tried to mask her uneasiness with a smile. First there was breaking news that the lead prosecutor in the case in which she was to testify was kidnapped, and now his replacement had called wanting to verify whether she was Dr. Celia Thomas-Cole.

"No, Gavin. I told you. Only my parents, brothers and grandmother know. And they would never give out any information about me."

"I don't want you to talk to anyone until I make a few telephone calls."

Her pulse quickened. "Who are you going to call?"

Leaning closer, Gavin kissed her cheek. "Someone who knows someone who hopefully will give me the answers I need," he said cryptically.

"You're not going to tell me?"

"Don't pout, baby girl," he teased when she pushed out her lips. "I'm bound by confidentiality not to reveal my sources."

"When are you going to call them?"

"It won't be until tomorrow," he lied smoothly. As soon as Celia went to bed he intended to call the Bureau.

Celia crawled into Gavin's lap, her arms going around

his neck. Instinctively, she knew he was hiding something from her. Why, she mused, had he wanted her to end the conversation without confirming who she was?

When he'd suggested they pretend to be married she'd thought it silly and sophomoric. It was something she'd done as a teenager when she and a boy referred to each other as husband and wife if only to establish themselves as a couple. But she wasn't fourteen and she was much too old to play games. However, the kidnapping and this creepy call from a stranger had her emotions spinning out of control.

If Gavin wanted a make-believe wife, then he was going to get one. She hadn't known him a week, but there was one thing of which she was certain. She believed him when he said he would protect her.

"I'm going up to take a shower," Celia said, nuzzling his ear.

"I'll join you as soon as I put away the game and make sure the fire is out."

Not only did Gavin want to extinguish the fire, but he also planned to check all the doors, windows and call Vera Sanchez to request background information on Elijah Morrow.

It took more than an hour for Vera to get back to Gavin. The Bureau analyst had confirmed Elijah Morrow's claim that he worked out of the Dade County's prosecutor's office. But that didn't explain why he'd called Celia in North Carolina if her cell phone was her primary number. He wanted to call Nicholas Cole-Thomas, but something told him that waking up the horse breeder would send him into panic mode.

Gavin decided to wait and then he would try to

connect the missing puzzle pieces that were becoming more and more difficult with each passing day. He checked the windows and doors before going upstairs.

It was after one when he slipped into bed beside Celia. She stirred briefly and then settled back to sleep. It would become the first time he would sleep with her in her bedroom.

Chapter 13

He'd gotten up at five—leaving Celia sleeping soundly—to call Nicholas, who'd expressed concern about the brazen abduction of Alton Fitch. Gavin had reassured Celia's brother that he would exercise extreme caution when it came to keeping her safe. The rain had stopped and pinpoints of sunlight pierced the watery clouds by the time Gavin entered Asheville's city limits.

He'd ended the call minutes before Celia had come looking for him. She'd greeted him shyly, and Gavin wasn't certain whether her reserved demeanor was the result of his unorthodox lovemaking the night before, or she was more unnerved by the report of the kidnapping than she'd said. After a short time they'd returned to bed.

Later that day, Gavin gave Celia a sidelong glance.

She hadn't said a word since they'd left Waynesville. "What's bothering you, sweetheart?"

Celia stared at Gavin. He appeared relaxed and unruffled while her stomach was churning. She'd wanted to believe the D.A.'s kidnapping was a random act, that it had nothing to do with the upcoming trial where she would become the plaintiff's only witness. She'd had almost a year to prepare herself to take the stand and recount what she'd witnessed.

"I keep thinking about Alton Fitch."

"What about him?" Gavin asked.

"What are the odds of the kidnappers—"

"Don't, Celia," he interrupted. "Please don't become fixated on something which may have nothing to do with you."

"How do you know it has nothing to do with me, or the upcoming trial?" she countered.

Gavin gripped the steering wheel so tightly the veins on the backs of his hands were clearly visible. "I doubt it, Celia. If it's retaliation, then there probably wouldn't be a ransom demand."

"Do you think his family will pay the ransom?"

"I'm certain they will. The Fitches own most of South Beach." He placed his right hand on her thigh. "Don't worry, baby. If anyone wants to get to you, then they're going to have to get through me. And I will shoot to kill."

Celia closed her eyes. "Please don't talk about shooting or killing someone."

Gavin gave her thigh a gentle squeeze. "Okay. Then I'll wound them and you can patch them up."

"You know I'm mandated by law to report a gunshot wound."

He wanted to tell Celia that he was the *law* and as a federal agent, his authority wasn't relegated to any given state but to all fifty states and U.S. possessions. "And I'm mandated to take out any son of a bitch who comes after you."

Fear, stark and very real, swept through Celia, a fear that surpassed the one she felt for Alton Fitch. Gavin's voice was cold, detached and deadly, and she found it hard to believe he was the same man who'd made the most exquisite love to her.

"No, Gavin. You're taking this bodyguard thing much too seriously."

"Wrong, Celia. I'm not serious enough. Your brother believes I am your bodyguard. It was also his suggestion we present ourselves as lovers."

"Which we are," she added.

Gavin wiggled his eyebrows. "That was before we did the nasty, baby girl."

"Not only are we lovers, but now we have to pretend to be husband and wife."

He removed his hand from her thigh. "I believe we're beyond the pretense stage, Celia. The only thing that's missing is a marriage license. Maybe if we survive the trial period we can try it for real."

"You're crazy as a loon," Celia spat out. "I'm not marrying you or any man—at least not for a long time."

Gavin grabbed his chest. "Damn, Cee Cee. You really know how to hurt a guy."

"Please, Gavin," she drawled, "spare me the theatrics. The only thing that's hurt is your ego because I turned you down."

"You don't think I'm husband material?"

Celia wanted to laugh, but the topic of marriage was

hardly laughable. She'd given Yale's proposal a lot of thought before she'd agreed to become his wife. It was only after he'd put the ring on her finger that she moved in with him.

"I don't know what to think, Gavin."

Signaling, he maneuvered on to a road leading to downtown Asheville. "Don't you have criteria for the man you'd want to marry? I assume you'd want him to be able to provide you with the basic necessities," he said, answering his own query. "He probably should also be sane and disease-free. Let's see. What else is there? It would help if he didn't have a criminal record." Gavin snapped his fingers. "No baby-mama drama. That has to be at the top of the list. Is there anything else, Cee Cee?" He hit his forehead with the heel of his hand. "How can I forget the very glue that can hold a marriage together? Sex! The sex must be smokin' hot!"

Biting back a smile, Celia stared out the side window. "Like jalapeño hot?"

Gavin shook his head. "Hotter."

"Scotch bonnet?"

"Hotter."

She turned, seeing the smirk on Gavin's handsome face. "Habanero."

He winked at her. "There you go. Now, take us. We're probably somewhere between jalapeño and chipotle, but before summer's end we should approach habanero heat."

"Is that a promise, Gavin Faulkner?"

"I usually don't make promises because some are impossible to keep. But, this is one time I'm going to do everything in my power to fulfill it."

Celia returned her gaze to the side window. She was

a scientist, a realist and usually not prone to flights of fantasy. But what Gavin proposed *and* predicted was nothing more than fantasy and perhaps wishful thinking.

She'd dealt with life and death on a daily basis, but having witnessed two murders had shaken her more than she could've imagined. Going into therapy had helped her cope with her personal grief, while her faith and escape into romance novels had kept her from an abyss of self-pity.

"What's the matter, Cee Cee? You have no comeback."

"Nope."

Chuckling, Gavin maneuvered into a parking space in front of a jewelry shop. "You're already learning how to be a good little wife. The first rule: don't argue with the big man."

"And the second rule: don't forget your *good little wife* is a doctor and she can hurt the *big man* in ways he could never imagine."

Gavin parked, turned off the engine and draped his right arm over the passenger-seat headrest. "Can you give me an idea of where you plan to hurt me?"

Celia flashed a facetious grin. "Since you were bragging about not having baby-mama drama, I'd like to help you out and make certain you'll never experience it."

"Oh, hell, no! You will not mess with my package. I'd like the option of whether or not I'd like to father a child."

"You want children?"

"Don't look at me like that, Celia. Why wouldn't I want children?"

She lifted a shoulder. "I don't know. You just don't seem like the paternal type."

"I could say the same thing about you," Gavin countered.

Pinpoints of heat stung Celia's cheeks. "I'd planned to have a child once I was married."

Gavin shook his head. "Now, that's a sorry-ass excuse if I ever heard one. You've lived with a man, Celia, and that's not what I would call traditional, so *I have to be married to have a baby* doesn't quite fit into that schematic."

"What if I don't want to be a baby mama?"

"What if you didn't know you were pregnant when your fiancé was murdered?"

"Then I'd be a baby mama."

Leaning closer, he angled his head and kissed her. "There you go."

"You're some piece of work, Gavin Faulkner," she whispered against his firm mouth. "You missed your calling. You would've made out like a bandit running a Ponzi scheme, because you definitely would've hustled lots of people out of their hard-earned money."

"And you know what happens to people who go into that line of work? They go to jail for a very long time." He kissed her again. "Let's go before the police cite us for public lewdness."

"We're not doing anything," Celia protested.

"Not yet, but all this talk about making babies is getting me aroused."

Her gaze shifted to the area below his waist, her eyes widening when she noticed the solid bulge in the front of his jeans. Groaning, she closed her eyes while exhaling audibly. "What am I going to do with you, Gavin?"

That's what Gavin had been asking himself for days. What was he going to do with Celia once his assignment was over? Would he continue to keep in touch with her? Or would he relegate her to his past like all of the other women in his life? He hoped that was a question he wouldn't have to answer for a while.

"I don't know. That's something you're going to have to figure out."

Celia continued to ask herself the same thing when she walked into the jewelry shop with Gavin. The first thing she noticed was the number of women staring at him, and she knew exactly what was going through their minds because the impact of coming face-to-face with him in the supermarket had affected her the same way.

Moving closer to his side, she slipped her hand in his. "What type of band do you want?"

"I'd prefer a simple band without a lot of bling."

Tilting her chin, she met his eyes. "Do you want matching bands?"

He smiled. "That would be nice."

Releasing her hand, Gavin put his arm around Celia's waist over a white man-tailored shirt she'd worn over a pair of fitted jeans. He didn't know why, but for a fleeting moment, he wanted what they were about to embark upon to be real. After he'd proposed they pose as a married couple, he chided himself for making the suggestion, but once he'd made love to Celia he knew his feelings had changed. He'd changed, too.

It was as if he'd tired of the undercover assignments and he had grown tired of telling one lie in order to validate another. Whenever he got a call from Bradley, he never knew where he would have to drive or jet off to. One year he'd been assigned to cases in Texas, Nebraska and Indiana. He investigated everything from civil rights violations to federal oversight of police abuse, and several elected officials who were accepting bribes for steering government contracts to several organized crime families.

Did he want to marry? Yes.

Did he want children? Again, the answer was yes.

He wanted them both, but not as a field agent. The memory of two agents wearing dark suits, white shirts and conservative ties and shoes standing in his living room and informing Malvina Faulkner that her husband had lost his life in service to the Bureau and his country was branded into his brain.

Malvina was either too shocked or she was expecting the news, because she exhibited no visible reaction. She thanked the agents, and then retreated to her bedroom, where she didn't emerge until the following morning. Gavin didn't know what to do, so he went into his own bedroom, closed the door and cried. It was the last time he'd cried, because he knew he had to be strong for his mother. Captain Gavin Tyrone Faulkner, Sr. was buried with full military honors at Arlington National Cemetery. For the past twenty-seven years Malvina had made it a practice to visit Arlington twice each year— once to mark her late husband's birthday and the other time to commemorate their wedding anniversary.

A conservatively dressed, middle-aged woman approached them with a warm smile. "I'm Bernice. May I help you?"

"I'm Gavin and this is my wife, Celia. We're looking for wedding bands."

"Would you like them in gold or platinum?"

Gavin shared a look with Celia, who'd raised her eyebrows questioningly. "We'll decide after we try on a few."

Bernice angled her salt-and-pepper head, her experienced gaze sweeping over the tall, attractive couple. Her dove-gray eyes hadn't missed the size and brilliance of the diamond studs in the young woman's ears. "Please come with me and I'll measure your fingers. I'm certain I'll have something you'll like."

Celia sat on a stool, while Gavin stood behind her, one hand resting on her shoulder. "Do you see anything you like?" he whispered in her ear.

"They're all nice," she said. And they were. Bernice had removed three men's gold bands. One was set with a circle of round diamonds, another in white gold with a pink stripe and the third white gold with two-toned bands. She took out matching bands for a woman.

Celia and Gavin alternated slipping bands onto each other's fingers and then placed their hands side-by-side for a comparison. She shook her head. "I'm not feeling these. What do you think, darling?"

Gavin dropped a kiss on Celia's hair. "Do you have something a little more conservative?" he asked Bernice.

Bernice replaced the rings in their slots and returned them to the case. "I have a platinum set. And, I also have another set in platinum with double milgrain. They're a little pricey for plain bands, but I'll let you in on a little secret," she whispered like a co-conspirator. "I saw the same rings in Tiffany when I went to New York."

Gavin winked at the salesclerk. "May we see them?"

Celia rested her head on Gavin's solid shoulder when Bernice went to the opposite end of the shop. "I'll pay for the rings, Gavin."

He stiffened as if she'd struck him. "Like hell you will."

"The tradition is the bride pays for the groom's ring and vice versa."

"What you don't know about your new husband is that he's anything but traditional."

Straightening, Celia stared up at Gavin. He was glaring at her. "What is your problem, Gavin?"

"My problem is I don't take money from women. The other problem is I need for you to keep a low profile. That's not going to happen if you start making big-ticket credit-card purchases—unless you happen to have several thousand dollars in cash stashed away in that suitcase you call a purse."

"What's wrong with my handbag?" she said defensively.

When she first saw the Louis Vuitton XXL tote in the Dadeland mall she'd been drawn to it like sunflowers and the sun. She'd hesitated only because it was much larger than the handbags she favored. The next day, she'd returned to the shop, picked up the bag, placed her credit card on the counter and fifteen minutes later walked out with her purchase.

A sensual smile curved Gavin's mouth. "It's large enough to hold an infant or a small dog. I wouldn't be surprised if you decided to carry Terry around in it."

Celia showed him the tip of her tongue. "I'll buy Terry a Louis dog carrier if you keep runnin' off at the mouth."

"No, no, no, baby. You will not turn *our* dog into a bitch by carrying him around when he can walk."

A frown settled between her eyes. "There's no need to get hostile."

"I'm not hostile, Celia. I'm just telling you what you're not going to do."

Celia saw Bernice coming toward them out of the corner of her eye. "We'll talk about this when we get home," she warned between clenched teeth.

Gavin ran a hand down the length of her back. "I

thought you were going to be a dutiful and obedient little wife."

She rolled her eyes. "Well, hubby, you thought wrong."

Bernice opened a soft felt cloth to reveal two pairs of wedding bands, smiling when Celia expelled a gasp. Reaching for a velvet-covered mat, she placed the rings on the black surface. She wasn't surprised when Gavin and Celia picked up the same set to slip the corresponding ring on each other's fingers. They'd chosen the double milgrain platinum bands. Not only were they physically compatible, but it appeared that their tastes were similar. They were even dressed alike in white man-tailored shirts, jeans and black boots. Gavin wore his shirt with the hem hanging out his jeans, while Celia had tucked hers in.

Celia and Gavin shared a smile. "We'll take it," they said in unison.

Bernice's smile was dazzling. "You both have wonderful taste."

"Thank you," Gavin and Celia chorused.

"Do you want to wear them, or should I wrap them up?"

"We'll wear them," Gavin said, reaching into his back pocket for his credit-card case and handing her a card.

Bernice glanced at the name. "Mr. and Mrs. Faulkner, if you take them off I'll have them cleaned for you." She signaled to a young man. "Please clean these for me." Turning back to her customer, she flashed her practiced professional smile. "I'll be back as soon as I process your payment."

Celia wrapped her arms around Gavin's waist, going completely still when she felt the outline of a holster clipped to the waistband at his back. The firearm was a constant reminder that their ruse wasn't all fantasy, that there could possibly be someone looking to keep her from testifying.

When she'd gotten up earlier that morning she'd made certain not to tune into any of the news channels. The report of Alton Fitch's abduction had rattled her more than she'd wanted to admit or acknowledge. As the star witness in a trial that would no doubt attract national news coverage, her testimony was vital for a capital murder conviction. Without her, the defendant would go free and there would be no justice for the families of the six who'd needlessly lost their lives. Of the four who were injured, Celia was the luckiest. The three others had sustained wounds that had left one with a shattered hip and the other two had suffered spinal cord injuries. One, a gang member, would be confined to a wheelchair for the rest of his life.

Resting her head on Gavin's chest, she breathed in the scent of the cologne clinging to his shirt. "What's up with you not letting a woman pay for something?"

Gavin cradled the back of her head. "I grew up with guys who thought nothing of asking and taking money from women. They were nothing more than unofficial pimps and they refused to understand why I wouldn't let a woman buy me gifts or let them pay for food whenever we went out to eat."

"What about for your birthday or Christmas?" Celia asked.

He smiled. "Those are the only exceptions. I suppose I feel so strongly about it because I have a female cousin who's a lawyer, yet she feels the need to buy a man. She's pretty and smart, but is a zero where it concerns men. She had one boyfriend who used to come to her office whenever he ran short. The one time she didn't have any cash on her, he went off on her in front of her colleagues and the firm's clients. One of the partners called her in and told her that if she didn't straighten out her personal life she would have to look for another position.

"I was at her house when the ignorant fool came around again with his hand out. When she refused to answer the door, he threatened her. That's when I opened the door and I told him in no uncertain terms that if he came within ten feet of her I was going to kick his ass. He must have known I wasn't blowing smoke because she never saw him again."

Easing back, Celia stared up at the deep-set dark eyes that warmed her in passion and froze whenever he turned his lethal stare on her. This time there was no warmth in the near-black orbs. "Why would she even want to support a grown man?"

"I don't know, Celia. Maybe it was something maternal, or it could be she didn't feel good until she cared for the less fortunate."

"Even though I've never taken care of a man, I'm always willing to assume the responsibility for my share."

Gavin shot her a warning look. "Let's not discuss money. It's so gauche." His voice, although soft, was layered with an icy edge. "Please, darling," he said when she opened her mouth to come back at him.

Celia didn't know if his reluctance to talk about money was because he'd disapproved of his cousin's relationship with worthless men, or he was intimidated by her wealth. Aside from the diamond earrings, which were a gift from her parents when she'd graduated medical school, she didn't wear or own priceless baubles, and she didn't drive a luxury car. Her tangible assets were her homes: the one close to the North Carolina–Tennessee border and the Miami beachfront mansion she'd purchased from her cousin.

She had her favorite charities and the organization where she'd generously volunteered her time and served as a board member. After working double shifts at the hospital and her philanthropic obligations, there wasn't much time for a personal life. That was the reason why she'd decided to date someone with whom she worked.

"Okay, darling," Celia crooned. Her apology was layered with a sticky sweetness that changed Gavin's expression from annoyance to shock.

Nichola Cole-Thomas may have reared her children in what they'd considered the old-fashioned way, but she'd instilled in her three children a sense of stalwart independence that intensified with adulthood. Celia had been reminded that money brought comfort, not happiness, and that she shouldn't look for someone to love her more than she loved herself and she shouldn't blame anyone but herself when she made bad choices.

It was Nichola's motto, *do not be beholden to anyone,* that Celia followed without question. Gavin had refused payment for his personal security services but she wasn't going to permit him to spend more than two thousand dollars for an unadorned platinum wedding band for her.

She had the name and address of his cousin's security firm, and she planned to mail a check, payable to Gavin Faulkner, in an envelope marked Personal and Confidential days before leaving North Carolina to return to Florida.

As the adage said, there's more than one way to skin a cat—even if that cat reminded her of a sleek, powerful and cunning black panther.

Chapter 14

Gavin maneuvered up a steep paved road, slowing when he spotted a large two-story log cabin with a wraparound porch in a nearby clearing. Celia had given him the directions to her closet neighbors, Daniel and Hannah Walsh. If he'd wanted to visit his neighbor, then he only had to walk about five feet to the next-door apartment instead of getting into a vehicle and driving there.

He'd found her unusually quiet and withdrawn after they'd left the jewelry shop, and he wondered if she'd been thinking about what it would've been like to exchange rings with her late fiancé instead of a stranger who'd unceremoniously invaded not only her sanctuary, but also her life.

Gavin was always cognizant that Celia could order him to move out of her house if he put too much pressure on her. After all, she'd moved in and then out of

Trevor-Jones's apartment and into her own home. What he'd longed to do was reveal who he was and why he was hanging out in the area.

He knew he was using her, using her to establish a cover and using her to pass the time when he would've been holed up in a lodge watching television, reading or hiking while waiting for Raymond Prentice to contact him. What he didn't want to acknowledge was that he was using her body. Whenever they'd lie together he'd wanted not to be Gavin Faulkner, undercover special agent for the Bureau, but Gavin Faulkner, field supervisor. He wanted to become a pencil-pushing bureaucrat until it came time for him to collect his government pension.

"Do you think we've picked up enough beer?"

Celia's dulcet voice broke into Gavin's musings. He gave her a quick glance. "Six cases of beer, a case of red and white wine and a dozen three-liter bottles of soda is more than enough liquid beverage for a cookout for every weekend of the summer."

"Hannah told me not to bring anything, but I just couldn't show up empty-handed."

Gavin turned into an area where sedans, SUVs and pickups were parked. He parked and shut off the engine. Shifting on his seat, he gave Celia a long, penetrating stare. "You're impossible."

"What are you talking about?"

"Your friend tells you not to bring anything and you do just the opposite."

"That's what I call being capricious and prepared, because Hannah is a local celebrity and their gatherings are nothing short of a pep rally."

"I'd say it's more like you being contrary. If things

don't go your way or how you believe they should be, then you try to correct it. Bend it to your will."

Her eyebrows shot up. "You're a fine one to talk, Gavin Faulkner. You came on to me at a supermarket under the guise you didn't know anything about cabbage. Then you have the balls to try and claim a dog that probably would've died if I hadn't operated on him. And don't forget you're living with me under the pretense we're—"

"I catch your drift, Celia," Gavin interrupted. "And wrong choice of word. You could've said audacity instead of *balls*."

"I used the right word, Mr. Faulkner, and you know it. You are ballsy."

"What I do know is that I can be a little heavy-handed."

"Heavy-handed," Celia repeated. "Do you realize how many times you've told me what I can and cannot do or say?"

He ran his fingers through her hair. "I'm sorry, baby."

"Sure you are until the next time."

Gavin unbuckled his seatbelt, lifting Celia effortlessly over the console where she sat half on and half off his lap. "I want you to stop me whenever I come at you twisted."

Staring up at him through her lashes, Celia bit back a smile. "Will it do any good?"

"You can always try," he teased, winking at her.

Instinctively, her body arched toward him, silently communicating how much she needed and wanted Gavin. She needed him to remind her that each time they lay together she was able to celebrate the essence of being born female. And, she wanted him because he made her feel safe, protected. Even if she were in one part of the house and he in another, she was able to feel his presence.

The exchange of rings the day before had affected her more than she'd wanted. For a brief moment, she'd fantasized it was Yale instead of Gavin who'd slipped the ring on her finger. However, what she'd found disturbing was she couldn't remember Yale's face. She'd wanted to cry, but couldn't—not in public and not when she'd have to explain to Gavin why she hadn't been able to keep it together.

As an intern, she'd survived the wrath of her supervisors and the many firsts that came with the intense training to become a medical doctor: delivering a baby, performing a tracheotomy and calling the time of death. The images were vividly imprinted on her brain like a permanent tattoo, yet the man she'd promised to marry hadn't been dead a year and she couldn't remember his face.

Gavin buried his face in Celia's hair, inhaling the floral scent clinging to the soft curls. "What's the matter, baby?"

"What makes you think anything is the matter?" she asked, answering his question with one of her own.

"You're shaking."

Celia knew she couldn't lie to Gavin any more than she could continue to lie to herself. She'd loved Yale when she wasn't in love with him. "Why can't I remember his face?" she said tearfully.

Gavin suddenly realized she was talking about her late fiancé. "Don't beat up on yourself, Celia. You not only went through medical trauma but also psychological distress. You saw two people murdered, not knowing whether you'd be next. It's a miracle you hadn't blotted out everything that happened that night."

"You don't understand, Gavin. I wasn't in love with

Yale. Did I love him? Yes. But not enough to set a wedding date, although I'd continued to wear his ring. We'd made love more when we didn't live together, and after I'd moved out, I'd unconsciously begun to withdraw from him physically and emotionally. What I hadn't wanted to do was accept it." She closed her eyes. "Yale knew, but I was in denial. I'd told myself we could continue the way it'd been, working together and planning a future that would never come. He'd wanted to have children right away, and I wanted to wait. He didn't want a long engagement, but I kept throwing up roadblocks because deep down inside, I knew he wasn't the man I'd wanted to spend the rest of my life with."

"Do you think it would've been better if you hadn't survived, because then you wouldn't be burdened with unsubstantiated guilt?"

Despite the overwhelming feeling of confusion, Celia managed to smile. "You sound like my therapist."

"You didn't answer my question."

She shook her head. "No. Yale's mother came to see me during a period when I wasn't heavily sedated and grief had aged her appreciably. If it hadn't been for her voice, I wouldn't have recognized her. She kept repeating that parents weren't supposed to bury their children. Yale was her only child and she'd looked forward to our marriage because she wanted grandchildren."

Gavin wanted to tell Celia that Yale had already made his mother a grandmother. The son Yale had sired at seventeen was now a twenty-six-year-old father of two, and that meant his mother was now a great-grandmother.

"Did you ever think maybe Yale proposed marriage so that he would give his mother grandchildren?"

"No."

Celia had said no when it'd suddenly dawned on her that Yale was fixated with her having his child. It'd reached a point where she no longer trusted him to protect her and had her ob-gyn fit her for an intrauterine device. Even that had become irrelevant because their sex life went from sporadic to nonexistent.

She and Gavin pulled apart at the sound of an approaching vehicle. "Are you ready to go in?"

Gavin traced the delicate curve of her cheekbone with his finger. "Are you okay?"

Turning her face, Celia kissed his broad palm. "I'm wonderful."

"Are you sure?" he asked.

"Yes."

He got out and came around to assist Celia, raising her left hand and kissing the band on her finger. "Let's go and meet your neighbors, Mrs. Faulkner."

Still holding hands, Celia led Gavin around to the rear of the house where a crowd had gathered. Many were sitting at picnic tables leading down to the lake, while others stood in line at an outdoor kitchen waiting for food or drink. Hannah Walsh, now an award-winning illustrator, had used her earnings to expand what had become her dream house. Erected on a hill, the cabin's location—surrounded by ancient oak and towering pine trees—overlooked a lake.

"The woman wearing the red, white and blue striped bibbed apron is Hannah. Her husband, Daniel, is flipping burgers," Celia whispered.

"She's pregnant," Gavin said matter-of-factly.

"She's very pregnant, darling. That's why I've been knitting every chance I get to finish the blanket for the layette before she gives birth."

"When…" Gavin's words trailed off when he noticed a short squat man with a reddish beard and strawberry-blond hair staring at Celia. The expression on the man's face was one he recognized immediately. It was adoration. "I think you have an admirer."

He didn't blame the man for staring at Celia because when she'd come down the stairs, he'd found it almost impossible to take his eyes off her. A pair of cropped stretch jeans hugged her hips like second skin, and the red-and-white-striped stretch top with three-quarter sleeves showed off her flat midsection and firm breasts. He'd been tempted to ask her if she planned to wear a jacket but then he realized Celia could possibly believe he was jealous. And a display of jealousy meant he was becoming emotionally involved and that was something Gavin wanted to avoid at any cost.

"That's Hannah's brother." Celia waved to the man gripping a longneck in one hand and a burger in the other.

Hannah Walsh turned when she heard a familiar feminine voice. A wide smile split her rounded face. "Celia, you made it."

She smiled at the woman who always had a kind word and friendly smile for everyone she encountered. Hannah, barely five foot, had a mass of reddish-blond curls that reminded Celia of Orphan Annie. Every inch of her round face was covered with freckles. The women exchanged air kisses.

"I told you I wouldn't miss this."

Hannah stared boldly behind the lenses of her sunglasses at the man with Celia. To say he was gorgeous was an understatement. There was something about his face that reminded her of Shemar Moore, the actor who played an FBI agent in *Criminal Minds*.

"*This* is turning into a spectacle. Daniel invited half his high school graduating class and their families."

Celia exchanged a knowing glance with Gavin. She hadn't bought too much. "I told you I was bringing a guest, but didn't tell you who he is because I wanted it to be a surprise. Gavin, this is our hostess, Hannah Walsh. Hannah, Gavin Faulkner, my husband."

The expression on Hannah Walsh's face was priceless when Celia introduced Gavin as her husband. The children's book illustrator opened and closed her mouth several times. She cradled her belly with both hands. "Omigosh! You're married!" Her expression changed again. This time it was a grimace.

"Are you all right?" Celia asked.

Hannah nodded. "I'm good. Every once in a while I have a few contractions. It looks as if my daughter…oops! The sex of the baby has been a secret until now."

"Gavin and I promise to keep your secret. Won't you, darling?"

"Oh, yes. Of course," he replied quickly, extending a hand. "It's a pleasure to meet you, Hannah. And congratulations on the baby."

Hannah accepted his handshake. "Are you two planning on starting a family right away?"

"No."

"Yes."

Celia and Gavin had spoken in unison.

"Which is it?" Hannah questioned, her gaze shifting from her friend to her new husband. "Yes or no?"

Gavin put his arm around Celia's waist, pulling her closer. "Celia wants to wait, but if it were up to me she'd already be pregnant."

Reaching out, Hannah took Celia's free hand. "The girls are going to have a little chat, but not before I introduce you to my husband," she told Gavin.

Gavin nodded and dropped his arm. "I'm going to need a couple of strong arms to help me unload some liquid refreshment from my truck."

Hannah glared at Celia. "I told you not to bring anything."

"Please, Hannah. Do you realize how many people are here?" The rear of the property was quickly becoming more crowded with newcomers. Many of the benches at the picnic tables were filled and some guests were sitting under trees and a few had gone as far as the lake. A loud roar went up when a group of men arrived carrying audio equipment.

"Last year, everyone complained because we didn't play music, so this year we asked some of the guys Daniel works with who deejay during their off-time to bring their equipment."

"It's a good thing your closest neighbor is far enough away so you don't have to worry about them calling the police," Celia teased.

Hannah winked at Celia. "That's the reason why I invited my neighbor, and if she were to call the police then her neighbor's husband would answer the call."

"Your husband is a police officer?" Gavin asked.

"He's a state trooper. Most of his close friends are law enforcement. Some are local and the others are state and federal."

Gavin followed Hannah into the outdoor kitchen, his mind going into overdrive. When she'd mentioned federal police, he wondered if he would recognize any of them, or if they would in turn recognize him.

Daniel Walsh was taking orders as to the doneness of hamburgers, franks, sausages and steaks. The outdoor kitchen was magnificent with a double grill, burners, oven and smoker. It also contained a sub-zero fridge, sink and icemaker. Styrofoam chests were filled with meat and fresh fish covered with ice. Fifty feet away was a portable bar, and judging by the number of people lined up in front of it, the two bartenders were being kept very busy.

Hannah tapped her husband's arm to garner his attention. "Darling, I'd like you to meet Celia's husband."

Daniel's green eyes grew wider in a deeply tanned face as he turned to stare at Gavin. His straight coal-black hair was a vivid contrast to the emerald-green orbs. His features clearly identified him as Native American.

"You and Celia married?"

Gavin flashed a half smile. He knew Celia's friends would be shocked by the announcement because there was no doubt they knew and had probably met Trevor-Jones.

"Yes, we are."

"Congratulations. I'd shake your hand, but if I take off the mitt, then I'm going to lose my momentum. I can tell you now that some of my buddies are going to be disappointed to hear she's no longer available. Most of them didn't like her fiancé and when we got the news that he'd been killed during that hospital shootout they said all the proper words out of respect, but I for one thought he was a puffed-up pain in the ass."

"I'm going to need some of your buddies so they can help me unload my truck. Celia decided to clean out the beverage store. After that, if you need help I'm willing to help you grill."

Daniel turned to a tall, skinny teenage boy with a flaxen ponytail. "What'll you have, Bobby?"

"Steak, medium-well."

Reaching into a cooler, Daniel took out a rib eye steak and placed it on the grill. He then took off the mitt, handing it and the long-handled fork with a digital thermometer to Gavin. "Show me what you got."

Smiling, Gavin put on the mitt and picked up another fork without the thermometer. "I don't need a fork with a read-out to tell me when a steak is medium-well." He inhaled the smoke coming off the grill. "Nice. There's nothing better than mesquite-grilled bone-in steak."

Crossing his arms over his chest, Daniel nodded his head. "So, you do know a little sumptin' about grillin'."

"Only a little," Gavin answered modestly.

His secret desire, once he retired, was to open a barbecue joint where he'd serve ribs, brisket, chicken, pulled pork and the requisite side dishes. If Celia had her college roommate and grandmother to thank for her culinary prowess, then he would have to pay homage to his maternal grandmother. Grandma Annie Mae Smith was an unofficial pit master, who'd learned the skill of smoking meat from her father. Whenever her church hosted barbecue fundraisers or a revival, everyone in Charlotte came out for the event.

Whistling sharply through his teeth, Daniel called out to three of his coworkers. "I need you to help with something."

Gavin relinquished the mitt and fork and shook hands with the men, none of whom he recognized. Although none were in uniform, he could easily identify them as law enforcement.

"You a cop?" asked a short, stocky black trooper Daniel had introduced as Smitty.

"Personal security," Gavin answered.

"You babysit folks like those crazy-ass Hollywood actors who have too much money, and don't know what to do with it?"

Gavin's impassive expression did not change. "No. I usually babysit the families of the invisible people who have enough money to buy private islands or run a small country."

Smitty's eyebrows went up a fraction. "The pay must be real good."

"The pay is commensurate with the risks."

Daniel slapped his colleague on the back. "Stop interrogating the man and go unload his truck."

Gavin gave his host a surreptitious wink as he led the way back to where he'd parked the Yukon. There was something Smitty had said that he found irritating. Not only had the man asked too many questions, but the questions were too personal in nature to ask someone he'd just met. Trooper Smith would bear watching closely.

Celia sat in Hannah's living room, holding her two-year-old son. The toddler had inherited his mother's curly hair, but the color was raven-black like his father's. His eyes were a beautiful hazel ringed by the longest lashes she'd ever seen on a boy. His coloring had compromised. It was a dusky peach with a spray of freckles over his pert nose and cheeks. Since picking him up, Daniel, Jr. had played a visual peekaboo with her. Celia felt sorry for the girls who would eventually become the recipient of his gaze.

Hannah sat on a matching club chair, supporting her bare feet on a footstool. She took a deep swallow of water, peering at Celia over the rim of her glass. "Are you going to tell me, or do I have to get into your business by asking what's up?"

Celia and Gavin had lain in bed earlier that morning concocting a story that would be consistent whenever anyone asked about their pretense of a marriage. "What do you want to know?"

"Where did you meet him, and does he have a brother?"

Celia shook her head in amazement. "You're incredible, Hannah Walsh! You're about to give birth, and you're talking about hooking up with another man."

A flush crept up Hannah's face to her hairline. "I'm not looking for me," she said. "I wouldn't trade my Daniel for all the men in the world—even if they came with a perfect face and body like your husband's."

It was Celia's turn to blush. She'd discovered Gavin didn't have to do a thing to attract stares from women. All he had to do was walk by or walk into a room. He'd caught her attention immediately when he'd approached her in the supermarket.

"He is rather nice on the eyes," she agreed.

"He's more than nice, Celia. I'm going to let you in on a little secret."

"What is it?"

"We Cooper girls like our meat either medium-well or well-done."

Celia covered her mouth to hold back screams of laughter. "Now you tell me," she said between her fingers. She lowered her hand when Danny gave her a puzzled look.

"I suppose you wouldn't have given Yale a second look."

Hannah shook her head. "Please. Not even if I was desperate. I'd always thought he was so wrong for you, Celia. He was too old, and if you hadn't been who you are you would've ended up as his doormat. Daniel said he only hooked up with you because you're smart *and* beautiful. It's too bad he had to die the way that he did, but if he had to check out in order for you to find someone like Gavin... I don't mean to sound glib, but such is life. Now, tell me how you met Mr. January, February, March and the other twelve months of the year."

Celia didn't want to believe that Hannah had echoed the sentiments of her family members. They'd called Yale spoiled, controlling and, at times, condescending. It was the attempt to control her that had them at odds with each other. She wasn't certain whether his need to control came from their age difference or his warped sense of entitlement because he was a third-generation physician.

"Either you're particularly horny, or you need some," Celia said, teasingly.

"Both. I've been spotting the past two months, so my doctor has Daniel on booty lockdown."

"Lockdown or lockout?"

"Both. Come on, Celia. Tell me how you met Gavin."

Taking a breath, Celia told Hannah that she'd met Gavin when he worked a security detail for one of her brother's Thoroughbreds when Nicholas transported the horse to a Florida racetrack.

"Nicholas came to see me before he drove back to Virginia. Gavin was with him because he was dropping him off in Charlotte. To say I was a hot mess was an understatement. I needed a haircut in the worst way and I was so thin I could've passed for a Halloween scarecrow, but when Gavin looked at me, I felt as if I were the only woman in the world. He asked if he could call me and I said yes. Whenever he wasn't assigned to provide security for a client, he would come and visit. And, as they say, the rest is history."

Hannah flashed a Cheshire-cat grin. "That's what I'm talking about! Although you're thinner than the last time I saw you, you're still stunning. Does he make you happy, Celia?"

She stared at the little boy who'd fallen asleep in her arms. "He makes me deliriously happy, Hannah."

Celia hadn't lied to her friend. She'd smiled and laughed more since meeting Gavin than she had in years. She felt closer to him than she'd ever felt with Yale. And sex had little to do with it.

"If that's the truth, then why do you want to wait to have a baby? Daniel and I were different because he wanted to finish college and get his career on track so he could support me and our children without having to penny pinch. Neither of us anticipated how much income my illustrations would generate, but even if I never illustrated another book we would still live comfortably. You're a doctor, Celia. Even if you decided not to go on staff at a hospital, you could always set up a private practice. You can either work out of your home or hire a nanny to take care of the baby when you're seeing patients."

"That is a possibility."

"What is a possibility, Celia?"

Both women turned at the sound of a man's voice. Gavin had come into the living room without making a sound. "We were talking about your wife having your baby," Hannah announced.

Gavin moved closer, staring at the little boy in Celia's

arms. It suddenly struck him that he and Celia were playing a very dangerous game. They'd concocted a story supporting their courtship and marriage, but they hadn't talked about children. Most people wanted to know if or when a newly married couple planned to start a family.

He'd never denied wanting to marry or father children. It was his undercover work that posed the problem, because he didn't want his wife to go through what his mother had experienced. Gavin didn't want agents coming to his home to inform his wife that her husband had sacrificed his life in the service of his country.

He had an obligation to his mother, himself and the Bureau to bring his brother back alive, and he'd also promised Nicholas Cole-Thomas he would keep his sister safe. Gavin Tyrone Faulkner, Jr. had pledged to help everyone, but whom could he turn to when he needed love and understanding? Celia was as close as he'd come to a life partner, and even their time together came with an expiration date.

"If you've changed your mind, then we can start tonight," he crooned.

Celia almost choked. "Can we talk about this later, Gavin?"

"Of course, darling. I just came in to ask you if you're ready to eat."

"Yes, I am." As much as she always enjoyed interacting with Hannah, the baby talk was making her very uncomfortable. She watched as Gavin closed the distance between them, scooped the little boy off her lap and cradled him to his chest. A lump rose in her throat when her eyes met Gavin's.

Her heart stopped, and then started up again in a

runaway rhythm. She'd tired of the lies only because she'd never been a good liar. Tell one lie and then she had to tell another to cover the first one. After a while, the lies escalated to where she wouldn't recognize the truth even if it meant survival.

"I'll meet you outside."

Turning on her heels, she walked out of the house and into the warm afternoon sun. Perhaps she'd be able to pull off the farce without the angst she was undergoing if she hadn't slept with Gavin.

She now found it almost impossible to differentiate between lust, passion, desire, infatuation and what she'd been afraid to acknowledge as another four-letter word…love.

Chapter 15

The aroma of grilled meat lingered in the air long after the sun had set behind the mountains. The DJ had packed up his equipment and the families with young children had left to return to their homes after an afternoon filled with food, music and a carefree frivolity. Strategically positioned floodlights had been turned on at dusk, illuminating the property as if it were nine o'clock in the morning instead of nine at night.

Gavin liked his hosts. He particularly liked Daniel. He was generous, unpretentious and completely without guile. Daniel reminded him of Celia. He was brutally honest. Gavin was also glad he'd come to the cookout with Celia, because it'd been a long time since he'd been able to kick back and do absolutely nothing but eat, drink and listen to music while watching others do the same. Little children had run around in wild abandon, teenagers had competed with one another in dance-offs. Their older siblings and parents were content to sit around talking or cooling off with a dip in the lake.

Gavin, who'd shared grilling duty with Daniel, sat on the man's back porch with him and four of his police-officer buddies. He'd sat sipping Wild Turkey bourbon from an old-fashioned glass and taking puffs from a quality cigar. He was half listening to the conversations going on around him, because he couldn't get the image of Celia cradling Hannah and Daniel's son out of his head.

Living with Celia had given him a greater advantage of becoming more familiar within a shorter span of time than if he'd dated her. He'd learned to gauge her moods, which ran the gamut, from defiance to annoyance, joy, tension and anger. What he hadn't glimpsed—until today—was serenity. The look on her face radiated peace, the emotion that probably had eluded her for almost a year. His gaze lingered on her as she sat with a small group of women sitting under a copse of trees. He smiled when she threw back her head and laughed with the other women.

"What's your take on the robbery, Faulkner?"

The query shattered his musings and he turned to stare at a middle-aged sergeant with a noticeable paunch, who'd passed on the bourbon to drink beer. "I'm sorry, Jimmy," Gavin apologized, "my mind was elsewhere."

"And I have a good idea just where your mind was." Isaac Smith had insinuated himself into the conversation.

Gavin ignored the gibe. He had no intention of discussing Celia with any of the men. "What were you asking?"

Isaac Smith took a deep drag of his cigar, blowing out a perfect smoke ring. "Jimmy Lee was asking about the gang that kidnapped and shot that gun dealer who's from around here."

A shiver shook Gavin, and he uncrossed his legs, stretching them out in front of him to camouflage his reaction to Smitty's reference to the gun shop owner's kidnapping, which had been a closely held secret. Who, he wondered, had given the trooper classified information, because the details as to the kidnapping were deliberately excluded from any Bureau, local police and newspaper reports.

"Have they caught the bastards?" he asked smoothly.

Smitty took another puff of his cigar. "Not yet. Fortunately, Dane Jessup was able to give the ATF folks a description of the shooter. Let's hope they catch him before I do, because I'd blast his ass and ask questions later."

Slouching lower in his chair, Daniel Walsh crossed his feet at the ankles. "I read an article yesterday that'd been printed in the *Houston Chronicle* about high-powered gun purchases at a Houston-area store by a Gulf drug cartel cell. They were smuggled across the border by the syndicate and were tied to fifty-five killings in Mexico, including the deaths of police officers, civilians and gangsters."

Gavin forced himself to relax as all of his senses came into focus. The reason he'd been ordered to hang out in Waynesville while waiting for Ray to contact him was to gather as much information as he could about the gun thieves, and it was more than luck that Celia's friend's husband was in law enforcement.

He shook his head. "It doesn't make sense, Daniel. The drugs flow north into our communities, contributing to more violence and compromising public health and safety, but we know weapons from the U.S. flow south and are used in violent attacks."

Smitty sat up straighter. "But, why steal guns when you can buy them legally?"

"Why buy the cow when you can get the milk free?" Daniel asked.

"Robbing gun dealers bypasses legal paperwork and background checks, which many wouldn't pass," Gavin interjected.

Daniel ran a hand over his hair. "That's true for some." Everyone stared at him.

"What aren't you telling us, Danny?" the sergeant asked.

"I have a cousin who works for the ATF Houston division, which also includes the Rio Grande Valley and the Del Rio, and he said agents inspected gun dealer records and knocked on doors of people who purchased guns that wound up in Mexico. Many said they were stolen, but there was one case that involved a small-town Texas policeman. He'd bought a few military-style rifles, left them in his car and on the same night forgot to lock the door. He's in a lot of hot water because he couldn't explain why he hadn't filed a police report or why he'd visited Mexico the next day."

Jimmy smothered a belch with his hand. "I guess you can say that that good ole boy can say bye-bye to his pension. The local police may look the other way, but not the feds."

Gavin nodded without commenting. The veteran police officer was right. The federal police had prioritized illegal gun sales. The file on Raymond Prentice included a report on the results of the Gun Runner Impact Team operation, which brought in one hundred agents from around the country for temporary duty. Two hundred seventy-six full-scale investigations were opened against weapons purchasers as well as a handful of firearms dealers.

Since it was illegal to own firearms in Mexico, and the U.S. had top-quality guns readily available, the cartels organized cells that recruited U.S. citizens with clean criminal backgrounds to purchase the weapons without raising red flags. ATF inspectors, who'd gone through the records of more than one thousand dealers, issued warning letters about compliance to more than seventy and revoked the license of one. Many problems were attributed to sloppy record keeping.

"It's not going to stop until our people stop buying the shit," Daniel sneered.

Smitty blew out a series of smoke rings. "I doubt if that's ever going to happen. As long as there are illegal drugs you're going to have people selling their souls to buy it, and those on the other end who will annihilate anything and anyone who get in their way of making a profit."

Jimmy Lee raised his longneck. "Preach, Brother Smitty." The other four raised their glasses in acknowledgment.

Gavin drained his glass, and then pushed off the chair. He extended his hand to each of the men. "Gentlemen, it's been good."

Daniel stood up. "How long are you and Celia hanging around?"

"We plan to spend the summer."

He slapped Gavin's back. "If you're not doing anything next weekend, then we'd like you to come on by."

"It can't be next weekend, but if the invitation's open

for the following one, then why don't you bring your family to our place?"

"That's a bet, providing Hannah doesn't go into labor before then."

Gavin gave the men a snappy salute before walking off the porch and down to where Celia sat. Her head popped up when she saw him. Reaching down, he helped her to her feet, waiting until she said her goodbyes.

"What's the matter?" he asked when she wrinkled her nose.

"You've been smoking."

"The boys and I had a cigar to go along with our bourbon."

Celia wrinkled her nose again. "Well, if that's the case then you can sleep with the boys tonight."

Holding her arm in a firm grip, Gavin led her around to where he'd parked his truck. "I had my fill of sleeping with *the boys* when I was in the army."

"Well, I'm not going to share a bed with someone willing to risk their health because of an addiction."

Gavin helped Celia up, and then came around to sit next to her. "I didn't know you cared that much," he teased.

"Yes, I care, Gavin. The problem is I care a little too much about you."

"You care too much as a doctor or as my wife?"

"That's something we're going to have to talk about."

He pondered her cryptic retort, starting up the vehicle. "What's on your mind, Celia?"

"There you go again."

A frown found its way onto Gavin's face. "What are you talking about?"

"Why do you have to come off so condescending?"

"You think?"

"I know," she shot back. "I want to talk to you about something and you make it appear as if I'm annoying you."

He wanted to tell Celia something was bothering him, but it wasn't her. It was Isaac Smith's reference to the group of gun thieves kidnapping the gun dealer. Dane Jessup was carjacked on the way to work, taken across the border into Tennessee then returned to North Carolina where the thieves cleaned out his store with the intent of leaving him for dead. The case would've fallen under the jurisdiction of the ATF if it hadn't been for the kidnapping, which was why the Bureau had become involved. Gavin had wanted to believe Jessup's abduction was Raymond Prentice's idea because he was apprehensive about his cover being blown. If not, then it was something new in the gang's repertoire of brazen holdups.

"I'm sorry, baby, if I came off sounding so insensitive. What do you want to talk about?"

Celia turned, staring at Gavin's strong profile. "I can't do this."

"Are you talking about our marriage?"

She nodded. "I can't keep lying, Gavin, only because I've never been adept at it. I'm flubbing the script, and whenever someone asks about our dating and how you proposed I have to mentally backtrack and try to recall what I'd said before."

Gavin's hands tightened on the leather steering wheel. He could understand Celia's exasperation because subterfuge wasn't a part of her psyche. "What else is bothering you, sweetheart?" His voice was soft, as if he were comforting a child.

"I can't stop thinking that Alton Fitch's abduction is somehow connected to the hospital shooting."

"And what if it isn't?" he asked.

Celia managed to force a smile through an expression of uncertainty. "Then I have one less thing to worry about."

"I don't want you to worry about anything, Celia."

"That's easy enough for you to say, Gavin. You're not the one who has to testify against a member of one of the most ruthless gangs in south Florida."

"Are you having second thoughts about testifying?"

Celia shook her head. "No. The only way I don't testify is if I'm dead, and I don't plan on dying in the very near future. I was spared for a reason, Gavin, and I believe it's to make certain the people who were murdered in that E.R. did not die in vain."

"That's my girl. For a minute, I thought you were going soft on me."

A pregnant silence filled the vehicle as she stared through the windshield. "I'm not afraid for myself."

"Even if you were, I'd still take care of you." Gavin knew his pledge to protect Celia hadn't come from his promise to Nicholas Cole-Thomas, but from some place that was totally foreign to him. Celia had admitted that she cared a little too much for him. Well if he was going to be truthful with her, then he would have to admit that his feelings were more intense than just caring about her well-being.

He didn't want to think about or believe that a woman he'd known a week had changed him completely—inside and out. Solitary by nature, he was used to living and working alone. Even when he'd had relationships of what he'd considered long duration he'd never asked a woman to live with him, and when they'd made the offer he hadn't hesitated to reject their offer.

Celia was different, though. It could be her independence and inner strength that drew him to her. She had her music, needlework, garden and cooking to keep her busy during the day, and when they shared a bed it'd become more than his making love to her. It'd become a time to heal, to love. Gavin wasn't certain if he was falling in love with Celia because he believed he'd never been in love. He'd known lust, but not love for a woman who wasn't a family member.

"Will it make you feel more relaxed if we make our marriage legal?"

"What?" The single word exploded from Celia.

"We can go to Virginia, where there's no waiting period, and we don't have to be a resident of the Commonwealth. We can get married the same day we procure the license."

"We can't, Gavin."

"We can do anything we want to do, Celia. I shouldn't have to remind you that we're consenting adults."

"But I'm not in love with you."

"You weren't in love with Yale, yet you'd agreed to marry him."

Celia wished she could've retracted her words when she admitted loving Yale, yet not being in love with him. There were times when she'd questioned her decision to accept his marriage proposal, but when she'd analyzed why she had it'd come down to doing what was the norm. She had a career and the next phase of her life was to get married and have children.

"It was different with me and Yale."

Gavin made his way slowly down the steep hill, stopping and looking both ways before driving onto the paved road leading back to Celia's house. "And it's going to be different for us."

"How different, Gavin?"

"The decision will be yours whether to annul the marriage or see if we can make a go of it."

Celia stared at Gavin, tongue-tied. She couldn't believe he could come up with such an absurd proposition. "You want to dump the responsibility in my lap." The query was a statement. "No, thank you, Gavin. I'm not that desperate to be married."

"What if I accept the decision as to our future together?"

"It still doesn't solve anything," she protested.

"Yes, it does, Celia. You can stop lying."

Somehow he'd turned the tables, and as they say, the ball was in her court. *She* was the one who had little or no skill when it came to telling lies. "Answer one question for me, Gavin."

"What is it?"

"Did any of the guys question you about me?"

"Nope. Why?"

"I got the third degree from the ladies about you. The only thing they didn't ask is whether you wear boxers or briefs."

"Would you have told them if they'd asked?"

"Hell, no. That's none of their business."

Gavin laughed as he drove into the driveway of the house. He pushed the button on the remote device and maneuvered into the two-car garage. It was a tight fit with the two SUVs but he didn't want to leave either vehicle out overnight. "The only thing guys want to know is how long did it take me to get the drawers."

Celia smiled and landed a punch on his shoulder. "That is so low-down."

"Whoa, baby. Hitting your husband can be interpreted as domestic abuse."

"No, it's not because legally you're not my husband."

Gavin shut off the engine and pressed the remote again. The door lowered automatically. A ceiling light illuminated the interior of the garage. "What's it going to be, baby girl? Do you want to stop lying, or continue the farce?"

"Okay. We'll do it. But when it comes time for us to split up, I don't want to have to deal with any histrionics from you."

"I guess you're going to want me to sign a prenuptial agreement."

Celia smothered an expletive. How could she have forgotten she was worth millions? "I'll call my attorney on Monday and ask him to draw up one. He can overnight it to Nicky's farm. We can sign it and send it back before we exchange vows."

"That sounds good. Remember, Monday we pick up Terry."

I've truly lost my mind, Celia thought as Gavin got out and came around to assist her.

Celia waited for Gavin to disarm the alarm. "I'm going to call my brother to let him know our plans have changed, and then I'm going to take a bath and go to bed. I'll try and wait up for you."

Gavin closed the door and reset the alarm. Reaching for Celia, he pulled her to his length. "We're going to do okay."

Curving her arms under his shoulders, she buried her face between his neck and shoulder. The lingering scent of his cologne was barely discernible. He smelled of burning wood and cigar smoke. Celia didn't know why, but she wanted what she'd shared with Gavin to be real, that when they did marry, it would be for all the right reasons.

But, then she had to ask herself if she'd agreed to marry Yale for all the right reasons when the only thing they had in common was medicine. Other than that, there wasn't much that they did together. Much to her surprise Gavin helped her inside and outside the house. He was not opposed to doing loads of wash or folding the clothes once they came out of the dryer, and he cooked and cleaned up afterwards, which left her time to clean the house.

Traditionally, when Coles married it was for life. The exception was her cousin Nathaniel. He'd married Kendra Reeves, agreed to a divorce after their daughter drowned in the family pool, but convinced her to give him a second try. They were now expecting another baby.

"Is that wishful thinking, darling?"

Easing back, Gavin stared at her upturned face. "Yes, it is." He smiled. "I'm going to hang out down here and watch the news and then I'll be up."

He'd said yes when he'd wanted to say it was a prayer. There was something about Celia that tugged at his heart the way no other woman had been able to do. He had no inkling what it was about her and hoped he would discover what it was before it came time for her to testify.

Going on tiptoe, Celia kissed his ear. "I'll see you later."

Gavin waited for Celia to climb the staircase and disappear from view before he reached for his cell phone. Walking to the back porch, he flipped a wall switch. Soft light from a table lamp and floor lamp illuminated the space. He reached for the remote and tuned the television to CNN, hoping for an update about the Florida prosecutor's abduction.

But, first things first. Gavin wanted to know how Isaac Smith came by the information about Dane Jessup's kidnapping. Was there a leak in the North Carolina field office? Had the loquacious state trooper overheard something he shouldn't have repeated? Or was he a dirty cop?

The questions nagged at Gavin until he punched the buttons on his BlackBerry that connected him to the Bureau. He identified himself to the analyst that answered the phone. Vera was either off or she was away from her desk. He gave the man Isaac Smith's name, asking him to get back to him as quickly as possible.

"Do you want to hold, Agent Faulkner, or should I call you back?"

"I'll hold."

Gavin stared at the television screen, reading the closed captions while he waited. He didn't have to wait long. Smitty, as he was known to the locals, had been under surveillance for more than a year.

The man was more than a dirty cop. Isaac Smith was a traitor.

He flicked off the television, plugged his cell into the charger and checked all of the doors and windows. Gavin's footfalls echoed dully on the staircase. He'd come to the Great Smoky Mountains to provide safe passage for an undercover agent, but had found himself involved with a woman that made him feel things he didn't want to feel; she'd gotten under his skin when he'd agreed to legalize a charade of a marriage.

Gavin could not have imagined that when he'd walked into FBI headquarters to meet with a Department of Justice task force he would become a player in a plot that was becoming more and more complex. He was protecting a witness, when it should've been someone from the U.S. Marshal Service; the prosecutor in the case where Celia was the key witness had been kidnapped in front of his home and unknowingly he'd made contact with a traitor masquerading as a North Carolina state trooper.

Fitch's abduction and Isaac Smith's clandestine activities were on the Bureau's priority list. Raymond Prentice and Celia Cole-Thomas topped his.

Chapter 16

Gavin walked into the bathroom, stripping off his clothes and leaving them in a large wicker hamper. Even though he'd begun sleeping in Celia's bedroom he hadn't used her bathroom. Natural flooring materials lent character and subtle coloration to the overall design of the space. The colors of taupe, tan and beige were dominant. There was a vintage-style sink, plank-wood walls and slate floors.

There was the requisite garden tub with a Jacuzzi, but what Gavin had found shocking was the sunken hot tub in a corner of the large room. French doors leading to the second-story wraparound deck provided an unobstructed view of the Great Smoky Mountains. The vistas from the second story were not only spectacular but awe-inspiring.

He'd stood on the deck earlier that morning, watching the sun rise and glorying in the cool mountain air sweeping over his nude body. There were no voyeuristic neighbors to observe his wanton display of flesh, just hawks and other birds soaring high above treetops. Celia had chosen the perfect location for her mountain retreat. It was where one could come to find peace and to heal.

Gavin brushed his teeth and rinsed his mouth with a mouthwash, trying to come to grips with the realization that he was to become a married man before next weekend. His rationale was that he was doing it as a part of his undercover; that he hadn't wanted to compound Celia's angst because she didn't like to lie, but knew he couldn't hide behind any of the reasons that were as transparent as water. He was falling for the woman—hard!

Everything about Celia appealed to his domineering personality. She was feisty, fearless and outspoken. He couldn't intimidate her, and he'd stopped trying. They'd become a couple—in and out of bed and he looked forward to going to bed and waking up with her beside him. Gavin had told himself it was the sex, but knew he wasn't being completely honest with himself. He could have sex with any woman and the result would be a physical release.

Making love with Celia had surpassed a simple slaking of sexual frustration. It wasn't just his body going through the motions of seeking to ejaculate, but his mind wanting to bring her ultimate pleasure before he'd take his own. So far, he'd managed to remain emotionally detached from the act, because it would make it easier for him to walk away at the end of the summer. Falling in love with Dr. Celia Cole-Thomas was not an option. Gavin walked out the bathroom, a towel wrapped around his hips at the same time Celia walked out of the bedroom with a towel tucked into her breasts. Light from her bedroom spilled out into the narrow hallway.

He smiled. "Where are you going?"

Celia returned the smile. "I was coming to look for you."

Gavin took a step. "Why were you looking for me?"

"I thought perhaps you'd fallen asleep while watching television."

Gavin's gaze swept over her damp hair, flawless face and the soft swell of brown flesh rising above the terry-cloth fabric. He made a face. "That was only one time, baby girl." She'd gone upstairs to bed, leaving him watching a movie that failed to keep his interest. Instead of turning off the television, he'd fallen asleep. It was two in the morning when Celia came down to wake him.

He moved closer, feeling the moist heat of her breath on his jaw. "Are you ever going to let me live that down?"

"I'll think about it, lover."

This was a Celia he liked—sexy and teasing. His hands moved up and he undid the towel, holding it open to view her naked body. He smiled. She'd put on weight. Her breasts and hips appeared fuller than when he'd first slept with her.

"Aye," he drawled in a flawless British accent, "the fair maiden hides her true treasure under a scrap of cloth."

Celia reached for the towel around Gavin's slim hips and removed it. "It is said that a man's strength is in his loins. How strong are you, milord?" The towel fell to the floor, her eyes growing wider when she realized Gavin was more than half-aroused. "What is that between your thighs, milord?"

Placing his hands on Celia's waist, Gavin lifted her

effortlessly off the floor. "It's something that gives pleasure, poppet."

He didn't give her a chance to react or protest when he pressed her back to the wall and guided his erection inside her hot body like a heat-seeking missile.

They stood in the dimly lit hallway, Celia's feet braced against the opposite wall, her arms gripping Gavin's neck, as they copulated. She was in heat and the only thing she wanted was the rigid flesh moving in and out of her quivering flesh.

The sounds of heavy breathing and the slip-slap of flesh meeting flesh sent her into a sexual frenzy. She couldn't get close enough. Arching her back, she bucked wildly as Gavin's hips slammed into her like a jackhammer.

Then it happened. The contractions became stronger and stronger, sweeping over her like a fire racing out of control. It ended when an orgasm seized her, holding her in a grip of ecstasy that singed her mind and body. It released her, only to grip her again, this one stronger, longer than the one preceding it. The muscles in Celia's neck bulged as she tried vainly not to climax. Making love without the barrier of latex sent her libido into overdrive.

Gavin felt the burning at the base of his spine and the tightening of his scrotum, and knew it wouldn't be long before the fiery pleasure scorching his mind and body would come to an end.

Did he want it to end?

No.

Did he want to pull out before he ejaculated into Celia?

Yes.

But his mind refused to follow the dictates of his brain when he knew getting her pregnant would complicate everything. As an agent working undercover he didn't want to risk losing his life and leaving his wife and child without protection. He'd remembered the number of times he'd heard his mother crying when she thought he was asleep. And at ten years of age, Gavin knew she'd missed her husband. It'd taken years for Malvina to begin dating again. She'd finally met a confirmed bachelor in their gated seniors-only community.

A primal scream and the rake of fingernails on his back made the hair stand up on the nape of Gavin's neck. Lifting her higher, his fingers bit into the soft flesh on her buttocks. Pressing his forehead to the wall next to Celia's thrashing head, he moaned in sweet agony as he released himself into the pulsing flesh pulling him farther and farther inside where he didn't know who he was. It ended when he slid down to the floor, taking Celia with him. Still joined, she straddled his thighs, their chests rising and falling in a deep, shuddering rhythm. A soft chuckle began in his chest before Gavin threw back his head and roared like a triumphant large cat.

Celia, enjoying the aftermath of a still-throbbing ecstasy, caught Gavin's earlobe between her teeth. "What's so funny?"

"You," he said in her ear. "Methinks the maiden is no maiden, but a she-cat wench. I'm willing to bet you left claw marks on my back."

Celia trailed her fingertips up and down his back, stopping when he gasped. "Let me up, Gavin."

"No. I don't want to move."

"But, you have to. I need to see if I broke skin."

"Look at it later." Cupping a firm breast in his hand, Gavin gently squeezed it, eliciting a gasp of breath from Celia. "Did I hurt you?"

She shook her head. "No, darling. I'm expecting my menses and my breasts are always tender before it comes."

Pulling back, Gavin tried making out Celia features. "When is it coming?"

"I'll probably see it tomorrow."

Cradling her face between his hands, he brushed a kiss over her parted lips. "What if it doesn't come, Celia?"

"Are you asking about you getting me pregnant?"

"Yes."

Lowering her gaze, Celia stared at the corded muscles and power in her lover's upper body. He'd lifted and held her off the floor with the ease of someone lifting a small child. His lovemaking, in various unorthodox positions, had her experiencing pleasure that defied description.

"I doubt if I am. But if you did, then it would complicate our agreement, Gavin."

"How's that, baby?"

"If you or I decide to annul the marriage, then there's the question of custody. Do I assume full custody, giving you liberal visitation, or would we share custody?"

The muscle in Gavin's jaw twitched when he clamped his teeth tightly together. "*If* I get you pregnant, there won't be an annulment. We'll live together as husband and wife and raise our child together."

"*If* will become a reality if you don't wrap up your meat."

A beat passed when Gavin stared at Celia. "No, you didn't just say that."

"Yes, I did," she said sassily. "I can't tolerate oral contraceptives, so I was fitted for an intrauterine device. If we're going to make love without using protection, then I'm going to have to find a doctor…"

"I don't want you to do it," Gavin interrupted. "I told

you before I'll assume the responsibility of protecting you. And I will."

Pressing a kiss along the strong column of his neck, Celia snuggled closer. "You will until we mate again like animals in heat."

Cupping her hips, Gavin pulled her closer. "You're the one who's in heat."

"And you're not?"

"I'm always in heat when I'm around you. It wasn't always that way with me and other women."

Celia felt his flesh stir inside her, and she feared if she didn't get up then they would have a repeat of their unbridled coupling. "Please let me get up so I can look at your back." Gavin stood in one continuous motion, bringing her up with him. He carried her into the bedroom to the bath, bending slightly until her feet touched the slate floor. The votives lined along a counter and around the tub flickered like stars.

Flipping a wall switch and flooding the bathroom with light, Celia stared at the raised welts on Gavin's back. Thankfully, she hadn't broken the skin.

"Wait here while I get my bag. I need to clean the scratches."

Shifting so he could see his back in the mirrored wall, Gavin snorted. "It's nothing, Celia."

"That's where you're wrong. Scratches can be ugly if they become infected." She walked out of the bathroom, returning with her medical bag. After washing her hands, she ripped open a packet with sterilized gauze, covering it with an antiseptic and dabbing it on the scratches. "I know it stings a little bit."

Gavin bit back an explosive curse. "It stings more than a little bit, Doc."

She blew on the four welts that looked like tracks. "Don't be such a baby, Gavin."

He glared at her. "Let me scratch you, then dab some of that liquid fire on you."

"I'd gladly agree but only if I can give you my menstrual cramps."

"No, no, no. I want no part of that business."

Celia closed her bag, leaving it on a side table in the bathroom. "I thought not. Are you ready to go to bed?"

Bending slightly, Gavin swept her up in his arms and carried her to the bed. "I'll be back as soon as I put out the candles." Returning to the bathroom, he blew out the many candles and then turned off the lights. He knew making love to Celia without using a condom was risky. What had surprised him was that she hadn't become hysterical. Did she want a child? Or did she know her body so well that she knew it was impossible for her to conceive at this time in her cycle?

He got into bed, pulling Celia until her hips were flush against his groin. "Good night, baby."

"Good night, love," Celia slurred.

Gavin lay in the darkness wondering if Celia did love him or if it was just a casual term of endearment. He wanted to tell her that he not only loved her, but that he was also falling in love with her. It was the only plausible reason why he'd elected to have unprotected sex with a woman he'd known and would marry within a span of two weeks.

Celia sat on the window seat in the alcove of the kitchen, holding the cordless phone between her chin and shoulder as Terry turned around on her lap until he found a comfortable spot to sleep.

"*¿Cómo estás,* Cee Cee?"

She smiled. "I'm good, Nicky."

"Please don't tell me you're not coming."

"Gavin and I are still coming, but we've decided to come down a couple of days early."

"That's good news."

Celia stared at Terry, exhaling a breath. She and Gavin had gotten up early to drive to Asheville to pick up the puppy. His wound was completely healed and he couldn't stop trying to lick her when she picked him up. Gavin had settled the bill while she bonded with her new pet.

"The good news is that Gavin and I are getting married."

There was silence on the other end of the line. "Are you sure you know what you're doing?" Nicholas asked.

Celia knew whenever her younger brother deliberately softened his tone it signaled the calm before a storm. "Yes, we do." Her gaze darted around the kitchen, praying Gavin wasn't within earshot. "I'm in love with him, Nicholas. And, what I feel for Gavin is so different from what I felt with Yale."

"Is it love or is it lust, Cee Cee?"

"Both!" She didn't care if Nicholas didn't like her tone.

"When and where are you tying the knot?"

"We decided to marry in Virginia, and I'd like you to be our witness."

There was another pause. "I'd be honored to stand in as your witness. Are you going to tell Mom and Dad?"

"Not right away. And I'd appreciate it if you wouldn't tell them until I do."

"Okay. But what's the rush, Celia? Are you pregnant?"

Celia shook her head although her brother couldn't see her. "Why did I know you would ask me that?"

"I asked because it's the most obvious question, *chica.* And don't get me wrong. I like being an uncle. As soon as Samuel's old enough I'm going to put him on a horse."

"Don't you think Diego and Vivienne may have something to say about that?"

"Both of them are all right with it. Now, am I to become an uncle for the second time?"

"No, you're not."

"Are you planning on starting a family? I'm only asking because you seemed vague about the subject of kids when you were with Yale."

Celia wanted to tell Nicholas she was vague when it came to setting a wedding date, so having a baby hadn't figured into the equation at that time. "I suppose we eventually would like to have at least one child." She knew for certain it wouldn't happen within the next nine months because her menses had come that morning. She and Gavin were given a reprieve.

"Do you know for certain when you're coming?"

"Hold on and I'll ask Gavin." Placing the puppy on the floor, Celia went in search of Gavin. She found him sitting out on the patio. He was so still that at first she thought he'd fallen asleep on the webbed lounger. When his head came around and he looked at her, Celia felt as if she were staring into the eyes of a stranger.

"Nicholas wants to know when we're coming."

Sitting up straight, Gavin stared at the woman who in a few days would become his wife. He couldn't have imagined a scenario like the one into which he'd been thrust even if a clairvoyant had predicted it. He swung his legs over the chair and stood up.

"Tell him we'll be there tomorrow."

Celia brought the receiver to her ear and walked back into the house. "Look for us tomorrow."

"¿Chica?"

"Sí, hermano."

"Congratulations. And tell Gavin the same."

"What's up, Nicky? Don't you want me to tell Gavin that smack you told Yale about ripping him a new one if he didn't treat me right?"

"I don't think so, Cee Cee. I'd never go one-on-one with someone built like your fiancé. I'd have to equal the odds with something like a—"

"Please don't say gun, Nicky."

"No. I was thinking more along the line of a two-by-four."

"I'm going to hang up now before I say something I'll regret."

"Damn, Cee Cee. You were never this defensive when it came to Yale."

"Maybe it's because Gavin and Yale are two very different men."

"Or maybe you realize you never really loved Yale," Nicholas continued. "I'm not going to belabor the point, but you know I never liked the man."

"And you like Gavin?"

"Yes. What's there not to like? You did real good this time, Cee Cee."

"We'll see you tomorrow." Celia ended the call, knowing she had to go upstairs and pack.

Gavin, cradling Terry to his chest, walked into the bedroom to find the bed covered with clothes. "How much are you taking?"

Celia's head popped up. "I'm trying to decide what to take."

"How many days are we staying?"

She counted on her fingers. "At least five, and I figure I'll change at least twice a day. So that makes ten outfits."

"Why don't you take five, and we can buy whatever you need once we get to Staunton?"

"Are we going to have time to shop, Gavin?"

He approached her. "We'll take the time, baby."

Going on tiptoe, Celia kissed him. "After spending what I think of as half my life in scrubs, I really enjoy going shopping."

"Are you going to buy a dress for the ceremony?"

She went still, her eyes widening at the suggestion. She and Gavin were legitimizing a sham of a marriage, and he was acting as if their union would be of long duration. *If* and only if she did become pregnant, then Celia would reconsider an annulment. Gavin had grown up without his father and she hadn't wanted the same for his child.

"I suppose it should be easy enough to find a dress befitting a daytime wedding."

Celia realized she would also need shoes, to have her hair styled and a mani/pedi. She'd always planned to marry once, and if her marriage to Gavin ended in an annulment, then she would've had the experience of being a bride.

Gavin angled his head, trailing kisses along the length of her neck. "I have a suit, but I'd like a new shirt and tie."

"If we get to Virginia early enough, we can pick up the license tomorrow. We can shop on Wednesday, and Thursday morning I'd like to get my hair styled before the ceremony."

"Is this your way of telling me we're going to marry on Thursday?"

Celia lowered her gaze as heat flared in her cheeks. She'd come off sounding like a tyrant, barking orders. "If you find yourself available Thursday afternoon, I'd like to invite you to *our* wedding, Mr. Faulkner."

"I'd like nothing better than showing up Thursday afternoon to become a participant in *our* wedding."

"You know you're silly, Gavin."

"No, I'm not. What I am is lucky to have found someone like you." Gavin winked at Celia. "I'm going to walk Terry. It's not too early to train him to do his business outside."

"Be careful with him, Gavin."

He gave her a level look. "Lighten up, baby. You're going to wind up turning Terry into a punk." He dropped a kiss on the terrier's head. "Come on, Bruiser. If left up to your mama she'll paint your toenails pink, tie a matching bow around your neck and instead of calling you Terry, you'll answer to Theresa."

"I'm not kidding," Celia said to Gavin's broad back when he turned and walked out of the bedroom.

Sitting on the bench at the foot of the canopy bed, she exhaled an audible breath. She had the house, the dog and before the end of the week she would marry a man who had her craving him as if he were a controlled substance.

Chapter 17

Gavin turned his SUV onto a private road leading to Cole-Thom Farms. Nicholas Cole-Thomas had warned him that the horse farm was like a fortress, and judging from the cameras and security checkpoint Gavin knew Celia's brother wasn't just blowing smoke. Stopping at the checkpoint, he nodded to the man in the booth. A high-powered rifle in plain sight was a definite deterrent for anyone attempting to bypass security.

A man who wore every year of his advanced age on his face slid back the window in the air-cooled booth. "May I please see your driver's license?"

Gavin reached in the rear pocket of his jeans where he kept his license, placing it in the outstretched hand, while strategically positioned cameras recorded his and Celia's image along with the vehicle's license plate.

They'd gotten up before sunrise because Celia

wanted to be on the road before rush-hour traffic. He'd loaded Terry in a crate, placing him and his doggie supplies in his SUV's cargo area. Once he'd loaded their luggage, they headed for the interstate highway. Gavin stopped once they crossed the state line from North Carolina into Virginia where he'd ordered breakfast to go, because they didn't want to leave the puppy in the truck with the rising temperatures.

"Follow the signs, Mr. Faulkner," the guard said, smiling and handing Gavin his license.

Gavin returned his license to his back pocket, shifted into gear and continued along the newly paved road. Towering trees stood along the roadway like sentinels. The mowed grass reminded him of baseball fields. "How big is this farm?" he asked Celia.

"Nicky said it's about almost four hundred acres. He claims it's much smaller than some of the other farms in the area."

"The landscaping is impeccable. It must take a week to mow the grass." He pointed to his right. "Look over there, baby."

Celia caught her breath when she spied several mares with their young. The sunlight shimmered on their deep red coats. "The foals are adorable, but I still don't want any part of them."

Gavin slowed to five miles an hour when he recognized what appeared to be a gray Arabian stallion racing across the meadow at breakneck speed in pursuit of a mare that kicked up her hind legs whenever he got too close.

"Isn't that just like a woman?" he said. "Why is she playing hard to get?"

Celia noticed the stallion was aroused. "Maybe she's not in estrous."

"I'm willing to bet she is or he wouldn't be all over her. See, I was right." At that moment the mare stopped and permitted the stallion to mount her. Gavin gave Celia a sidelong glance. "One of these days we're going to try that position."

She was saved from replying when a trio of chimneys came into view. As Gavin maneuvered up an incline, Celia gasped when she saw the three-story antebellum great house at the end of a live oak allée. A full-height, columned porch wrapping around the front and sides of the magnificent Greek Revival mansion made her feel as if she'd stepped back in time. When Nicholas talked of spending most all of his inheritance to start up a horse farm she'd thought him frivolous, but he'd proven her wrong.

Her smile was dazzling. "It looks as if my little brother is doing the damn thing."

Gavin shook his head in awe. "Nice." He maneuvered around to the rear of the house where sedans and SUVs and pickups were parked.

Celia was out of the truck as soon as Gavin cut off the engine. Arms outstretched, she met her brother when he came forward to meet her. "You fooled me, Nicky," she said, kissing his cheek.

Nicholas's dark eyes swept over his sister. She looked wonderful, and there was no doubt her bodyguard was just the medicine she needed to heal from the ordeal that had turned her life upside down.

"What are you talking about?"

"You told me you bought a *little place* in Virginia, while most of your money went into buying horses."

"The house came with the land. It was abandoned and dilapidated and I spent more renovating and trying to restore it than I did buying horseflesh. If it hadn't been for Aunt Parris buying furnishings at wholesale I probably would've declared bankruptcy."

Celia's smile turned into a scowl. "You know you could've come to me if you needed money."

"No, I couldn't. Remember, you needed your money for that free clinic you planned to open in Miami." Reaching for her hand, he squeezed her fingers. "Do you intend to go through with your plans?"

She nodded. "Yes. I've decided not to return to the hospital." It was a decision that hadn't come easily for Celia, but she knew she would never be able to walk into the E.R. without reliving the trauma of that fateful night.

Nicholas glanced over his sister's head to see Gavin approaching with a dog on a leash. "We'll talk later." He offered his free hand. "Welcome to Cole-Thom Farms."

Gavin shook his soon-to-be brother-in-law's hand. "Thank you. This place is beautiful."

"Thank you," he said modestly. "And I want to thank you for convincing my sister to come for a visit."

Celia rolled her eyes at Nicholas. "If you'd told me it was like this I would've come sooner."

"I tried to tell you, Cee Cee, but you wouldn't listen." He bent over and patted the terrier's head. "Hello, handsome. There are some dogs around here that would be glad to show you the lay of the land." Nicholas straightened. "Is he old enough to mate?"

"No! Terry's still a puppy."

Nicholas exchanged a look with Gavin, who lifted his shoulders. "That's what I thought about a stray runt until he got one of my bitches pregnant."

"That's not going to happen with Terry," Celia said, "because I plan to have him neutered."

"You will *not* take his manhood," Gavin stated emphatically.

"Did I say something wrong?" Nicholas asked.

Celia glared at Gavin. "No, but Gavin did. Do you have any idea of the number of stray dogs that are put down each year because people don't neuter or spay their pets?"

Nicholas preempted Gavin from answering. "You two must be exhausted after the drive. Come inside and let me show you to your rooms. If you brought a crate for the dog with you, then he can stay in the room with you. Otherwise, you can board him with the other dogs, all of which have had their shots."

Gavin spoke first. "He can stay with us tonight. Tomorrow he's going to have to hold his own against the big dogs."

"I wouldn't worry too much about him," Nicholas said over his shoulder as he led the way around to the front of the house. "Terry may decide that he prefers living on a horse farm to hanging out in the mountains or in Florida."

Celia wondered if Nicky was referring to himself. He preferred breeding horses to working for ColeDiz. And yet, no one would ever question Nicholas's business acumen. He'd become a master when it came to negotiating a deal.

The day he'd exchanged his custom-made tailored suits, imported footwear and expensive sports cars for jeans, boots and a pickup was the day Nicholas Cole-Thomas had found his niche. Her brother, four years her junior, had established himself as a breeder of note within Virginia's horse country, while she'd floundered in an attempt to find her own professional footing.

Celia knew the shooting had changed her life; however, she'd allowed it to slow down her life. She'd vacillated about whether to return to the hospital or follow through with her plan to open the clinic. Gavin coming to live with her represented a return to normalcy, while she was reminded that she'd spent much too much time alone.

Marrying a stranger was anything but normal, but she realized that she was more comfortable living with Gavin than she had ever been in her three-year relationship with Yale. Gavin respected her personal space and the time when she preferred being alone to do the things she liked doing. But then when they did come together to cook, eat, watch a movie, play a board game or take a walk, she knew she'd found her soul mate.

Wiping her feet on a mat inside the entry hall and walking into the living room, Celia stared up at the massive crystal chandelier suspending from the ceiling rising more than twenty feet above a parquet floor bordered by an intricate rosewood inlaid pattern. Twin curving staircases leading to the second story were a scene out of *Gone with the Wind.*

She recognized her great-aunt's decorating trademarks with a collection of candlesticks on the fireplace mantel, the elegant fabrics on love seats, sofa and chairs and the collection of framed prints featuring horses.

"This is more than I ever could've imagined." The only house she'd seen that was comparable to Nicholas's house was the one her great-grandfather had built for his wife and children. The twenty-four-room West Palm Beach mansion overlooking a lake was filled with priceless artifacts and had become nothing short of a showplace.

"Amen to that," Gavin said.

Nicholas stopped at the staircase. "I can't take any of the credit for what you see. My great-aunt designed the rooms, her daughter Regina the gardens, and another cousin who's an architectural historian selected the antiques. Everyone asked if I was going to give the house a name, so I decided to call it Cole House because it was Cole women who did what they do best."

"They sound like incredible women," Gavin said.

Nicholas gave Gavin a long, penetrating stare. "You should know that firsthand. After all, you're marrying one."

Gavin returned the stare. "I don't need you to tell me that."

Celia's gaze shifted to Nicholas, then Gavin and back to her brother. "Please don't start that male posturing nonsense or there will be no wedding."

Nicholas waved his hand in a dismissive gesture. "Cole women give their men a lot of lip until they become mothers. After that, they go into 'yes, dear' and 'no, dear' mode."

Gavin winked at Nicholas. "That's something I'll keep in mind."

Celia folded her hands at her waist. "Nicky, why do you always want to start something?"

"Love you, too, Cee Cee." Turning, Nicholas made his way up the staircase, Celia and Gavin following. "I'm putting you in the west wing because the sun doesn't reach that section of the house until late morning. I'm at the opposite end in the east wing." He opened a set of double doors and then stepped aside. "You have a bedroom, private bath, sitting and dressing area. There's a wet bar in a chest in the sitting room and if you need anything let me know and I'll have someone bring it to you."

Shifting Terry to his left hand, Gavin wrapped his right arm around Celia's waist. "Celia and I would like to take you out for dinner tonight. That is, if you don't have any other plans." His fingers tightened on her waist.

"Please say yes, Nicky," Celia chimed in as if she and Gavin had discussed it beforehand.

Nicholas reached for the cell phone attached to his waist. "Let me make a call first."

"Why don't you have *her* join us," Celia said perceptively, "unless you don't want me to meet your girlfriend?"

"Peyton's not my girlfriend."

Celia's eyebrows shot up. "*Her* name is Peyton?"

Nicholas angled his head. "Her father wanted a boy. I'll call and let her know we're going to have company."

"What time do you want us to be ready?" Gavin asked.

"Seven. See you guys later."

Celia waited for her brother to close the door before glaring at Gavin. "Let me give you a word of caution, Gavin. Please don't get into it with Nicholas, because he likes nothing better than verbal confrontation. And, he's not above backing it up with his fists."

"Stop trying to protect Nicholas, Celia. He's not your little brother anymore. In case you've forgotten he is a grown man."

She ran her fingers through her hair. "You're right, *m'ijo*. Nicholas doesn't need me to fight his battles. Just take a look at this house, the farm. My younger brother has succeeded when most of us believed he would fail."

"Did anyone tell you that you couldn't be a doctor?"

"Not really. But, it was my older brother, Diego, who always had my back."

"You don't have to have your brothers' protection, *m'ija.* Now that's my responsibility."

A beat passed as Celia stared at the man with whom she'd fallen in love. "You're really serious, aren't you?"

There came another pause. "You just don't know how serious I am," Gavin said. He approached Celia, handing her Terry. "I'm going down to the truck to bring up his crate before he ruins your brother's priceless Persian rug."

Turning on his heels, he walked out of the bedroom suite. Gavin hadn't lied to Celia. He'd promised to protect her and he would—with his life if the situation called for it. He would forfeit his life because he'd fallen in love with her.

As ordered, he'd called his supervisor to let him know he was in Virginia. Mac informed him there still was no further communication from Raymond Prentice, but if the undercover agent did contact the Bureau, then a jet would be standing by to fly Gavin back to a North Carolina regional airport or private airstrip.

Come on, O, call me. He felt that if he'd mentally willed it, then his brother would contact him. He wanted to bring Raymond Prentice in, and then concentrate on trying to make his marriage to Celia work without a list of conditions.

Celia waited for Gavin to fall asleep before she slipped out of bed, dressed and tiptoed out of the bedroom. Terry, curled into a ball on the fleece mattress in the crate, was also sleeping. The bedroom she'd been assigned overlooked a beautiful English garden. It'd been Christmas when she last saw Regina Cole-Spencer. The landscape architect and her pediatrician husband had traveled from Brazil to Mexico to spend time at the home that had once belonged to Regina and Aaron's father, before they came to West Palm Beach to celebrate Christmas with the ever-increasing Cole clan.

Walking along a stone path, she stopped under an archway covered with climbing pale pink roses. The plantings were mixed, roses set among perennials, presenting a riot of color. She continued, smiling when seeing a wooden fence with a doorway that reminded her of one of her favorite books—Frances Hodgson Burnett's *The Secret Garden.*

Suddenly it hit Celia. She didn't want to be married in a cold, sterile courthouse with a clerk officiating at what was to be one of the most important days in her life. She wanted a minister or a priest to marry her and Gavin in her brother's garden.

From her second-story bedroom window she was able to see the half a dozen cottages where full-time, permanent farm personnel lived with their families, a larger building that was the mess hall and in the distance, the stables where the horses were bedded down for the night. She knew that horses were social animals and were kept outdoors during the day to graze and run to release pent-up energy. She'd noticed men on horseback and others in pickups patrolling the property. All were armed with either handguns or rifles.

Celia bumped into Nicholas as she walked into the large, ultra-modern kitchen. "I was just coming to ask you something."

"And I wanted to give you this." He handed her several pages. "They came in on my fax machine."

When Celia had called her attorney to let him know she needed a prenuptial agreement, he suggested faxing the papers would be quicker than sending them overnight. She had to call Nicholas to get his fax number. "That's the prenup I asked my lawyer to draw up for me."

The nostrils of Nicholas's thin nose flared slightly. "You know this is a first, Cee Cee."

"What are you talking about, Nicky?"

"You're the first Cole to have a prenup."

"It wasn't my idea."

"Whose idea was it?"

Celia bit her lip. "It was Gavin's. He was the one who suggested a prenup."

Nicholas narrowed his gaze. "What's the matter? The two of you don't plan to stay together?"

Reaching for her brother's hand, she pulled him over to a stool at the cooking island. "I have something to tell you, and if you repeat it then I'm going to jack you up, Nicholas Bennett Cole-Thomas."

Nicholas gave her an incredulous look. "Damn, Cee Cee, it must be serious if you're calling me by my full name."

"This is serious, Nicky."

He sobered. "Okay, I'm listening."

Celia told him everything from her initial meeting with Gavin to their decision to make their farce of a marriage legal. What surprised her was that Nicholas's impassive expression did not change.

"What, no comment?" she taunted.

Nicholas threw up his hands. "What do you want me to say, Celia? When a man proposes marriage, it usually means he's tired of chasing skirts and wants to settle down and have a family of his own. Consider yourself blessed, because you're getting someone who's willing to commit without feeling as if there's a noose around his neck. And I really admire the brother for suggesting a prenup, but something tells me you're not going to need it."

"What makes you think that?" she asked.

"The man's in love with you."

"That's where you're wrong, Nicky. Gavin may like me, but I know he's not in love with me."

"Oh, because you say so?" Nicholas asked.

"Because I know so," Celia retorted.

"That shows how much you know, Doc."

Nicholas and Celia turned at the same time to find Gavin standing barefoot under the entrance to the kitchen. A pair of jeans rode low on his hips and the T-shirt stretched over his broad chest appeared to be a size too small. Celia wanted to be anywhere but in the kitchen with Gavin glaring at her as if she'd defamed his character.

Crossing muscular arms over his chest, Gavin leaned against the door frame. "What's the matter, Celia? I've never known you to be at a loss for words," he taunted, ignoring her gasp.

Nicholas, feeling the tension rising in the kitchen like a hot breeze, stood up. "I'm going to leave you two to hash this out."

"Stay!" The command was crisp, sharp and Nicholas sat back down. "You need to hear this," Gavin said, his voice calm and softer. "I didn't propose to Celia out of some perverted sense of duty and honor, but because I'm in love with her. It wouldn't have mattered if she had a problem pretending to be my wife, I still wouldn't have agreed to make it legal. I know what she's worth and I suggested a prenup because I don't want or need her money.

"Tell me now, Celia, if we're going through with

this. If not, then I'll head back to North Carolina. I'll pick up my stuff from your place and leave your keys with Daniel and Hannah." He glanced at the clock on the microwave. "You have exactly one minute to give me your answer."

Celia closed her eyes and bit down on her lip to stop its trembling. "I…" Her words trailed off.

Nicholas popped up. "Look, man, you're not going to pressure my sister like that."

Gavin lowered his arms. "And what exactly are you going to do about it? This is between your sister and me. I'd asked you to stay because I want you to hear me out, not interfere."

"*¡Bastante!* Nicholas," Celia screamed.

"It's not enough, Celia," Nicholas countered.

"Yes, it is. Gavin asked me a question and he has a right to get an answer." Her eyelids fluttered wildly, matching the runaway pulse in her throat. She'd balked, refusing to set a wedding date with Yale, but she was determined not to make the mistake twice. A smile trembled over her quivering lips. "Yes, Gavin."

His eyebrows lifted a fraction. "Yes what, Celia?"

Her eyes shimmered with unshed tears. "Yes, I will marry you."

Crossing his arms over his chest again, Gavin angled his head. "Why?"

Rising to her feet, Celia walked over to Gavin and placed both palms over his heart. "Because not only do I love you, but I'm also in love with you. I want to go to bed and wake up with you beside me. And if you want a house full of babies I'm willing to push out as many as I can before I'm too old."

Gavin picked up Celia, fastening his mouth to hers

as her arms went around his neck. He kissed her, silently communicating the depth of his love for her. "We can start as soon as we're married," he whispered against her moist parted lips.

Nicholas stood up. "Come on, guys. Take that stuff upstairs." He walked over to the couple still locked in a passionate embrace. He placed a hand on Gavin's shoulder. "I only let you order me about in my home because of my sister. You need to remember that when you're lord of your own castle and someone gets in your face."

"I don't think so, Brother Thomas. Not too many men are crazy enough to get in my face."

"So, it's like that, Mr. Elite Special Forces?"

"You got that right, rubber ducky."

"Stop it!" Celia shouted, waving her arms above her head. "I'm not going to have my brother and my fiancé at each other's throats because of some silly military competition."

Gavin and Nicholas bumped fists, and then pointed at Celia, while laughing uncontrollably. "Gotcha!" they chorused.

At that moment Celia realized she'd been duped. "You guys are sick," she spat out. She pulled away from Gavin, walked over to the countertop and picked up the printed pages and tore them into strips, then returned to throw them at Gavin. "That's what I think of your freakin' prenup. And I don't want to get married in the courthouse." She turned her angry glare on Nicholas. "I want you to find a minister to marry me and Gavin here at the house. I don't care how much you have to bribe him to perform the ceremony, just make certain he's here Thursday evening."

Nicholas waited until Celia stalked out of the kitchen to look at Gavin. "Are you certain you want to get hooked up with my sister?"

Gavin smiled. "I've seen her worse."

"And you still want to marry her?"

Gavin sobered. "When you find yourself in love with a woman you learn to ignore a lot. She's funny, sensitive, kind and generous. I know you don't want to hear this being that you're her brother. But, the girl is sexy as hell."

"If you say so," Nicholas drawled. He leaned in closer to Gavin. "I know who you are and what you do."

Gavin pretended ignorance. "What are you talking about?"

"I have a cousin who works in Langley who called his friend at Quantico. And I don't want to know what you're doing in North Carolina."

"And I'm not going to tell you," Gavin shot back.

"Whatever it is, I don't want my sister in the line of fire. She's been through enough this past year."

"Don't worry about Celia. The marshals are ready to step in at a moment's notice." Nicholas offered his hand, but Gavin ignored it and gave Nicholas a rough hug. "Do you think you can find a minister for Thursday?"

"Blackstone Farms has a resident ordained minister, who I'm certain would be happy to officiate. I'll call Reverend Jimmy Merrell and ask him. Maybe we can have a little something afterward to celebrate the happy occasion. I'm warning you in advance, that the Coles expect you to repeat your vows New Year's Eve."

"Why New Year's Eve?" Gavin asked.

"It's become a family tradition, dating back to when my great-grandfather married my great-grandmother in Havana, Cuba, that we marry on the last day of the year."

"It sounds like a wonderful way to welcome in a new year."

"The Coles tend to get a little raucous, but it's all in good fun."

Gavin smiled. He was looking forward to meeting Celia's family, but he knew that wouldn't happen until after he was reunited with his brother.

Chapter 18

Celia discovered two hours after Nicholas picked up Peyton Blackstone at Blackstone Farms that it wasn't a date but a business meeting. The first hint should've been that Peyton looked nothing like the women Nicholas had dated, and the other was she referred to Nicholas as Mr. Thomas. She stood in the powder room with Peyton at a Staunton steakhouse, reapplying a coat of lipstick.

A pair of large smoky-gray eyes met hers in the mirror. "You thought I was your brother's date."

Celia capped her lipstick. "I did until I heard you call him Mr. Thomas."

The petite woman removed a comb from her purse, pulling it through thick, blunt-cut, honey-blond, shoulder-length hair. "I want a position as an assistant veterinarian, and coming on to Nicholas Cole-Thomas will definitely not endear me to him."

Celia picked at her curls. "You like him?"

Peyton blushed. "What's there not to like?"

"I'm biased, so I'm not the one to answer truthfully." She felt sorry for the newly licensed veterinarian. Over dinner she'd discovered Peyton had graduated from Western College of Veterinary Medicine in Saskatchewan, Canada, lived at Blackstone Farms, but decided she wanted to establish a reputation as a veterinarian without using the Blackstone name.

"Have you applied to any of the other farms in the area?"

"Yes, but with no luck. I'm willing to work as a vet tech, but everyone claims they can't afford to add another employee to their payroll."

"Has Nicholas said he couldn't pay you?" Peyton shook her head. "Why don't you offer to volunteer? Nicholas would be crazy to turn down free medical care for his horses." Celia barely had time to react when the veterinarian hugged her.

"That's an ingenious idea, Celia." She blew her an air kiss. "Thank you." Peyton cut a dance step, and then stopped when she saw Celia looking at her in amusement. "What are you thinking, Celia? That I'm some horny chick who wants to lure your brother into the sack and kill two birds with one stone."

"I'm not thinking anything, Peyton. I only know what I see."

"And, that is?"

"You're in love with my brother and you're frustrated because he acts like you don't exist."

The tears Peyton had suppressed from the time Nicholas arrived at Blackstone Farms with his sister and her fiancé fell. She'd asked Nicholas to have dinner with her to discuss employment possibilities *and* find out whether his indifference was real or imagined. She had her answer. It was real.

Celia felt completely helpless as she watched Peyton cry. It reminded her of the time when she'd come home sobbing into her pillow because her first boyfriend had cheated on her and didn't care if she knew it. There was no one to console her, or dry her tears. No one to tell her that the cheating SOB wasn't worth her tears. But it was different with Peyton. Nicholas had related to her as if she were a stranger, a face in the crowd of millions.

She took a step, pulling Peyton into a comforting embrace. "I'm not one for matchmaking, but I'm going to try to help you out. Gavin and I are getting married Thursday afternoon. Nicholas has agreed to be our witness, but I'm going to need an attendant. I'm going shopping tomorrow for a dress. Will you come with me?"

Peyton sniffled, then reached for a tissue from a box on the countertop and dabbed her eyes. "You'd do that for me?"

"I've been where you are, Peyton, crying my eyes out over a man. Only the man I shed tears over wasn't worth the gum that was stuck on the sole of my shoe. Nicky's different. He's one of the good guys. I've never known him to mess over a woman."

"But why me, Celia?"

"It's not so much you, but for sisterhood. Now, clean your face so we can tell the men that you've agreed to be my maid of honor."

Gavin and Nicholas stood up when Celia and Peyton returned to the table. Nicholas pulled out the chair for

Peyton, seating her. "Are you all right?" he asked, noticing her red puffy eyes.

"I'm okay now."

Nicholas leaned closer. "What happened?"

Peyton fluttered moist spiky lashes. "Celia asked if I would stand in as her maid of honor, and I got a little emotional."

Resting an arm over the back of Peyton's chair, Nicholas winked at Celia. "If Peyton's going to be your maid of honor, then I guess that'll make me Gavin's best man."

"Peyton and I are going shopping for gowns after Gavin and I pick up our licenses."

Gavin ran a finger around the rim of his wineglass. "Well, if the ladies are going to get all dressed up, then that means we men have to step up. Nicholas, do you happen to have a tailor on speed dial?"

Reaching into the breast pocket of his jacket, Nicholas took out a cell phone. "As a matter of fact, I do."

Three pairs of eyes were fixed on Nicholas when he told his personal tailor what he needed on very short notice. He ended the call and smiled. "Brother Faulkner, we have an appointment at one. Will that give you and Celia enough time to pick up a license?"

"We plan to get to the courthouse when it opens."

Nicholas smiled at Peyton under lowered lids. "Dr. Blackstone, now that we're going to be hanging out together for the next few days I'd like you to call me Nicholas."

"I will if you stop calling me Dr. Blackstone."

Reaching for his wineglass, he touched it to Peyton's. "Hello, Peyton. Allow me to introduce myself. I'm Nicholas."

Picking up her glass, she nodded demurely. "It's nice meeting you, Nicholas."

"I know what you're up to, *m'ija*," Gavin whispered in Celia's ear.

"Silencio, m'ijo," she whispered. Reaching under the table, Celia placed her hand on Gavin's thigh. She heard him suck in a breath when her fingers inched closer to his groin.

"Okay, baby, okay," he gasped.

Celia kissed his ear. "I thought you'd see it my way."

Celia stared up at Gavin as she repeated her vows. When she'd walked down the garden path at Cole-Thom Farms, she'd nearly lost her composure when she saw Gavin waiting under the arch of climbing roses, breathtakingly handsome in a tuxedo, pale pink silk tie and matching rose boutonniere.

She'd tried on a number of gowns before selecting one that didn't have to be altered. It was a platinum silk sheath with embroidered tulle, a sweetheart neckline, short cap sleeves, beading, sheer back and a sweep train. A stylist had blown out her curls, pinning them into an elaborate chignon on the nape of her neck. Tiny pink rose buds tucked into the coil of hair took the place of a veil. Peyton was ravishing in a similar gown in a darker gray that matched her large eyes.

Nicholas had invited two neighboring farms, and the owners and their employees were already in a party mood because of the upcoming weekend open house festivities. The owner of Cole-Thom Farms sister's wedding was an unexpected prelude to what was billed as an inexhaustible supply of food, drink and music.

There was an exchange of rings, a kiss sealing their troth and then it was over. Rev. Merrill had pronounced them husband and wife to the thundering applause of nearly two hundred guests who showered the newly-weds with birdseed and flower blossoms.

Nicholas had hired a party planner who'd performed a minor miracle when she had dozens of white tents erected in a pasture on the south end of the property. A caterer—with a staff of more than fifty—was on hand to take orders, keep the liquid refreshment flowing and serve cook-to-order meals. The DJ had something for everyone, and even before Celia walked the garden path, people were up on their feet dancing.

Celia held the train to her gown in her left hand. Then she placed her right in Gavin's as he led her to the portable stage for their first dance as husband and wife. She was surprised when she recognized Foreigner's "I Want to Know What Love Is" coming from speakers. As she listened to the lyrics she suddenly realized the depth of Gavin's love for her.

She rested her head on his shoulder. "Please tell me I'm not dreaming, Gavin."

He tightened his hold around her waist. "Believe me, you're not dreaming, baby girl. And I'm going to prove that to you tonight. We'll have a wedding to remember."

"Does that mean I'm going to have two wedding nights?"

Pulling back, Gavin gave her a look of confusion. "What are you talking about?"

"We're going to have to do this again for our families. I know my father is going to go off when he finds out that he wasn't given the honor of giving his only daughter away in marriage. And I'm certain your mother isn't going to take kindly when you unexpectedly present her with a daughter-in-law."

"My mother will love you. She's been haunting me and my brother relentlessly about grandchildren."

"Is your brother seeing someone exclusively?"

"I never know with Orlando. He'll see someone for a while, and then when I ask about her he'll pretend he doesn't know who I'm talking about."

"He probably adheres to out of sight, out of mind."

"That sounds like my brother."

Gavin stared out over Celia's head. There wasn't a day since he'd been called into the meeting—what now seemed so long ago—that he hadn't thought about Orlando. The fact that there was a contract out on his life frightened Gavin.

He and Orlando seldom discussed their undercover assignments, preferring instead to talk about sports and politics. And as long as he hadn't known what his brother was involved with or in, Gavin was able to make it through the day without the added burden of worrying about Orlando. He never asked his mother if she'd heard from her younger son because Malvina refused to broach the subject. It was as if she feared the worst, or she was waiting for agents to come to her door with the news that either one or both of her sons had sacrificed their lives serving their country.

"When am I going to meet your mother and brother?"

Celia was asking questions he wasn't able to answer truthfully. "I'm not certain about my brother, but I'll introduce you to my mother before the end of the summer."

"Is she retired?"

"Yes. She retired earlier this year. She still has another year before she turns sixty-five, but she claims she's burned out. I didn't have the heart to tell her she was burned out twenty years ago, but Malvina Faulkner is one of those unrealistic social workers who believes she could change the world one client at a time."

"She's probably more idealistic than unrealistic, Gavin."

"Same difference," he drawled.

Gavin felt a tap on his back. He spun Celia around to find Nicholas grinning at him. "I guess you want to dance with your sister?" He released Celia's hand, bowed elegantly from the waist and extended his hand to Peyton Blackstone.

Celia gave her brother a tender smile. She admired his close-cropped hair. He and Gavin had gone to a unisex salon where they had haircuts, facials and professional shaves. "I can't believe you pulled this off with only two days' notice."

"I hadn't planned to host an open house this year, but you marrying Gavin gave me the perfect excuse to usurp the other breeders. With the exception of Sheldon Blackstone, the other owners consider me a brash upstart with an overblown ego."

"Why are they hatin', Nicky?"

Nicholas's expression became a mask of stone. "It's probably because they had to start from scratch to get to where they are today. I'd heard talk that I'd outbid someone for the property, so their plan was to gang up on the new guy in town. Then when I brought the Arabian stallion all hell broke loose, and there were rumors that someone was going to steal El Hajji. That's when I hired added security, because I was negotiating the sale of an Arabian mare. This is private property, and if anyone attempts to trespass, then I'm not responsible for what happens to them."

"I thought horseracing and breeding was a gentlemen's sport."

Nicholas snorted. "Gentility goes out the window whenever there's competition."

"But, your horses aren't competing."

"It's not about winning purses, but stud fees, Cee Cee. I've made a small fortune putting New Freedom out to stud."

The beginnings of a smile softened Celia's mouth. "You've made it as a successful breeder, now what about your love life?"

"What about it?"

"You have a twelve-room house you need to fill up with a few little CTs."

"I'll think about a few little Cole-Thomases after you have one."

"I'm sorry, brother. My children will be Faulkners, not Cole-Thomas. You and Diego will have to carry on the name."

Nicholas swung his sister around and around, until she pleaded with him to stop. "I told the housekeeper not to come down your wing of the house tomorrow in case you and Gavin want to sleep in late. And don't worry about Terry. I'll take care of the pup."

Her whole face spread into a smile, dimples deepening. "Thank you, Nicky."

"Don't party too hard tonight, because we're going to have to do this again tomorrow at Blackstone Farms and Harridans Farms Saturday."

Celia entered the bedroom, stopping when she saw Gavin filling flutes with pale bubbling champagne. He'd put on a pair of black pajama pants, but had left his chest bare. His exposed skin glistened in the glow of lighted pillars in hurricane lanterns spanning the length of the fireplace mantel. He'd showered while she'd soaked in the Jacuzzi to ease her tired legs and feet. They'd tried to sneak away from the wedding reception once the sun had set, but whenever she tried to escape, someone grabbed her to dance.

The scent of a familiar perfume wafted in Gavin's nostrils and he turned to find Celia standing near the bed in a white silk lace-trimmed nightgown that reminded him of her wedding gown. She'd taken the pins out of her coiffed hair and the ends were curling softly around her face.

He smiled, walking over to Celia and handing her a half-filled flute. "At last," Gavin murmured, "I can get you all to myself." Celia giggled when he nuzzled her neck. "Did I tell you how much I love you, Mrs. Faulkner?"

Celia giggled again. "Not enough, Mr. Faulkner."

"I love you. I love you and I love your life," he crooned in singsong. Gavin knew he would have to wait a few more days before he was able to make love to Celia. Her period couldn't have come at a worse time, but he knew waiting to consummate their marriage would make their coming together even more unforgettable. "After we renew our vows I'm going to take you on a real honeymoon."

Celia's heart swelled with a love she hadn't thought possible. Her free arm went around her husband's neck, holding on to him as if he were her lifeline. "Hush, *m'ijo.* We can honeymoon when we get back to North Carolina."

Gavin pressed a kiss under her ear. "You don't want to go to the Greek Isles or the French Riviera?"

"It doesn't matter where we go as long as we do it together."

"Nicholas told me you're a workaholic, so if we make plans to go away I don't want drama, Celia."

"You won't get drama." She touched her flute to his before taking a sip of the premium vintage.

Gavin stared at her fresh-scrubbed face. He still hadn't processed that Celia was legally his wife. This time there would be no pretense, no need to lie and lie again to cover the previous lie.

What had surprised him was Nicholas's disclosure that he suspected his brother-in-law was a federal agent. *Langley* and *Quantico* were buzzwords for the CIA and FBI. Gavin knew whoever Nicholas's relative contacted at Quantico probably told him of his inability to disclose any information on Gavin Faulkner, leaving the other to draw his own conclusion.

Peering at his wife over the rim of the flute, Gavin drained the glass. He eased the stem of Celia's glass from her loose grip, placed it on the sideboard, then swept her up into his arms and carried her to the bed.

The lay together, talking quietly while planning their future. By the time the last pillar sputtered before burning out, they had fallen asleep.

Chapter 19

"Celia, baby, we're leaving."

Celia dropped a kiss on the top of Terry's head, then placed him in his crate and secured the latch. "I'm coming."

Gavin walked into the bedroom. Terry was whining and jumping up, trying to get out of the crate. "Why don't you let him hang out with the other dogs down at the stables?"

Her gaze swept over Gavin. They were going to Blackstone Farms and he'd chosen to wear a white shirt, black slacks and slip-ons. "Do you think he'll be all right?"

Extending his hand, Gavin helped her stand. "He plays with them all day. Of course he's going to be all right." Celia still refused to go anywhere near the stables or close to where the horses were exercised or grazed.

"Okay, you can take him. I'll wait for you on the porch."

Celia walked over to the dressing area and picked up a small purse with a shoulder strap, looping it over her body. The light from a table lamp glinted off the band on her left hand. Although she no longer had to lie and pretend Gavin was her husband, she wanted to tell her parents of the change in her marital status—not by phone but in person.

Even if she'd wanted to return to Florida, she knew it was better to remain out of the state until the police solved Alton Fitch's disappearance. It had been more than a week since the prosecutor had gone missing and so far the family hadn't heard a word from the kidnappers other than they were willing to return the D.A. alive if the family paid a ransom. There were news reports that the amount of the ransom still hadn't been set, and the longer he was missing, the odds were against him being found alive.

The heels of her stilettos were muffled in the rug as she walked out of the bedroom and down the hall to the staircase. All of the employees at Cole-Thom were invited to the Blackstone get-together. The exception was security personnel who were scheduled to work that night.

Nicholas turned his head so Celia couldn't see his grin. It'd been a long time since he'd seen her bare so much skin. A black off-the-shoulder dress, ending at her knees, fit her body like second skin, while a pair of black stilettos put her close to six feet. One thing he always liked about his sister was that she was very secure about her height.

"We're going to pick up Gavin at the stables." He opened the door and led Celia out into the warm air. It was dusk, his favorite time of the day.

Celia looped her arm over the sleeve of Nicholas's raw silk black shirt. "You look very dangerous dressed all in black."

Nicholas wiggled his eyebrows. "I feel dangerous tonight."

"Dangerous or reckless?"

"Both."

"Watch out, ladies. Nicholas is on the prowl tonight."

"My male employees like interacting with Blackstone Farms because they say the women over there are much prettier than the ones here."

"I hope they're not talking about their wives."

Nicholas laughed. "If they are, then they're in for a world of hurt. I've witnessed a few marital spats, and they weren't nice. The difference between this farm and Blackstone is that we don't have small children. Of course, their farm is a lot bigger than this one."

"How big?" Celia asked, once she was seated in the Lincoln.

"Blackstone Farms is about ten thousand acres. They operate like a small town. They have a church, and a couple of years ago they chartered their own school. So, the kids never have to leave the farm to attend classes."

"I suppose they never have to close the school because of snow."

"You're right about that. Last year we had record cold and snowfall totals."

Nicholas drove away from the house along a road leading to the stables. Streetlamps were coming on, lighting up the area as if it were daytime. He tapped the horn lightly, garnering Gavin's attention. Slowing, he waited for his brother-in-law to get into the rear of the sedan before driving in a westerly direction toward Blackstone Farms.

"You have to come and visit during the fall. Halloween is really special around here. We have hayrides and bonfires and the little kids are allowed to stay up until midnight. Sheldon hosted Halloween last year and it's my turn this year."

Celia stared at her brother's profile. She'd found it uncanny how much he resembled their paternal grandmother, Nancy Cole-Thomas. Then there were those in the family who claimed Celia had inherited her grandmother's candor. If it came up, then it would come out.

"What about the older kids?" she asked.

"Believe it or not, they seldom leave the farm. Everything they'd want is there. Those who attend schools away from the property form friendships with other kids, most of whom wish they could live on a working horse farm."

"What about dating?"

"I haven't lived here long enough to know those statistics, but I do know that Jeremy and Tricia Blackstone grew up together and eventually married. You'll probably get a chance to see their triplet daughters tonight."

Celia wanted to ask Nicholas about Peyton Blackstone. She'd noticed them talking and dancing during the reception. When she and Peyton had gone shopping for gowns, Celia saw another side of the quixotic veterinarian who'd grown up with an overbearing, alcoholic father who never let her forget he'd wanted a son. It wasn't until she was an adolescent and she'd searched the Internet that she'd discovered another branch of the Blackstone family tree. Acting on impulse, she'd e-mailed Sheldon Blackstone at the farm who'd been able to confirm they were cousins and therefore related.

Peyton had convinced her father to let her spend her summers at Blackstone Farms, and it was Sheldon who underwrote the cost of her college education once she'd expressed interest in veterinary medicine. It wasn't what Peyton said but what she hadn't said about growing up in a home with a mother who was too frightened to defend herself or protect her daughter during her husband's alcohol-induced tantrums that led Celia to believe that not only had Peyton been verbally abused as a child, but physically abused, as well.

She'd discovered the vet had a wicked sense of humor that had kept her laughing when they'd had dinner at a restaurant frequented by college students. Some of the young men tried hitting on the attractive natural blonde, but Peyton easily parried their advances with a look that scared off the most persistent admirer.

All thoughts of Peyton fled when Nicholas stopped at a pair of electronic iron gates emblazoned with a bold letter *B*. Leaning out the driver's side window, Nicholas stared into a camera and gave his name. Within seconds, the gates opened and closed behind them as he drove through. There was still enough daylight for Celia to see white rail fences, stone walls and verdant landscaped grassland.

The road diverged into four directions, but Nicholas followed the sign pointing the way to the main house. A towering flagpole with an American flag flying atop a black-and-red one lifted in the slight breeze. Teenage boys were doing double-duty directing traffic and parking the many vehicles in an area set aside for parking.

Celia had been introduced to the Blackstone men and their wives the day before, but hadn't had an opportunity to talk with them other than to accept their warm wishes for a long and happy married life. She remembered Sheldon Blackstone because he'd passed his incredible good looks on to his sons Ryan and Jeremy. Tall and solidly built with salt-and-pepper wavy hair, high, slanting cheekbones, an aquiline nose and light gray eyes, the middle-aged Blackstone patriarch had married a woman twenty years his junior and had become a father for the third time. There had been the titillating news circulating throughout Virginia's horse country that Sheldon's daughter was younger than her nieces and nephews.

Gavin alighted from the rear of the car to assist Celia as she placed one foot on the ground, then the other as he pulled her gently to stand. He would be the first to admit that Celia was stunning in the revealing dress, but he also didn't want to deal with other men lusting after his wife. The day before she appeared the vestal virgin in white and now, twenty-four-hours later she'd morphed into a vamp in black, and a mass of curls had replaced the sophisticated chignon.

Taking her hand, Gavin tucked it into the bend of his elbow, following Nicholas and a swelling crowd over to large tents with dozens of tables that were covered with white linen. Folding chairs, swathed in white organza, were tied with either black or red satin ribbon, representing the farm's silks.

The Blackstones, resident veterinarian Dr. Ryan Blackstone and his wife Kelly, who had set up the farm school, were on hand to greet their guests.

Jeremy Blackstone, who'd taken over the daily operation of the vast horse farm, stood with his arm around his wife Tricia while two identical little girls clung to the legs of their parents. All of the Blackstone grand-children had varying shades of gray eye color.

Peyton stood in the receiving line, holding the third Blackstone triplet. She was resplendent in a one-shoulder black dress that ended inches above her knees. Four-inch pumps added height to her diminutive frame, and also called attention to her legs. She pulled her hair back and tied it with a black ribbon. Celia watched Nicholas as his gaze traveled from Peyton's face to down her compact body before reversing itself. He reached for her hand and pressed a kiss on her knuckle before moving on.

"Don't you dare say anything," Gavin whispered in Celia's ear.

"Do you think he likes her?" she whispered, ignoring his warning.

"Leave it alone," he warned again. Celia narrowed her eyes at her husband. "Glare at me all you want, I'm not going to gossip about your brother."

"I'm not gossiping, darling."

"Yes, you are, Celia. We're leaving here tomorrow and Nicholas and Peyton know where to find each other."

Gavin's cryptic rejoinder spoke volumes. Men talk just like women talk and Celia was willing to bet Nich-olas's indifference to the pretty veterinarian was a de-fensive ploy not to get involved with the owner of the neighboring farm's cousin.

When Peyton had tearfully revealed bits and pieces of her childhood, it served to reinforce Celia's attitude that she had truly grown up blessed. It wasn't her family's money that had set her apart from some of the other girls with whom she'd gone to college and worked, but it was the sense of family first.

Any Cole, whether legitimate, illegitimate or adopted

garnered full family backing. If you hurt one Cole, then look for the wrath from the others to descend upon the hapless perpetrator. Whenever she argued with Yale, Celia never involved her family—especially her brothers, who were looking for any excuse to "jack" him up. Trust funds aside, the men were one rung above thug status.

Celia exchanged air kisses with Peyton. "You look incredible, girlfriend."

Peyton blushed. "Thank you. So do you for a newly married woman." She leaned closer. "I'll never be able to thank you enough for asking me to be your bridal attendant."

Celia winked at her. "Are you practicing?" She pointed to the toddler who was an exact copy of her sisters.

"No. It's going to be a while before I think of becoming a mother. This little muffin will hang with me until the music begins. Then she's going to bed. Maybe we can get together later and talk."

A moment later, Gavin greeted Peyton. Then he pulled Celia gently over to a table and seated her. He leaned over her head. "Are you satisfied, Mrs. Faulkner?"

She smiled over her shoulder at him. "Totally." Celia pressed a hand to her throat. "Could you please get me some water?"

"Do you want anything else?"

"No, just the water, thank you," she said.

Celia watched Gavin walk, her gaze lingering on his retreating figure. They'd slept in late, waking at noon. They shared a shower for the first time, stopping short of making love. Whereas other women had their menses from three to five days, hers lingered for eight. The delay in consummating their marriage only served to heighten the anticipation of making love to her husband for the first time. She and Gavin had decided to forego Saturday's gathering at Harridans Farms and return to North Carolina.

Once the partying began in earnest, Celia realized her wedding reception had served as the kickoff at Blackstone Farms that had become the New Year's Eve, the Super Bowl, Kentucky Derby and the Fourth of July rolled into a massive tailgate party. She ate, danced and drank much too much. The hands on the clock inched past midnight, the unofficial time for the celebrating to end, but no one headed to the parking area to retrieve their vehicle.

Celia sat barefoot on the grass, sprawled between Gavin's outstretched legs. "I think you're going to have to be the designated driver tonight."

Gavin nodded in agreement. "I believe you're right. Nicholas appears to be a little unsteady on his feet."

"Nicky's not much of a drinker."

"Neither is his sister," Gavin countered.

"There are a few teetotalers in the family, not because they're in recovery, but because they can't tolerate alcohol."

"Four is my limit."

Celia smiled at Gavin over her shoulder. "I've never been able to finish two before I fall asleep."

"You're a pervert's fantasy. Get the girl drunk and take advantage of her."

"That's not nice, *m'ijo*."

"It is what it is, Celia. I've known guys who'd deliberately get a woman drunk just to have sex with her, because under normal circumstances she wouldn't think of sleeping with him."

"I know, because I've treated enough rape victims who come into the E.R. for an AIDS test. It's only after I have a consult with them that they admit to being date-raped. Some of them refuse to name their attacker, but after the urging from a female social worker or rape victim advocate, they give up the name. That's when the police get involved and with DNA as evidence, the piece of garbage is charged with rape."

Gavin buried his face in her hair. "What's the most bizarre situation you've ever encountered?"

"There are too many to count, but the ones that stand out are when patients are brought in with foreign objects lodged in the most unlikely orifices."

"Ouch!"

"You've got that right. Most times I have to sedate the patient to remove the object." She looked thoughtful. "I miss treating patients."

Gavin closed his eyes, enjoying the soft warmth of his wife's body. It was the first time he'd heard her talk about her profession. He opened his eyes. "How serious are you about opening that clinic?"

"Very serious. I own the building. Before I left Florida I was to meet with the contractor to go over the plans so he could begin renovating the space."

"How much space is there?"

"Fifteen thousand square feet."

Gavin whistled softly. "It's pretty big."

"It takes up about a quarter of an abandoned strip mall. I plan to have a reception area, waiting room for patients, a play area for children, then there's the examining rooms. I want to offer emergency internal medicine and pediatric care. Future plans include a pediatric dentist, ob-gyn services and a nutritionist. Obesity has become a major health issue in this country. If we're able to get kids to eat right, it will prevent more serious health problems before they become adults."

"It sounds like a monumental undertaking, but I know you can do it, baby."

"Thank you."

Gavin angled his head, kissing her neck. "You're welcome. I want you to know even though I may not agree with everything you say or do, I'll always have your back."

"And I'll have yours."

Celia felt her eyelids grow heavy as she forced herself to stay awake. In the end, sleep won out and she didn't remember Gavin gathering her off the grass or carrying her to Nicholas's car. She woke when he climbed the staircase to their bedroom. She stayed awake long enough to wash her face and brush her teeth before succumbing to a deep, dreamless sleep.

As planned, Celia and Gavin left Virginia Saturday morning to drive back to North Carolina. A softly falling rain slowed traffic along the interstate and it was late afternoon when the house came into view.

Gavin entered the house first, checking to make certain it was secure. He unloaded the luggage and Terry. Interacting with the dogs at the horse farm had helped the puppy act like a dog. He no longer soiled the paper in his crate, scratching and whining when he wanted to be let out to relieve himself. The crate was placed in the mudroom with the door ajar and clean wee-wee pads in a far corner.

Gavin called the Bureau to report his return to the base of operation. Then he checked his e-mail for new messages. He sent one e-mail to Bradley MacArthur, informing him of a change in his marital status. A smile tilted the corners of Gavin's mouth when he typed in the name of his spouse. He'd wanted to be a fly on the wall when Mac opened and read the e-mail.

Powering off the laptop, he returned it to the carry-on, returning the bag to the back of the closet in the guest room. Taking long, determined strides, Gavin walked down the hall to the master bedroom. He paused to strip off his clothes, leaving them on the floor near the door, and entered the bathroom. The sound of running water and Gloria Estefan singing "Don't Wanna Lose You" greeted him. He froze when he heard Celia's beautiful modulated contralto singing along with the talented Miami-based performer.

Celia's voice was lovely and the words to the song so poignant that it gave him pause. *I don't wanna lose you now. We're gonna get through somehow.*

Were the lyrics prophetic? Would they find love only to lose it?

Gavin approached the shower and opened the door. He knew he'd shocked Celia when she emitted a small gasp. "May I?"

A sensual smile softened her lips. "Yes, you may."

He stood under the spray of an oversized showerhead, staring down at moisture beading up on his wife's flawless brown face. Lowering his head, he brushed his mouth over hers, as he pulled her to stand between his legs.

Water washed away shampoo and body wash as Gavin pressed Celia against the wall of the shower stall. Slowly, deliberately, he fastened his mouth to her breasts and suckled her until the nipples were erect and hard as dried beans. One hand searched between her thighs, causing her to rise on tiptoe.

Celia opened her mouth to force more air into her lungs. Gavin's thumb moved back and forth over the swollen nub at the apex of her thighs, making it hard to breathe. Hiccupping sounds were torn from her constricted throat as the fire that began between her legs spread throughout her body like the back draft from a jet's engine. Her arms went around Gavin's head, holding him fast.

Gavin hardened quickly, his blood-engorged penis swinging heavily between his thighs. If he didn't get inside Celia he knew for certain he would come in the shower. Using all of his strength, he lifted her with one arm while his free hand guided his erection inside her.

And, as they had during their last coming together, he mated with her. He slammed into her, then without warning he pulled out and turned her around to face the wall. He reentered her, this time from the rear. Gasps, groans, moans and the rhythmic slapping of her buttocks against his belly created a sexual symphony unlike any either had experienced.

Gavin felt his lungs burning, his heat slamming against his ribs, but he still refused to let go of the passion singeing every inch of flesh from his scalp to the soles of his feet.

Celia pounded the tiles with her fists as tears mingled with the water falling over her head and body. Gavin felt so good that she feared losing her mind. And if she were to go crazy then she wanted it to be in the throes of the most exquisite pleasure she'd ever known.

The flutters began, growing stronger and stronger until she knew she could hold back no longer. She closed her eyes, threw back her head and let out a trill-like sound that sent shivers up and down her body as an orgasm shook her violently.

Gavin felt the walls of Celia's vaginal canal squeeze his hard flesh, release him, then squeeze him again—harder and longer. Tightening his hold on her waist, he pulled her back against him, and not permitting her motion, released himself inside her still-pulsing body.

Spent, they slid down to the floor of the shower and waited for their pulses to return to normal. He heard a sound and at first he thought Celia was crying, but recognized it as laughter.

"What's so funny?" he asked, forcing himself not to smile.

"Why is it whenever we have mind-blowing sex we're never in bed?"

This time Gavin laughed. "Call it spontaneity."

"That's what I think I'll call our first-born."

"Yeah, right. And you'll have to accept blame when he or she comes home from school after kicking some kid's behind for making fun of him or her."

"Maybe it can be his or her middle name."

"We'll talk about baby names when you find yourself pregnant."

"What if I can't conceive?"

"It doesn't matter, Celia."

"But don't you want children?"

"Yes, I want children, but if we can't have our own, then we'll adopt. My mother adopted my brother after my dad passed away."

Celia tried to move, but Gavin's weight was pressing her down. "Please let me up."

Although he was reluctant to pull out of her warm

body, Gavin did. He came to his feet and turned off the water, then reached down to help Celia stand. "What is it?" he asked softly when he saw the strange expression on her face.

"You never told me your brother was adopted."

"That's because you didn't ask."

A swollen silence ensued, before Celia said, "You're right, Gavin. I didn't ask."

Chapter 20

Celia was unusually quiet as she sat on the patio crocheting a border of shells on the blanket she'd knitted for Hannah. Using a tiny pair of scissors, she cut the yarn, and then wove the loose end into the stitches, giving the garment a clean finish. Gavin sat nearby with Terry asleep in his lap. She folded the blanket, placing it in a large box lined with dark green tissue paper. The knitted hat, sweater and booties were placed atop the blanket. She placed a small card, indicating the gift was from her and Gavin, in the box and covered it with a hand-painted top.

"I'm going over to Hannah's to leave this for her."

Gavin pushed to his feet. "I'll take you."

"It won't be necessary. It's only down the road."

"I'll still come with you. Wait here for me."

Celia knew it was pointless to argue with Gavin when

he got this way. His voice was completely void of emotion. He knew she was upset because he hadn't mentioned that his brother had been adopted, and it was more blatant than ever that she knew very little about the man she'd married and to whom she'd pledged her future. She'd closed and locked the pocket doors when he returned.

"I put Terry in the mudroom," Gavin said. They still didn't trust the puppy to have the run of the house because he still had accidents.

They had just reached the front door when the house phone rang. Celia was galvanized into action by the time it rang a third time. She glanced at the display seconds before picking up the receiver. It was her grandmother.

"Hola, abuela."

"Celia, you have to come home."

"Why, *abuela?*"

Gavin saw the fear in Celia's eyes as her hand tightened on the cordless receiver. He couldn't hear what whoever had called had told her, but he knew instinctually it wasn't good news.

"Mama died in her sleep this morning."

Celia couldn't stop the tears filling her eyes. "No, no, no, *abuela.*"

Nancy Cole-Thomas's voice was very calm when she said, "Martin is making travel arrangements. He wants you at the Asheville Regional Airport by six tonight."

Trance-like, she nodded. "Okay, *abuela.* I'll be there at six." It was a full minute before she could bring herself to hang up. She placed the box on the side table. "I have to go back to Florida."

Gavin closed the distance between them, his hands going to her shoulders. "Why?"

"My great-grandmother passed away this morning. My uncle is sending the corporate jet to pick me up at the Asheville airport at six."

Cradling her face, he kissed her forehead. "I'm sorry, baby."

Celia blinked back tears. Her great-grandmother would've turned one hundred six if she'd survived the year. Although she'd expected Marguerite-Joséfina Isabel Diaz-Cole not to survive too many more years, the fact remained she didn't want to lose her.

"Thank you, Gavin." Resting her head on his chest, she counted the strong, steady heartbeats. "I need you to take the box over to Hannah and let her know that I had a death in the family, and that I hope to see her before the baby comes."

Even before he could ask whether she wanted him to accompany her, Celia indicated she was going back to Florida—alone. Gavin knew she didn't need a bodyguard because the Coles would take the steps to protect their own. They were sending a private jet to take her back to Florida, and no doubt she probably would be met with a security detail comparable to those of the Secret Service.

"You better go upstairs and pack. We're going to have to leave within half an hour if you want to make it to the airport by six."

Celia gave him a trembling smile. "Will you take care of Terry for me?"

Gavin gave her a look that said he couldn't believe she'd ask him something like that. "Of course I'll take care of him." He patted her behind. "Go and pack, baby."

Gavin made it to the airport with time to spare. He showed the police officer outside the terminal his shield and FBI picture ID when he parked his SUV at the curb. "I'll be right back as soon as she's boarded," he said softly.

The police officer nodded. "No problem."

Taking Celia's hand, he led her into the terminal and to a section of the airport that led to an area where private jets landed and took off. They walked down a gangway and out to the tarmac where a sleek Gulfstream G550 stood, engines revving. The ColeDiz logo was emblazoned on the side, and aircraft-identifying numbers on the tail. A tall man wearing a business suit stood outside the aircraft talking to a flight attendant. He turned and stared at them.

Celia moved closer to Gavin. "That's Diego."

Gavin stopped. "This is as far as I go." He handed her the single piece of luggage.

Celia turned, her gaze searching her husband's impassive features under the brim of his baseball cap. She dropped her bag and twisted the platinum band off her finger. "Hold this for me until I come back."

Staring at the ring on her outstretched palm, Gavin took it and slipped it into the pocket of his jeans. He leaned over and picked up her bag, handed it to her, then turned on his heels and retraced his steps. *Hold this for me until I come back.* Her parting words echoed in his head like a litany.

Celia watched Gavin until he disappeared from her line of vision, then she turned to see her brother coming closer and closer until she found herself cradled in his protective embrace.

"Who was that, Cee Cee?"

"My...my bodyguard." She'd almost slipped and said her husband.

"Let's board. We still have to stop in Mississippi and pick up Tyler and his family."

Diego took her bag while she climbed the steps and walked into the aircraft. Her New Mexico cousins filled half the seats. They were asleep; reminding her they were on a different time zone. The Coles always gathered in West Palm from Christmas Eve to New Year's Day. There were smaller reunions during the summer and Thanksgiving. Then there were the unexpected reunions that usually meant a death in the family. This was one of those times.

Celia leaned against Nicholas, praying she wouldn't break down. The funeral mass for their great-grandmother was conducted in Spanish, as per wishes. M.J., as she wanted to be called, was in control, even in death. She knew she shouldn't cry for a woman whose life had spanned more than a century, but with M.J.'s death that meant the man and woman who'd created a family with accomplishments that far exceeded their expectations were gone forever. But what they had left were memories of their stalwart determination to beat the odds.

Everyone had come to West Palm Beach except Nathaniel and Kendra, who was due to give birth any day now. The children of her Las Cruces, New Mexico cousins were growing so quickly she hardly recognized them. All of the Coles were dark-haired and dark-eyed. The only exception was Emily Delgado's son, Alejandro. The thirteen-year-old boy had inherited his grandfather's platinum-blond hair and startling light green eyes. Looking at the adolescent was like staring at a picture of Joshua Kirkland at that age.

Martin Cole stepped forward and placed a rose on his mother's gunmetal-gray casket. Nancy Cole-Thomas was next, and then Josephine Cole-Mitchell and following her was David Cole. Joshua Kirkland placed his flower on the casket of the woman who had been the bane of his mother's existence when Teresa Kirkland had tried to woo Samuel Cole away from M.J. One by one Coles, Kirklands, Spencers, Delgados, Grayslakes and Lassisters lined up to pay their respects to the woman who'd been their matriarch and *abuelita*.

Celia felt detached from her family and she knew she should've asked Gavin to come with her. She would celebrate her thirty-fourth birthday come August, and she was hiding the fact that she married like a girl whose parents had forbidden her to see a boy they disapproved of.

Her head popped up when a shadow blocked out the sun. "Hi, Daddy."

Timothy Cole-Thomas smiled at his daughter. "May I sit down?"

She patted the seat of the stone bench in the Japanese garden of the West Palm mansion where Samuel and M.J. had raised their four children. "Of course." She leaned against her father's shoulder. The CEO of ColeDiz for more than three decades, Timothy had finally retired at sixty, turning the reins over to Diego. His eldest son had taken the company in a direction that defied everything Samuel Claridge Cole proposed.

Timothy's hair was no longer salt-and-pepper but white. It was an attractive contrast to his dark unlined face. He'd inherited his mother's delicate features, features he'd passed on to Nicholas.

Putting an arm around his daughter's waist, Timothy pulled her closer. "I'd like you to stay in Florida."

"I can't, Daddy."

"*¿Por qué no?*" he asked, lapsing easily into Spanish. "Why?" he repeated in English when she paused.

"I feel at peace in North Carolina."

"You can feel at peace here if you stay with me and your mother."

"You don't understand, Daddy."

"I do understand, Celia. My hair has turned white worrying about you. Your house in Miami was broken into—"

"When?"

"A couple of weeks ago."

Celia felt a rush panic that made her lightheaded. "Why didn't you call and tell me?"

"And what would you have done, Celia? Jump in your car and drive back to Miami?"

"I…I don't know."

"Let me tell you what I do know. Alton Fitch's kidnapping was no random act. Even his wife and children have gone into hiding. And it has everything to do with the trial where you're the state's star witness. Last I heard was that Elijah Morrow asked to be taken off the case. Rumors are he was threatened."

Celia slumped against the back of the bench. Elijah Morrow had called her and she'd refused to speak to him. "Who's replacing him?"

"No one knows. And I'm willing to bet they're not going to get anyone willing to sit on a jury. No jury, no prosecutor means that son of a bitch will walk."

"How can that happen if they have a witness willing to testify?"

"If you live, Celia."

She shook her head. "This is ludicrous. A known

drug dealer comes into a hospital E.R. and kills two people before he's shot, and he gets a free get-out-of-jail card."

"It's all about drugs, guns and money, sweetheart. These people are ruthless and they don't care who they have to eliminate to get what they want."

"He gets to walk and what happens to me? Do I have to look over my shoulder every time I step out of my house, praying the crazy bastard isn't waiting for me?"

"I don't know what to tell you." Timothy kissed the top of her head. "I want you to stay here until the FBI finds Fitch. Right now he's a key piece to a puzzle that is becoming more bizarre with each passing day."

"Can't Merrick find out something?" Her cousin Alexandra had married a man who worked for the Central Intelligence Agency.

"The CIA doesn't deal with domestic issues. The FBI does."

"I'm certain he must know some FBI agents."

"Stop it, Celia! That's crazy talk. I just buried my grandmother. Please don't make me have to bury you, too."

Celia froze. It was the first time in years that she'd heard her father raise his voice. "What do you want me to do, Daddy?"

"Stay here until there's word on Alton Fitch. One way or the other," he added.

She wanted to tell her father that she'd left her husband, and he was expecting her to come back to him. "I'll think about it."

"When are you going to let me know?"

"Tomorrow," she said quietly.

Shaking his head and blowing out his cheeks, Timothy stared at the ground. He'd raised his daughter to be strong, but he hadn't realized how strong she was. If she hadn't gone into medicine he was certain she would've become the first female CEO of ColeDiz International, Ltd.

Waiting until her father walked back to the house, Celia reached into the pocket of her slacks and took out her cell phone. She had to speak to Gavin. She didn't know his cell number, but she prayed he would answer the house phone. It took five rings before Gavin answered.

It took less than three minutes to explain her position and why she'd decided to stay in Palm Beach with her parents. Much to her surprise, Gavin agreed with them. He gave her an update on Terry and told her he would call her every night at ten. He hung up without saying "I miss you" or "I love you." Celia stared at the tiny phone as if it was something she'd never seen before. Then she pressed the end button.

Chapter 21

The days and nights blended into one continuous span of time as Gavin waited in the house in the mountains. He waited for Raymond Prentice to contact him and he waited for Celia's return. It was as if Raymond and Alton Fitch had dropped off the face of the earth, never to be seen again.

June passed, then July and now it was the middle of August. The only things that kept him from going completely stir-crazy was his having to take care of Terry, who was quickly losing his puppy appearance. He spoke to Celia every night, refusing to tell her the dreaded three little words because he knew if he told her then he wouldn't stay and finish what he'd been ordered to do.

He was sitting on the patio reading when the chiming of the doorbell echoed throughout the house. Reaching for the automatic resting on a table, he slipped it into the small of his back. When he opened the door, he was surprised to see Daniel Walsh. He was in uniform. Hannah had given birth to a healthy girl and Daniel had invited him to a small gathering at his place to celebrate the event.

Gavin smiled. "What's up, Daniel?"

"May I come in?"

Gavin stepped aside. "Sure."

Daniel walked in and closed the door. "I have a cousin who lives on the Eastern Cherokee Reservation who told me there's someone on the res asking for you."

"Does this person have a name?"

"Ray. But you know him as O."

Attractive lines fanned out around Gavin's eyes when he smiled. "Tell your cousin to tell Ray to stay put. As soon I make a few calls I'll come and get him."

Daniel smiled for the first time. "How's the wife?"

"She's good. Thanks for the message."

"Anytime, brother."

Gavin felt his heart beating outside his chest. Raymond Prentice was hiding out on federal land. He'd found his way to an Indian reservation. Retrieving his cell, he called Bradley MacArthur with the news that Raymond Prentice had made contact. Mac's triumphant laugh came through the tiny earpiece. He told Gavin he would call him back as soon as he called the North Carolina field office to dispatch a team of agents to bring in one of America's Most Wanted.

Gavin whistled through his teeth, and Terry came running. Picking up the dog, he swung him around and around. "We're going home, boy."

Celia sat in bed in the bedroom where she'd grown up, watching the late news. She stared, unblinking, as the likeness of her husband filled the screen. He stood behind an FBI spokesman, a shield hanging from a chain around his neck.

Placing a hand over her chest, she sank down to the pile of pillows cushioning her back. Her pulse quickened when Gavin stepped forward to explain that a team of agents had uncovered the man responsible for kidnapping and the attempted murder of a gun dealer, and that he was shot and killed when he'd resisted arrest after he'd been spotted hiding out on an Indian reservation in western North Carolina.

Minutes later her cell rang. "Did you see the news?" asked Nicholas.

"I'm looking at it now."

"My brother-in-law is somethin' else."

"Your brother-in-law is going to get the business when I see him."

"Don't be so hard on him, Cee Cee. I think it's kind of nice having a special agent in the family. With Gavin and Merrick we have all the bases covered."

Celia's eyes narrowed. "Why don't you sound surprised to find out that Gavin was an undercover agent?"

"I've known for months that he's with the FBI."

"And you didn't tell me? Nicholas, you should be the one I should cuss out."

"Bye, Cee Cee."

A curse slipped past her lips when she realized her brother had hung up on her. "Who the hell is it?" she screamed when she heard someone knock on her bedroom door.

The door opened and her father stood in the doorway with an expression of shock freezing his features. "I know your mother didn't raise you to talk like that."

She dropped her gaze, thoroughly embarrassed. "I'm sorry, Daddy."

Timothy struggled not to laugh. "I'll excuse you this time. I came to tell you that there's someone here to see you."

"Who?"

Timothy stepped aside and Gavin filled the space where her father had been. "Your husband."

Celia's mouth opened and closed, but nothing came out. "How can you be here when you're…" Her words trailed off when she pointed at the television.

Gavin walked into the large bedroom, kicking the door closed with his foot. "It was prerecorded."

She stared at the man dressed in a suit that made him look even more delicious than the first time she saw him in the supermarket. "You know you're going to get the business for lying to me."

"I couldn't tell you," Gavin said as he approached the bed. His gaze never left hers as he removed his jacket, leaving it on the bench at the foot of the bed. The silk tie was next, then the shirt. Celia's ring was suspended on a chain around his neck.

"What are you doing?" she asked, when he kicked off his shoes and pushed his trousers and briefs off his hips.

"What does it look like, *m'ija?* I'm about to make love to my wife."

Celia attempted to slip off the bed, but she wasn't quick enough when Gavin's arm went around her waist over the cotton nightgown. He stopped, his eyes filled with wonder and shock. "You're pregnant."

She pounded his shoulder. "And you're a special agent," she countered.

Easing her down to the bed, Gavin buried his face

between her neck and shoulder. "Why didn't you tell me? We talked every night and you still didn't tell me."

"I wanted to, Gavin, but you never said that you loved me. Even if you'd told me that you missed me, I would've told you."

He placed a hand over the slight roundness. "When are you due?"

"Early March."

"Have you ever spent the winter in the mountains?"

"Yes. Why?"

"I've been offered a supervisory position in a North Carolina field office. No more undercover work."

"What about my house in Miami? Or my clinic?"

"We can use the house in Miami for vacations or when we come to visit your family. As for the property where you plan to open your clinic, I found out it's going to be razed to put up low-income houses. That means the county will pay you fair-market value, which is probably more than what you paid for it."

"I didn't buy it. Yale did. So, whatever they give me I'll turn over to his parents. But, aren't you forgetting something?"

"What am I forgetting?"

"I still have to testify."

"No, you don't, Celia. I'm going to tell you something that cannot go any farther than this room. Now I want you to promise me you will never repeat it."

The seconds ticked by as he waited for her response. "I promise."

Celia listened, not interrupting when Gavin told her the man who reportedly was killed resisting arrest was his adopted brother who was working undercover for the ATF. They'd faked his death, using movie-making technology, and Orlando Wells Faulkner was vacationing in Puerto Rico. Once he returned to the mainland he, too, would transfer to desk duty, much to the delight of their mother.

The Bureau had staged Alton Fitch's abduction because of a death threat. A jailhouse snitch told the warden that the E.R. shooter bragged about getting another gang member to take the D.A. out. His cell was wired with a listening device and the egotistical killer couldn't stop talking about whom he worked for and how many he'd murdered. When they played back the tape, he decided to accept life in prison without the possibility of parole, instead of a trial at which he was certain to get the death penalty.

"You're safe and D.A. Fitch is safe. And because your little friend with the pit bull tattoo used a gun that was stolen from a federal facility, and he was trafficking in drugs, the feds decided they wanted him for themselves. He's now in a federal maximum security prison in Wyoming."

"I can't believe it's over and I don't have to testify."

"That's over, but for us it's just beginning. I'll hang out here for a couple of days to meet your family, and then we'll drive down to Miami and have a mini-honeymoon before we go back to the mountains."

"Where's Terry?"

"I left him with Daniel and Hannah. I caught him humping a pillow, which means the boy needs some like I need some."

"What did you do these past two and a half months?"

"You don't want to know. I was all right until I heard your voice, then it was hard…" Gavin said through gritted teeth. He shook his head. "I don't believe I just said that."

"Let me take off this nightgown and let Dr. Faulkner see what she can do to relieve you of your problem."

Reaching up, Gavin removed the chain from his neck and opened the clasp. He took off the ring and slipped it on her finger. "I don't want you to ever take this off again."

"And I won't."

He removed her nightgown, and then trailed kisses over her ripening belly. When they tired of foreplay, Celia opened her legs to her husband and welcomed him into her body. He'd come home, and she was home as waves of ecstasy throbbed through her, making them one with the other.

Gavin breathed out the last of his passion into her mouth, chanting, "I love you. I love your life."

* * * * *

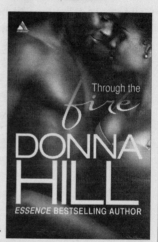